F*ck the Mommy Wars

A Novel

BY

By Ezmé Purvis

Acknowledgements

This is for Ashley.

This is for Jennifer. This is for Krista-Lee. This is for Phillipa. This is for Dorotea. This is for Abby. This is for Christina. This is for Bethany. This is for Abigail. This is for Nora. This is for Bonnie. This is for Sophia. This is for Jill. This is for Erin.

This is for every woman who is keeping all of the balls in the air. This is for every woman who doesn't want to be this angry. This is for every woman who has gotten out of bed every day because her family needs her, even though she hurts so much she feels like she might die. This is for every woman who has set aside her dreams because they were an inconvenience to everyone. This is for every woman who is beginning to awaken.

This is for all of their husbands, fathers, and sons. Some people might read this book and think that it is all man-bashing, but that couldn't be further from my intention. This life is so very hard, for men and women, and the only way to get through it is together. But for some reason, too many of the men of this generation find this openness impossible. They shut down, push us away, stop communicating, hide behind alcohol and drugs, or jobs, or screens, or sex. We just want you to be here! To be present, in the moment, riding the roller coaster alongside us. We love you, and we need you. Your children need you.

Also, I'd like to add: it was terrifying to put this out there. Moms have immense pressure to get it right ALL THE TIME. With no room for error. Our children's lives are in our hands! So we all pretend that we are doing better than we are. We don't tell anyone about the worst of it: our parenting failures become a guilty secret that eats away at our souls.

And here I am, telling the world about the worst of it.

I know that many people will read this and think: "What a horrible mother. She should never have had kids." I say that to myself all of the time. But this book is not for you. This book is for the mother that is working her ass off, and some days she's an awesome mom, and some days she feels like she is failing at everything. This book is for her.

You are not alone. Forgive yourself for your failures. Keep trying your hardest. That is all that you can do.

I want to thank Dorotéa for being my first reader, and the other dozen amazing friends who edited and encouraged me along the way. I want to thank Gina for letting me run up the electric bill at her cottage while I finished this book during a blizzard in November. I want to thank Craig for supporting me every day of my journey to be a writer, even though it meant airing much of our dirty laundry before the world. I want to thank the women in my life, who inspire me and support me and love me, through good times and bad. I can't begin to express how much you mean to me.

Trigger Warning

Abuse. Rape. Child loss.

Character List

- ## Alisha
  - Nickname: Lish
  - 34 years old
  - Daycare Operator. Former Anthropology Professor
- Partner: Isaac. 42 years old. Hotel Manager
- Children: Hana and Ari, both 2

- ## Andrea
  - Nickname: Drae
  - 34 years old
  - HR Administrator with a degree in English Literature
- Husband: Damien. 35 years old. Serial Entrepreneur
- Children: Wallace, 6, and Zachary, 3

- # Maja
  - 33 years old
  - Stay-at-home Mom. Former Software Designer
  - Husband: Nate. 34 years old. Software Designer
- Children: Eloise, 6, and Claire, 2

- # Sofia
  - Nickname: Sof
  - 38 years old
  - Midwife
  - Husband: Colin. 36 years old. Construction worker
  - Child: Greyson

3:00 am

Alisha

"Meow. Meoow. Meeeeeeeow." The cat leaps onto the bed, landing squarely upon one of the sleeping toddlers beside me.

"Get the fuck out of here!" I hiss at the creature and push her away, praying that she won't wake the babies. After some resistance the cat leaps back to the ground and proudly walks away, flicking her tail and throwing me an angry glance over her shoulder.

I settle back down between the two warm little bodies, their soft arms and legs quickly rearranging around my arms and neck, pinning me to the bed like an affectionate hostage situation. I hope I can get back to sleep. My heart is thumping in my chest from that sudden awakening. And I have to pee.

I try to focus on the gentle breathing of Ari on my right and Hana on my left. His breath is even and steady when he sleeps, where hers is erratic. Sometimes she holds her breath long enough that I'm inclined to nudge her, but then she exhales with a long, slow sigh and I relax again. Both little mouths are hanging open slightly as the air goes in and out. It is such a lovely thing, sleeping next to these two sweet little bodies.

But I'm never getting back to sleep. If I stay in bed I'll just get more and more bitter with every minute that ticks by until I finally drift off at the exact moment when the twins wake up and then I'll be so angry that I'll want to burn the house down and stab every person who looks at me sideways all day.

Best to just get up.

And now I can feel a hot flash coming on, so I need to get away from these two adorable little furnaces, pronto.

I carefully extricate myself from the twins' limp grasps and creep from the queen size mattress on the floor that acts as our family bed. Before my feet even hit the carpet the twins have shifted soundlessly into one another's arms, seeking each other's comfort even as they sleep.

My heart swells. They are so fucking sweet. It is hard to see in the daytime, because they don't stop moving long enough for me to notice how sweet they are, but when they are perfectly still like this, oh the love. It is too much.

I sneak across the hall, careful not to step on the squeaky parts of the floor, to the bathroom. Rather than turn on the bright light I leave the door open and pee by the glow of the night-light in the hall. Then, without flushing the noisy toilet or washing my hands under the squeaky taps, I creep down the hall to my step-son Kai's empty bedroom.

Two days a week this is Kai's bedroom, but as sleep has become more and more elusive it has morphed into my room as well. In addition to his single bed with a Minecraft bedspread, there are bookshelves and a small desk littered with Captain Underpants books, Marvel comics, and heavy academic books on human psychology. In the corner there is a tub full of lego and misplaced action figures, but also a bag full of small blue-and-white crochet squares. The bedside table is piled high with books, both Kai's and mine, fiction and non-fiction. I turn on the bedside lamp and cuddle up in the pile of pillows and grab my phone from the side table where I left it last night.

There are two notifications:

Email Notification

From: Mitchell Wellington
Subject: Refugee Paperwork
Hey There! I was wondering, if it isn't too much trouble....

Ugh, I don't even want to read that. The refugee paperwork is stressing me out just way too much.

Ignore, but don't forget. I fall into that trap way too often.

There's also a message from Maja:

Maja

Thursday, 8:22 pm
Hey! Are you guys still up for the park tomorrow?

Maja sent that last night but I didn't see it. I recently read a book about sleep which went on and on about all of the ways that screens mess with your sleep cycle. So now I'm so paranoid that I've banned myself from my phone after eight pm. Poor Maja will be wondering what is happening today. But I should not be looking at my phone right now! I can reply to both at a reasonable hour.

Insomnia vs willpower: one point to willpower!

I put the phone back on the table and reach for the book on the top of the pile – "Unconditional Parenting" by Alfie Kohn. Possibly my favourite parenting book ever. This is my third read and it still has the power to turn my day around.

Which I need right now. It has been a hard month, and this has been a hard week, and today will be a hard day, especially if I'm doing it on five hours of sleep.

I swallow my rising anxiety, breathe deeply, and start to read.

> By contrast, the unconditional approach to parenting begins with the reminder that my child's goal is not to make me miserable. She's not being malicious. She's telling me in the only way she knows that something is wrong.

I need to write this down. And post it somewhere highly visible.

Like on the kids' foreheads.

5:30 am

Andrea

Shit that was some dream. All the hairs on my body are standing on end. My skin tingles all over. I feel warm inside at the memory of that feeling of being passionately in love.

And then I remember my real life and feel instantly sick to my stomach. How do I get back into that dream and stay there forever?

Down that path, madness lies.

Out of bed. Damien's side of the bed is made, the blanket pulled tight and folded crisply over the pillow. If he was up very early or if he never came to bed at all I don't know.

And I don't really care.

I put on the bright overhead light and strip off my pj's (not really pj's, but a comfy pair of boxers and a t-shirt) and then I grab my running clothes. Sniff. Yeah, I can get another run out of these. I hurriedly put them on in the chilly room, warming my dark flesh which prickles with goosebumps. Damien keeps the house so cold, and, although I really like that keeping the thermostat low saves money, I hate that any time I turn it up he teases "this is

Canada, it is cold, put on a sweater" as if I just arrived from Africa last week.

I should really make the bed.

Fuck the bed. Mr. Perfect can make the bed.

Pee. From the toilet I can see the light shining from beneath the door of Damien's office. I can hear the rhythmic click, click, click of the keyboard. Exactly as it was last night when I went to bed. Exactly as it was yesterday morning when I went for my run.

I don't want to think about how lonely that makes me feel. I much preferred the feeling in my dream.

I'd like to peek in on my sleeping boys, but if they wake up now it will ruin my run, so I resist the urge to creep in and kiss their sweet little dreaming faces.

Shoes on. Out the door. I run down the eight flights of stairs to the lobby and out into the crisp fall morning.

I run down the hill today. Some days, when I'm really angry and want to punish myself, I run up the hill. But today I'm thinking that I want to run along the river and watch the sun rise from behind the autumn colours. That seems therapeutic.

I am aware that I am trying to run away from my problems, but how else does a person begin to cope with the monumental bullshit that has been dumped on me?

"Two years." The oncologist's voice still rings in my ears, even two weeks later. How the fuck does someone even begin to deal with that?

I run harder.

6:00 am

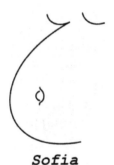

Sofia

How long have I been watching this spider crawl across my bedroom ceiling? What time is it?

It is dark outside. The hall light shines brightly enough through my open door that it illuminates the small black spider clearly as it scurries back and forth above me, trailing his web from the curtain to the wall and back again.

Are all the lights on? Is the door locked? Is it swinging wide open on its hinges? When was the last time I was out there?

Across the hall is an empty crib.

Without even thinking about it, I reach for the lighter and the half-smoked joint in the ashtray on the bedside table.

My breasts are getting hard with milk.

I smoke the rest of the joint, each inhale is like a breath of relief as my mind numbs and I return to watching the spider, my thoughts blissfully silent.

6:10 am

Maja

"Get up get up get up get up get up get up get up" Eloise chants softly in my ear. She knows better than to wake Nate, but I am fair game.

"Shhhh" I say anyway.

I open my eyes. It is still dark, but I can see Elle's long little face and blue eyes just inches from my face. I feel like I only fell asleep twenty minutes ago. My feet still hurt. My back hurts. I am not supposed to sleep on my back, but I always end up there.

Fuck this.

Here we go again.

With a deep breath I roll to my side and I feel the weight of the baby within me shift, stretching skin and muscles, pressing ribs and pelvis. I sit up slowly and gently rise from the bed.

Elle is immediately hanging off my hand and wrapping her legs around my leg. I try to shake her off quietly, but she is not budging.

Oh My Fucking God this child.

I grab my robe and slippers and creep out into the hallway, pulling the door shut behind me.

8

I remember a time when Nate was the morning person and I was the one who couldn't get out of bed.

But he drinks a lot more now.

Understatement of the year. I can see the pile of empty beer cans on the kitchen counter from here.

With Eloise still hanging from my leg, I pull Claire's door closed almost tight. She might sleep for another hour if I can keep Elle from waking her up.

Down the half-flight of stairs to the kitchen, still dragging my five year old on my leg. Now she's telling me, in a whisper thank God, about her dream about a unicorn and a dinosaur and the northern lights and something about a butterfly with a tiara.

Fuck this kid is heavy. It isn't enough to be carrying a baby in my belly, I have to drag this fucking fifty pound monster of a child around first thing in the morning. I feel a scream rising in my throat: get off me!!!!!!!! But I swallow it down. No yelling. I will not yell today.

At least she is being quiet.

Way to think positively, Maja. Keep that up.

Once we are in the kitchen Elle finally unlatches herself from me and speaks at a normal volume: "Can I watch *My Little Pony*?" Ugh, fucking *My Little Pony*.

I gesture to a pile of cardboard and ribbons on the living room floor, "What about your crafty thingy that you were making?"

This kitchen counter was cleared when I went to bed. Now there are beer cans, five empty glasses, plates, a frying pan, the remains of several meals... Fucking slob. Fucking drunk slob.

Eloise looks dissatisfied, "It was supposed to be a castle but the glue wouldn't hold the q-tips. Can I use the glue gun?"

I start with throwing the half-eaten egg sandwich, bowlful of soggy cereal and the pizza crusts in the garbage. "Sorry Peanut, I don't want you to use the glue gun. If..."

"Get me the glue gun!" Her face contorts into an angry scowl. She is so quick to anger.

"Dude, if you let me finish." Keep it light. What is that saying? Be the calm in their storm.

"Get me the glue gun!" Asshole.

I never swore until I had kids.

"Eloise, please take a breath and try talking to me like a person, not your servant." Maybe that was too harsh.

The bottom lip comes out. That means she'll be pissed at me all morning. Sigh. Let it go. "Elle, can I have a cuddle? I'm sad and I could use some love." She smiles and comes running to me. We soften into each others arms. Phew. Disaster averted. "I think the baby could use a cuddle too." Eloise loves the baby. She's so excited about a new sibling, and nine months is a lifetime when you are five years old. She kisses my round belly. "Ok, what I was going to say before you flipped out on me, was that I will get the glue gun out after breakfast and I can teach you how to do it. BUT you can't use it alone, ok? I have to be there."

"Yes, Mumma!" she smiles happily at the successful negotiation.

"Now, what would you like for breakfast?"

"I want to watch *My Little Pony*."

Ugh, fucking *My Little Pony*! Breathe. I will not yell today. "Sure, whatever." I go back to the mess in the kitchen and Elle settles down in the cool blue glow of the TV.

7:20 am

Alisha

The babies are giggling in their bed. The birds are singing outside my window, and the sun is creeping across the wall toward me.

I must have fallen asleep in Kai's room. My book is still open in front of me, and there's an empty box of crackers at the foot of the bed.

The last I remember it was five am, so I maybe got seven hours total? That is good enough!

The twins' giggles had started quietly but quickly rose in both volume and pitch: first Ari, then Hana, then Ari.

I wonder what they are giggling about?

Hana snorts and Ari squeals with laughter.

What a great sound to wake up to.

But I need to get my ass moving. Ruby is supposed be here in ten minutes, Chuckie and Zach will be here in a half hour, and I need to shower and get dressed and get breakfast for the twins and I...

Oh, shit! I should reply to Maja about today.

Maja

Thursday, 8:22 pm
Hey! Are you guys still up for the park
tomorrow?

Alisha

Today, 7:20 am
Yes! Sorry I didn't reply sooner. I'm a mess!

Today, 7:20 am
I have the screamy baby today, though, so just
a short one.

My whole body groans as I get out of bed. I've been pushing too hard and not taking care of myself and it is really starting to pile up. Everything hurts. But there's no time for stretches again today. Looks like I keep pushing through.

On the way to the bathroom I pass the cat in the hall. She flirts with me as if she has no idea that she's the jerk responsible for me losing two precious hours of sleep. "You are on my shit list, cat." I whisper and point an accusing finger at her innocent face.

Straight into the shower. My hair isn't even wet before little hands start to pull at the curtain. God forbid I get one shower alone. Isaac can be in here for hours without anyone whipping open the curtains and asking awkward questions about his genitalia. Me? Ten seconds max. I manage to pin the plastic liner to the tub with my foot so that no water escapes onto the floor.

"Mama! Mama!" Hana beams from under the fabric.

"Mama! Mama!" Ari appears beside her, two pairs of dimpled cheeks and glittering eyes. To me they look so similar, with their round faces, broad noses and wide-set eyes, but everyone else only sees that Hana has brown skin and black hair like her daddy and Ari has pale skin and blonde hair like his mommy and they gush about how cute it is that we made one of each of us. And every person says it as if they are the first to notice, and it is all I can do to force a smile.

"Hey babies! Do you want to go ask Daddy to get you some Cheerios?" Both two-year-olds grin even wider and, dropping the shower curtain back in place, they toddle off to find daddy, shouting "tsee-oohs, tsee-oohs".

Sweet. That doesn't usually work so easily. They're in a good mood today. Let's ride that wave straight through till bedtime.

Thump. Ari fell. I know it is Ari because it always is. But he's back on his feet without a peep and races off after his sister.

Seven hours of sleep, showering alone, and its FRIDAY! It's going to be a good day. Bring it on!

7:22 am

Andrea

Showered, dressed, hair, make-up, oats on the stove, tea in hand, newspaper spread out before me, kids are still in bed. I should feel good. I've checked all the boxes for a good morning. Yeah, my run wasn't nearly as uplifting as I'd hoped. Mainly because it was still pitch black out when I got home, so I didn't get my colourful autumn sunrise. Otherwise it has been a smooth morning. Yet I feel twitchy: I don't want to sit down. I don't want to read the paper. It is just full of shitty news about shitty people doing shitty things, and I already have enough shit of my own.

There's that light shining out from under Damien's door. I feel rage bubbling up within me.... Why is he even here?

Fuck it, I'm waking the kids up.

The boys share a room. Six year old Wallace on the top bunk and three year old Zachary on the bottom. When we converted this room from a guest bedroom I painted the walls a soft grey colour, almost white, and little by little I've decorated the walls with my own illustrations of the bedtime stories that I've been making up since Wallace was small. It makes this my favourite room in the condo.

Actually, it is the only room that I don't hate.

"Wallace" kiss and a shake, "Zach" kiss and a shake, "time to get up boys."

They both wiggle and blink.

I turn on the light right away. I should wait until the boys are a bit more awake, but I just don't have the patience for that today.

Just plow straight ahead and don't stop to look or pause to think. That seems to be my default head-space these days.

Thankfully I haven't set them off with my abrupt awakening, and two sleepy, happy little pink faces smile at me.

They look so much like their father. Which kills me. I mean, he's handsome and all that, sure, but I love my dark skin, a deep shade of black that isn't common in North America, and I would have loved to have shared it with them. Often when I go out with the boys, people assume I'm Damien's nanny, which is super ironic considering how I do ALL of the parenting and then he gets all of the credit. But I do recognize the benefits of looking like their dad: they won't stand out the way I did, which gave me such misery when I was young. The kids on the playground won't stare at them and ask stupid questions, their teachers will cut them more slack, and I won't have to talk to them about being careful with the police and other authority figures. So, as fucked up as it is, it means an easier life for them, really. But I also love who I am, and I draw a lot of strength and pride from my blackness, so I have a lot of conflict over it.

Although, they've both got awesome little afros. I'll have to be content with that.

I'm digging in the drawers below the bunks: "Wallace, love, do you want to wear blue or grey pants?" I need to buy more long pants now that it is getting cooler.

"Mom, do tsunamis happen on lakes?" Wallace asks.

"Blue or grey, Pickle?"

Rubbing his eyes, "Blue."

"Do you think tsunamis happen on lakes?" I've taken to replying to all of his questions with a question since I realized that most of the time he already knows the answer, and when he doesn't he is pretty good at thinking it through and answering himself. This way, I don't have to use my brain but he does: win-win all around. Blue pants with his white polo shirt, and white socks.

"Weeeellllll...." Wallace's face scrunches up when he's thinking. It is adorable. "I guess it would depend on if the lake is on a fault line, because a tsunami is caused by an earthquake, and earthquakes only happen on fault lines."

"Nice thinking. I'll bet you're right. OK, Zachary, blue or black pants?" Zach has plenty of hand-me-downs from Wallace, but they're all so worn-through from daycare.

"Mommy I want an aquarimum so I can bring home a fog."

"Blue or black, Bean?"

"Chuck and I taught a fog but Lish said that we had to put him back tetause we had nowhere for him to wive. But we tould teep him if we had an aquarimum."

"Blue or black, Bean?"

"Do I have anyfing gween? Chuck awways wears tuff with tictures on it, like *Lunasaurs* and *Nija Tunnles*. I want fog pants."

Chuck's parents do all of their shopping at Walmart, Bean.

"I have a green shirt with black pants?" I offer. Of course there's nothing wrong with shopping at Walmart, I just don't want my kids to be walking advertisements for Disney.

"It's a deo!" Zach jumps out of bed and throws some fake punches at his brother, who does a fake fall to the ground, complete with over-dramatic death face.

These kids crack me up. But Zach is about to dive on top of his brother and that will just descend into wrestling and I can't have that shit. They'll never come back down from that high.

I catch Zach mid-air and say, "But no, you can't have a pet frog here. You'll have to talk Alisha into it. She loves that sort of thing." They have a dog, a cat, whatever that thing in the basement is – a rabbit? gerbil? She's much better at embracing the natural world than I am. The best I can do is not scream and run away from whatever critter Zach picks up. Wallace couldn't care less about nature, but Zach has enough enthusiasm for the both of them.

Pj's off, with Zach dancing around while I cram his wiggling arms into his shirtsleeves. He has never so much as lifted a finger to dress himself in his whole three years, whereas Wallace insisted upon dressing himself when he was one and a half, long before he had the fine motor skills to pull it off. I honestly prefer Zach's way – waiting for Wallace to put on pants required tremendous patience, something I rarely have.

"Then we'w have to get Lish an aquarimum." Zach reasons. His attention pivots again, toward the bed and his stuffed penguin and seal.

It would, however, be really nice if Zach paid attention

even just a little bit, while I dressed him. I'm trying to change his diaper while he leans against the bed. Trying to put his pants on when he won't lift his feet. Trying to put his shirt on when he won't let go of his toys. I talk him through it but he's giving me nothing. Alisha once told me that kids just have a really, really long response time and I need to be patient, but today I feel like that response time is about five minutes.

Wallace has been dressed for a while now and is reading this chapter book that he couldn't put down last night, and Zach is clearly looking to stir shit up with him because he keeps throwing his stuffies toward his brother. Luckily Zach is a lousy throw, and I can head it off before it gets out of hand: "OK, oats are ready boys. We need to get a move on: I want to stop at Sofia's on the way." Wallace's face doesn't leave his book. Fight averted.

"Because her baby died?" Zach asks, turning his cherub face toward me.

The way he says it so bluntly is unsettling, but I manage a sad smile and say, "Yes, because her baby died. And she's very sad. And we always help our friends when they're sad." I can feel the pain rising up in my chest but I push it down and usher the boys to the kitchen table.

Don't stop to think about how much life sucks, just keep moving forward.

7:28 am

Maja

I'm still staring at my phone. I've been staring at it for ... too long. Just mindlessly scrolling through the pictures and news articles. Why am I even on my phone right now? I was supposed to be cleaning the kitchen, but somehow I'm sitting on my ass and this damn thing is in my hand again.

Oh, right. Lish sent me a message.

Alisha

Today, 7:20 am
Yes! Sorry I didn't reply sooner. I'm a mess!

Today, 7:20 am
I have the screamy baby today, though, so just a short one.

"MOM" Elle is shouting from her spot in front of the TV.

Maja

Today, 7:28 am
Yeah, that's ok with me!

"MOM!

Maja

Today, 7:28 am
George's or Oxbow Park?

"MOM MOM MOM MOM MOM!"

"Yes, Peanut?" I toss the phone on the table and re-assess the kitchen mess. I cleaned half of it, and then ignored the rest while I checked Twifagram, and got lost down that hole. Today the stink is about teachers getting laid off and schools getting shittier, about powerful men getting away with whatever they want, and about giant islands of garbage floating in the ocean, and about flooding in the Philippines that has killed 1000s – only about 100 kilometers away from my mom's family's town.

"Can I have waffles?"

"Yes, but not in front of the TV."

"Why noooooooooot." Oh that whiney voice just makes me cringe.

"Because waffles are messy and because I like to eat breakfast together because I love your face." I smile at her. She is still so sweet and young but she's in a grump this week and everything she says is a demand, and I feel like I'm her slave. And I'm in a grump this week too, so it takes epic effort to not take everything she says personally. I don't know who was in a grump first, but we just feed off each other's anger until we explode.

I'll do better today, I swear.

And I'm so tired. My back hurts. My pelvis hurts. And I feel like I never sleep anymore. I'm so done with being pregnant.

And there's still seven more weeks to go.

And once the baby comes, I'll be even more tired. It will only get worse.

"OK," Eloise brings her counter-offer, "I'll eat in the kitchen but I want maple syrup."

"I'm ok with that as long as you eat some berries too."

"I'm ok with that." Elle smiles proudly. I know that she doesn't want to be a rude little asshole with me. It just takes a lot of practice. Years, apparently. Heck, her dad is 30 and he still hasn't managed it.

"Deal." I look in the freezer and see an empty box of waffles. There were definitely two in here yesterday.

Did that asshole eat the last two waffles and then put the empty box back?

I shuffle around the freezer drawer in case they fell out of the box. "Crap. Bad news, Elle." She knows without me saying another word, and I can see the universe crumbling before her eyes. "Hold on, girl! Don't freak out..."

"But I want waaaaaaaffles...." The pitch of her voice so

shrill that she could give Mariah Carey some real competition.

Fucking drunk Nate.

"Elle, breathe. Breathe. I'm not in a rush today, I don't mind making some waffles."

Her tear-stained face lights up with hope. Oh, such big emotions in that little body. She gets so swept away by them. "You can make waffles?" as if I have magic powers. HA! Thank God someone gave me a waffle maker for a wedding gift. It is up above the cupboards covered in dust: let's hope it works!

"Do you want to help me?"

"YES!"

"OK, grab a chair." Except the table is covered with as much crap as the counter.

Shit I wish this kitchen was cleaner.

It would be if I hadn't been sucked down the wormhole of Twifagram memes and politics.

Or if my husband wasn't a fucking pig.

I pick up his laptop, a pile of papers, his dirty socks, a pair of jeans, his coat, and with my arms loaded I head toward his office in the basement, but I trip on his shoes at the top of the stairs and nearly go crashing down, saved only by dropping the coat and grabbing the railing. In my mind I envision the fall that could have been... the baby...

For a moment my mind flashes to our darling Sofia and her baby.

And then back to Nate.

Fucking oblivious slob. It isn't enough that you don't help me, you have to make everything harder, too?

I stomp down the stairs, and I throw his things on the floor just inside the door. My best defense is a passive-aggressive one, sadly. And he probably won't even notice.

He'll just assume that he put it there and won't even know that I'm pissed at him or that he nearly killed me. Like that time that I dumped all of his beer down the sink in a fit of rage, and he just assumed he drank it.

Deep breath. Calm down. Deep breath. I'm not going to lose my temper today.

As I'm returning from the basement I hear "Mama?" from the upstairs hallway. There is Claire in her *Lunasaurs* pj's, rubbing her eyes. She's so cute. Her face is round and her features soft and her brown eyes are huge. I can see the Filipino features in both of my girls, but most people can't. My parents hate that I married a white man but they love that my kids can pass for white. I am so disgusted with them for this, and I wish they'd stop saying it in front of the girls before they start to hate themselves.

"Good morning Bunny! Did you have a good sleep?"

She smiles at me from behind her soother, "Hand!" she raises her hand for me to hold while she bump, bump, bumps down the stairs on her butt.

"Elle and I are making waffles, do you want to help?"

"Yeah." The-two-year old has such a completely different personality than her sister. Where Elle is easy to panic, Claire is calm. Where Elle is shy, Claire is quick to stand up for herself. Where Elle is talking all the time, Claire is quiet but watching and thinking. Where Elle needs me like she needs air, Claire couldn't care less who is taking care of her as long as there are goldfish crackers available.

In the kitchen, I help Claire onto a chair beside her sister, and grab a big bowl and a measuring cup and a spoon for them to entertain themselves while I Google "easy waffles". Immediately Claire screams because Elle has taken all the dishes.

"Elle, what can Claire play with?" Elle ponders this question and reluctantly hands her sister the spoon.

I pick a recipe that looks easy and begin to gather the ingredients. Claire is screaming because she dropped her spoon. Elle is banging the dishes together like a drum. Claire is opening the flour and it puffs up all over the place. Elle is shouting because Claire has taken her measuring cup. I get another bowl, measuring cup, and spoon. Claire is shouting "Mama! Mama!" because she dropped her spoon again. Elle is loudly speaking every thought that passes through her mind. Clanking dishes, screaming Claire, chattering Elle. My head is spinning and it's only... 7:29.

Only thirteen hours to go.

The baby in my belly kicks me in the ribs so hard that I flinch.

Nate will be late for work again. He refuses to set an alarm, and if I wake him up he gets pissed, but if he's late for work he gets pissed.

Fuck him, I'm not his mother.

My phone beeps.

Alisha

Today, 7:30 am
Let's do Oxbow. It is less work. I can make
9:30?

Maja

Today, 7:30 am
Sounds good.

I put down the phone, but then pick it up again and add:

Today, 7:31 am
I see you are stirring up shit on Twifagram
again.

I set down the phone to grab the eggs from Elle before she can drop the whole box on the floor.

"Ok, the first ingredient is three eggs."

"Can I crack the eggs, Mamma?"

"What if I give you the whisk and you can mix the eggs, but I do the cracking? Remember the muffins with eggshells in them?"

She laughs, "Yeah, they were crunchy!"

But of course Claire wants the whisk and starts screaming. "Claire, you can put in the milk." I hand her the measuring cup.

"I want to pour the milk!" Elle yells and rips the measuring cup out of Claire's hands, and Claire bursts into tears, collapsing on her chair and nearly falling to the floor, and now she's screaming even louder from fear.

And I'm going to have three of these? Fucking hell.

7:34 am

Alisha

Still wet from my shower, towel around my head, I check my phone.

Isn't that a sign of an addiction? That I'll stand here dripping wet and freezing cold while I check out how many messages I've got?

I shouldn't be so hard on myself. I could have a message from one of my clients.

I don't. But I could.

Maja

Today, 7:28 am
I see you are stirring up shit on Twifagram again.

Oh, right. I forgot about that. I was struggling to concentrate on the book I was reading last night with all sorts of thoughts swirling around in my head about political bullshit – which I really should avoid in the evenings because it always keeps me awake – so I put a rant on Twifagram.

Alisha

I personally know 3 women who have been raped. I know 2 men who are rapists. I know 3 women whose lives have been destroyed by rape. I don't know any men whose lives have been destroyed by a rape accusation. I #BelieveWomen

15 Likes   7 Comments

Alisha

I have no doubt that I know more victims of rape who haven't confided in me, and more perpetrators who've just continued to get away with it and live among us smug and dangerous

René

It is so infuriating. I always knew that rape culture was a problem, but I can't believe how many men don't know it. How many actively deny it. It is terrifying.

Maria

Things are changing, but not fast enough!

Ellen

Well said!

Kristy

Well said! #BelieveWomen

Heather

I know 4 women who've been raped. I used to
know 2 rapists. I've never known any men
falsely accused of rape. I #BelieveWomen.

Jake

I know 3 men whove been falsely accused of
rape. 1 of them lost his job. I dont know any
women whove been raped and I dont know any
men whove committed rape. So should I write
#believemen?

Oh, for fuck sake, Jake. Always so righteous, aren't you?

I throw the phone down on the bed in anger, and
furiously towel myself off. I can feel the blood rushing
to my cheeks and it triggers a hot flash, tingling warmth
rushes to the surface from my head to my feet, and
suddenly I'm thankful that I'm naked.

But yes, Jake, you do know a woman who has been
raped. And a rapist. Mutual friends from our Master's
program. Jake just doesn't know that the guy was a creep
because he wasn't warned to stay away from him like all of

the girls were. I'll bet Jake thinks that guy is just a good old boy , incapable of rape.

Jake was always an asshole, even in school. One of those devil's advocate types who argued with the prof about everything. We used to joke that he'd be that anthropologist lecturing his subjects on how wrong their traditions are.

But I'm running super late, so telling him off will have to wait until later.

God, I should know better than to post shit on Twifagram. It always gets me so riled up.

I can see myself in the mirror as I pick out my clothes. This body that has been through the wringer more than a few times: 34 inches of scars – Isaac and I measured them once. The oldest are the twelve inch and four inch scars from the spinal fusion that I had when I was fourteen to repair my scoliosis. They are now faded to a pale pink. I once convinced Isaac's ten year old nephew in New Zealand that they were from a polar bear attack. Ha! Across my chest are two diagonal five inch gashes, one for each mastectomy. It is like my chest has angry eyebrows where my boobs should be. The brightest and newest scar (and sloppiest, big thanks to the student OB who was working that day and who apparently needs sewing lessons) is the five inches from the c-section. My two lovely babies came out of that hole, followed shortly afterward by my uterus, cervix, fallopian tubes and ovaries. And then I have a variety of little scars from drainage tubes and mole removals, plus one small burn scar on my arm from a bread-making incident in my waitressing days. But my favourite scar is a really cool spiral mark from a jellyfish tentacle that I got in New Zealand when Isaac took me to meet his parents for the first time. That scar is fading faster than I'd like (of all the scars, couldn't that one be bright red?). Besides the scars, there's the deformed rib cage from scoliosis, all the more noticeable without breasts to hide behind, saggy stretch-marked belly, butt and thighs from carrying the twins.... To think, my body was once as smooth and flawless as Hana's.

I know I'm supposed to have body image issues. At least that is what the doctors kept saying while trying to talk me into having breast reconstruction surgery. But I really don't have any strong feelings about how it looks. It looks like it has overcome some really epic challenges, that's how it looks. Being sexy isn't really a high priority at this point. Being alive. Juggling the responsibilities of children, a household, and a business. Those are important things. Don't get me wrong, I hate my body, but I hate it because it keeps trying to kill me, not because it isn't pretty. Pretty is a luxury that I don't really have the time or energy for.

Moisturizer, deodorant, yoga pants, *My Little Pony* t-shirt (since we're seeing Eloise today, I'll wear her favourite), pony tail.

That is the extent of my beauty regimen. Done. 7:38. Boom. I've only been out of bed for eighteen minutes.

But it is a good thing Ruby's dad is running late again. He's been coming for three weeks and has never made 7:30 once.

In the kitchen the twins are in their highchairs eating dry Cheerios. No dairy. No fruit. No protein. I'm guessing Isaac forgot to give them their vitamins too. But I won't say anything because I'm working really hard on this positive reinforcement thing: if he feels better he'll do better, and he won't feel better if I'm always telling him how many mistakes he makes. It works for the kids, surely it will work on a 42 year-old man! HA! I wonder if I can take the same approach with potty training and table manners....

Where is Isaac, anyway? I'm glad we're not overly paranoid about our kids choking to death and hover over them while they are eating or anything like that...

"Hey you two cute little monkeys!!"

"Tsee-ohs in my mouth, mommy!" Hana is pointing out the obvious, sputtering wet Cheerio bits across her pj top. No bib. That's ok. He got out of bed and fed them so I could shower in peace, the details are not important.

"Do you want some banana too?"

"Bana! Bana!" they shout in unison. Then giggle. Hana bobs her head back and forth and Ari copies her. Then they laugh again.

Little comedy duo. They are so happy all of the time. If I could have just a fraction of their joy...

Everybody would be suspicious. Nobody trusts a joyful adult. Ha!

I give them each a half banana and then unlock the back door before getting my own breakfast: Raisin Bran, since I'm constipated again.

Perfect timing, of course: just as I sit down to eat, the back door opens.

"Good morning" I call out to Ruby and her dad. He looks frustrated and overwhelmed, as usual. Juggling her bag and coat and shoes in one hand and the bucket car seat in the other. The one year old is crying already. Three weeks of this routine and she knows exactly what it is all about and she's not getting any less unhappy about it. Apparently nobody told her that kids should acclimate to daycare after one week.

"There's milk in the bag," he mumbles without so much

as a hello, "I've gotta run. Buh-bye Ruby." He sets the car seat on the kitchen floor and is out the door.

Brilliant.

"Bana, bana!" the twins are shouting, throwing their cheerios on the floor. Ruby is having a full-blown panic attack in her car seat, her face practically blue from screaming, and now the dog is barking to go out.

Where the fuck is Isaac?

Quickly, since I've done it a hundred times before, I grab the cloth baby carrier from the hook by the door where I left it last night, strap it around my waist, snap open the buckles of Ruby's car seat, lift her onto my hip and then, balancing the screaming baby carefully, I rotate the whole baby carrier around to my back, and fasten the clips that keep her in place. Then I grab another banana, half to each twin, and call Sheba, the dog, to clean the Cheerios off the floor, all the while bouncing gently to calm the tearful Ruby.

Silence. Blessed silence.

Mom win.

I head down the hall to see if I can find Isaac. He's not in our bedroom but the door to Kai's room is closed. I peek inside and see an Isaac-shaped lump in the daybed that I just made this morning.

If you would just go to bed at a reasonable hour...

"Isaac, the dog is waiting for you."

Grumble, grumble, groan from the bed.

I'm in bed at 9:30 every night and spend half the night getting woken up by you laughing at the TV until one or two in the morning, and then you get to sleep in while I juggle the morning routine. And you wonder why I start every day pissed off...

But I don't have time for that. And I'm trying to be

positive, so I have to let it go. "And don't forget that you are supposed to pick Kai up from his mom's on your way home from work tonight." He groans again and I shut the door, pretty certain that he will forget. Then Kai will be hurt and Melanie will be pissed and our fragile peace will be shattered.

But there's not much I can do about it.

Back in the kitchen, I eat my breakfast while dancing to keep Ruby from crying. I guess my Twifagram fight will have to wait until afternoon nap. I'm not even half finished my cereal when Chuck and his mom pull into the driveway.

Ah, well. I hate Raisin Bran anyway. And pooping is totally overrated. Move over pumpkin spice: constipation is the new fall trend.

Bowl in the sink, wet cloth to quickly wipe the twins' banana fingers, out of the high chairs and I lead them downstairs to the daycare in the basement singing "Chuck is here" all the way. Thank God they're feeling cooperative today. Some days they get that mischievous look on their faces and play the "run away" game. That is one of my least favourite games. It is right up there with "chocolate or poo?" and "does this fit in my mouth?"

A minute later Chuck comes blustering down the stairs. Almost four years old and he's only slightly less clumsy than he was as a toddler. Chuck has always been huge. He was already in size six diapers when he was one. And with his sandy hair and blue eyes he looks like a mini all-American high school football player. He's a good-natured little dude, and easy to take care of, and his parents always respect my rules and pay on time. But, like Ruby's dad, they never ask about how he is doing, what he's been up to all day, or where he's at emotionally when they pick him up. Instead of excitedly greeting their children at the end of a long day apart, they are distracted, impatient, and tired. Their kids are just one more item on a busy to-do list, which makes me so sad. I don't think they are bad parents: I know that they love their kids, and they are working their asses off. I just regret that we live in a world where parents have to spend so much time providing for their kids that they don't have time to enjoy them.

I guess I'm fortunate there. Having cancer is one way to put it all into perspective: I quit a pretty great job as a Professor at the university to run a daycare so that I could be with my kids. But it meant a $50,000 pay cut, and abandoning fifteen years worth of research, teaching and publishing, and I understand that most people don't want to go that far.

It also means that we're back to struggling to pay our bills again, like we were when I was a student. Which Isaac is particularly bitter about.

But no regrets here.

Well, maybe some regrets, I think as Ruby begins to scream again.

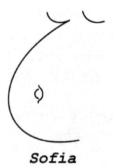

Sofia

Holy fuck my tits hurt. They are big and hard with bulging lumps where the glands are so full of milk that they threaten to block up. I have to hold them in each hand tenderly when I sit up in bed, and my shirt is soaked through on both sides. Where the fuck did I put the pump? The black bag blends in perfectly with the piles of dirty laundry and discarded dishes and – oh that's a pile of sheets stained with postpartum blood that I think I'll just throw out. I'd have an easier time if I opened the curtains, but I can see bright sunlight out there so there's really no chance of me doing that.

There's the breast pump. Under the towel, still wet and sticky from the milk that I spilled last night. Yesterday. Two days ago. This morning.

I scurry across the room, grab the pump, and rush back into bed with the damp pump bag that reeks of sour milk. Once back in bed I can breathe again, as if the world beyond the safety of my mattress were under water.

The pump is a loaner from Drae, the best pump on the market, she said.

What a waste, giving it to me.

I find it difficult to get a seal between the hard plastic breast pump and my hard, lumpy breast, and every bit of pressure sends sharp, stabbing pain through my breasts like an electrical current, but eventually I get the left side pumping, and then the right, and after some wincing and groaning, the pain eases a bit.

Wheeze, wheeze, suck, suck, goes the pump.

I wonder what real breastfeeding feels like. I wanted that so badly.

How can a heart so empty hurt so much?

The plastic bottles dangling from the pumps fill quickly. I don't pump too much because I don't want to increase my supply, but I also don't want it to dry up. I had decided to donate my milk – it would be nice to turn my pain into someone else's solution, but so far all I have is a week's worth of cannabis infused milk in my freezer that is no good to anyone.

I should just pour it all down the sink. But I can't. It is his milk. I made it for him.

My body doesn't know that he's dead.

I need to roll another joint. A joint so fat and so strong that I sleep all day.

I pry the pumps from my breasts carefully so I don't spill the milk everywhere. Again. I turn the machine off, remove the little bottles from the pumps, set them gently on the bedside table, and sink back into the pillow, a mess of pumps and pipes and boobs.

That is it. That is all I have for today. I'm not moving again unless the house is burning down. And maybe not even then.

I wish the joint would roll itself. Or I could just eat it. All of it at once. Just to numb this pain.

There's an empty crib across the hall. Crisply folded onesies in the drawers. Stacks of perfect newborn-size diapers on the changing table. A diaper genie that smells of new plastic.

The doorbell rings. I don't know how long I've been lying here. I cannot move, even if I wanted to. A knock. A key in the door. If it is Colin I cannot move. If it isn't... well I still can't move.

"Sofia?" it was Drae. "I'm coming in even if you don't want me!" I can hear her designer heels clicking on my tile floor, down the hall. "Colin's truck isn't here so I'm just going to walk straight into your bedroom." And she did. "Shit, Sofia, please tell me that you are still breathing."

When he wasn't breathing.

"I'm still breathing." A whisper is all that I can manage. It has been so long since I used my voice for anything except crying that it forgot how to work. But I sit up and straighten my damp shirt and bedsheets, as if I could hide how much I'm falling apart right now.

Drae is standing in the doorway, a vision of fall fashion perfection, coffee in one hand and a bag of take-out food in the other. She looks as out of place in the threshold to my room as she would in a WWI trench.

"Oh, honey. This place is fucking disgusting. Where is your self-respect?" she says in the most lovingly sarcastic tone. I do intend to laugh, but instead I exhale through my nose like a horse.

Drae ventures into the dark room, stepping strategically around some clothes and garbage and abandoned dishes. She clears some space on the dresser to set down the take-out bag and goes straight to the window, throwing the curtains open like someone banishing a vampire. I feel myself draw back as if the sun itself was causing my agony.

"Don't get me wrong, Sofia," Drae carries on, "you can be as tragic and broken as you need to be, but I'm not going to let you sit in the dark all day, eating nothing but tears and pain. I brought you coffee and breakfast. Eat." She puts the take-out food in front of me and the coffee on the bedside table, removing the two bottles of breast milk: "Is this fresh?" I nod my head, and she disappears into the kitchen with them. While she's gone I move the take-out food to the side.

From the kitchen: "Your sister told me that everyone went home on Tuesday and that you and Colin seemed to be holding it all together." She came back into the room, "But there is zero edible food in your fridge and your bedroom looks like a college dorm, so I'm thinking she was mistaken about your stability. Where is Colin, anyway? Surely he's not back to work already?"

Lump in my throat. "He left."

Drae's face goes cold. "What the fuck do you mean, he left? When?" Drae is one of those women who never got the memo about being passive and amenable. She is a good person to have on your side during a fight.

"I don't know when. Yesterday? The day before? He said it was too much and he left." 'I can't deal with this,' he said. *And you think I can?* But he'd rather just pretend none of it ever happened. I'll bet he's even at work today.

"That is the dumbest fucking thing I have ever heard in my life. Too much? What is too much? Supporting the love of his life through the loss of a child? Or doing the laundry and dishes while she mourns alone? Where is he? I'll slap him straight."

Yes, that is exactly the mama bear response I expected from her. My heart warms up just a bit. Like a tiny spark in a giant empty cavern.

But I'll never be happy again because my baby is dead. And my husband is gone. And I'm alone.

I don't know what to say to Drae.

"Do you want a hug?" she asks.

"Drae, you hate hugging." My gravelly voice is hard to hear. "But thank you for offering. It means a lot."

Drae sits on the edge of the bed and looks at me with a mix of heartbreak and pity. This is the look that other mothers give me now. The 'I can't even imagine how much this hurts, I'm going to hug my kids extra hard' look. "The boys are in the car so I can't stay, but I'm coming back after work with dinner, since the only food in your fridge looks like it will give you salmonella. Can I bring you anything else?"

Not what I really need.

"I think I'm out of toilet paper." I shrug.

"Done. Oh, and where the hell is your phone? I texted you like four times and you didn't reply to any of them."

"Bathroom? Kitchen? It's probably dead." I don't think I've used it since yesterday when I gave up on Colin calling. Drae looks around the room a bit, and then disappears through the door, returning a few minutes later.

"Bathroom." She smiles and plugs the phone into the charger beside my bed.

"Now you need to reply to my messages so I know you are still breathing. That is all you need to do for now, keep breathing. I'll take care of the rest, ok?"

Even that seems like such a monumental task. Tears well up in my eyes.

Drae sighs. "I can take the day off. You shouldn't be alone."

I'm such a mess. "I really would like to be alone." I

whisper, "I promise I won't off myself today. At least not until you come back with dinner."

"I guess I'll have to be satisfied with that for now. I feel like an asshole leaving you alone like this, but you know how people are about leaving kids in cars. I don't want to get lynched by your neighbours."

I laugh. How can I laugh when my baby is dead?

"Go. I'm ok. Thanks for the food."

And she goes. Drae is never one to equivocate.

And I'm alone.

And the joint still needs to be rolled.

And the crib is still empty.

8:20 am

Alisha

Sheba is upstairs barking her face off so I know Drae is here with Zach. You'd think the house was being swarmed by zombies, but no, it is just a good friend who is literally here EVERY DAY.

I'm in the midst of wrestling with Ari over a diaper change. It isn't enough that he poops at least three times a day, but like some sort of pint-sized asshole he has to wriggle and giggle and grab and squirm his way through every diaper change. I've tried stand-up diaper changes, so that he can watch TV or play with toys while I clean him, but it just makes his escape that much quicker, and suddenly I have poop on the couch, the walls, the toys, other kids, his mouth!... And there's no way in hell I'm using the changing table. It doesn't matter if you use the clip – lamest safety precaution in history – he'll launch himself off of that thing if you look away for even a second. Sometimes Hana will help him by threatening to throw something important in the toilet and then I have to choose between stopping Hana or holding down Ari. Now I have a sheet – an actual full-sized queen bed sheet that I lay down on the daycare floor, and I'll put my knee (yes my knee, don't judge!) on his chest to pin him down. And if I have the wet wipes already pulled out of the box before I even start, then I can get him clean enough that when he runs away without a diaper he doesn't get poo everywhere. Getting the diaper on before he runs away is some Gold Level Advanced parenting skill that I have not attained yet. Of course for three weeks I've been doing this with Ruby strapped to my back, crying and grabbing the flesh of my neck and my hair any time I pay attention to a kid who isn't her, so I've been prevented from really developing my technique to its full potential.

We were at the 'running away with a bare (clean!) ass while Lish has another hot flash' part of the process, when Drae and Zach come down the stairs into my basement daycare. They are both immaculately dressed, as always, which reminds me that my kids are still in their pj's. Again. Well, except for Ari who is bare-assed and gleeful.

"That one still crying non-stop?" she points at Ruby on my back, whose cries have reduced to a whimper now that the diaper change is over. Drae lifts Zach over the baby gate and he makes a beeline for the toy cars that are still lined up by colour, exactly how he left them last night.

"Yup, unless I hold her." I bounce instinctively to sooth her whimpering.

"And how is that working for you?" Drae hangs up Zach's stuff: top quality, brand name stuff. Drae values good quality things, no sweat-shop crap for her. I do too, but as I mentioned, I took a $50k pay cut, so it is hand-me-down sweatshop merch for us.

"Well, I had that migraine for eleven days. I think I've beat that now, but my insomnia is kicking off hard-core. Ruby's anxiety is more contagious than chicken pox."

Drae smiles sadly. "Oh, honey."

I change the subject: "How about you? How's work?" Drae should really be a children's author but instead she settled for an office job because someone needs to pay the bills while her husband chases his latest get-rich-quick scheme. I mean, I don't fault a guy for having dreams, but he's never contributed a penny in the seven years they've been married. Maybe it is time that he gets a job and Drae chases her dreams. She's probably the most talented out of all of us: her illustrations are incredible.

"Work is mind numbing. In an eight hour shift I probably spend six hours on Twifagram and two hours at the gym."

Ugh, Twifagram. I waste far too much of my life with that. And it is bad for my anxiety. Just knowing there are so many people in the world who are cruel, selfish, stupid and violent is bad enough, but thanks to social media I can hear all of their voices shouting over each other at once, and it makes me feel a bit sick.

"After six hours on Twifagram you'd need at least two hours at the gym, just to work out your rage."

Ari streaks past me with his bare ass, which I've been waiting for and I manage to catch him and wrestle him into a diaper while talking to Drae. Life skills that my PhD never prepared me for.

"OMG, I know, right? If I have to witness one more white dude mansplain rape I think I'll explode."

"But Drae, this is a man's CAREER we're talking about! A MAN'S CAREER! That is way more important than a woman's health and well-being or reputation or, you know, her life. I mean sure, rape is bad, but do there really need to be consequences?"

I joke because I can't really express how infuriating it all is. When I was fifteen I would have been horrified to be called a feminist – I thought we were all equal and feminism was irrelevant. I was so naive. Now I find myself getting angrier and angrier all the time as I see just how wrong I was: the world is still pretty fucking sexist, and a lot of people are perfectly ok with that. Of course my PhD started me down this road: I was looking at gender norms across several indigenous societies. That study taught me that a lot of the gender differences which I took for granted as biological were really born out of culture. But what really set me off was breast cancer and then becoming a mother, and suddenly it was like all of the lies I'd been told about myself, my body, my weakness, and my worth, just crumbled and I was reborn as some beautiful, powerful, furious creature.

I went from 'not feminist' to 'Angry Feminist' in four years.

Drae rolls her eyes. "Kill me. Twenty bucks says that he not only gets away with it, but he'll be running the country in two years." She finishes her coffee and I take it from her to toss into my garbage.

"I can believe that. Anything is possible in this broken world." It is no wonder everyone has depression.

Ari and Hana are now playing their favourite game – step off the couch and hope they don't break a leg. Drae looks horrified but I've seen them do it enough that it doesn't faze me anymore. "Are you serious? Your kids are insane. How are any of you still alive?"

"Ah, their bones are still mostly cartilage at this age. They pretty much bounce." I hope she knows that I'm joking.

Drae laughs: "My God, you have the patience of a saint."

People keep telling me that, but they don't know how often my patience runs out. Drae and Maja and I all pretend I'm the one who is the most successful at being the mom they want to be, but it isn't true. I actually think Drae is the best of us. She is the most patient. I don't think she's ever lost her temper so badly that she hit her kids, while I've hit Ari in anger more than once, and I know that Maja has hit Elle.... And when you consider that Drae had a pretty shitty role model in her narcissist mother, that makes it even more impressive.

I change the subject again, "Have you spoken to Sofia?" Drae and Sofia have always been close, even when we were all living together in our first year of university. As we came and went on our various adventures over the years, Drae and Sof were the glue that held us all together. Only in the past few years did Maja and I develop a similar bond, once we had children in common. So, as much as my heart aches for Sofia, I've really let Drae take the lead on how to support her through this.

"Yeah, I just came from there," Drae shakes her head sadly, "she's a mess. Colin left."

"What do you mean he left?" Colin is a man of few words and very shy. He and Sofia haven't even been together for two years, so none of us know him well at all. She met him on a dating app, and twelve months later they were married and pregnant. I don't think he's spoken more than a dozen words to me in that time. From the stories that Sofia tells it sounds like he was raised by a bunch of hillbillies, but has a heart of gold and tries really hard. I guess that is really the best that any woman can hope for: a man who tries hard. But if he's run away, maybe he's not trying so hard after all....

"I don't really know. Sofia seemed pretty out of it. I'm going to bring her dinner. Do you want to come? I think we need to do an intervention or something."

"Yeah, for sure. I'm in." Sofia has helped me through so many difficult times: when I had cancer, and when the twins were born. I'll do anything to return the favour. "I'll mention it to Maja. We're going to the park today."

"Nice. Say hi for me. I'm jealous of you two chillin in the park all day."

As if we're just chilling. "I'm jealous of you not getting treated like a personal slave all day." I hope she knows that I'm joking. But also not joking...

"You make a good point." She smiles. She gets it. We are both envious, but neither of us really wants to trade places. Maybe for a day or two, I do really miss adult company, but working in an office would be soul-sucking. And I wouldn't be able to wear yoga pants.

"OK, I'm off." Drae announces, "We'll be in touch about tonight. Goodbye Zach!" He doesn't turn away from the cars. "Zach! I'm going to work! Come give me a kiss!"

Zach sets down the green car, his favourite, runs to the gate, kisses Drae, then runs back to his cars before the twins can smash his arrangement. He really needn't worry: the twins are fighting over who gets to sit in the doll stroller. Hana, in her patented move, has grabbed Ari by the collar of his pj's and is dragging him backward across the room. I'm about to intervene but then Ari starts giggling so I just leave them be.

"OK, thanks Alisha. Have a good day!"

"You too!" I call as Drae rushes up the stairs. Wallace is probably still in the car. She must have had everyone ready and out the door before I even started breakfast. Sounds exhausting.

I should message Sofia.

Alisha

Today, 8:33 am
Thinking of you. Sending hugs. Drae told me
about Colin. Want me to drag him home by his
ear like Maja's mom would? I will do that for
you. I can do it with or without the
obscenities. Your choice. HUGS.

The big room in my basement is now alive with the work of children. As usual, Zach and Chuck are playing cars side-by-side, and the twins have moved on to another of their favourite games: race each other from one end of the room to the other while giggling and squealing. They chant "1-2-3 go!" but neither of them wait for 'go', and nobody cares who wins. It is the running and falling that they enjoy. Ruby is squirming and fussing to be put down, which I'd love to do but then I'd have to stay within two feet of her or else she'll have a panic attack, and right now I need to get ready for the park.

Starting with my twins still in their pj's.

While the kids are all playing nicely I run upstairs – the added weight of Ruby making my thighs burn and my pelvis, back and shoulders ache – to the twins' room to get some clothes.

Hot flash. Baby wearing certainly isn't helping me.

On my way back to the daycare I pass Isaac as he heads out the door. He looks sullen and tired. He's not taking very good care of himself these days. His dark skin looks chalky, his black hair looks oily, and I swear his gut has doubled in size this year.

"Good morning! Did you walk the dog already?"

"No."

"Can I get a goodbye kiss?" He shuts the door without a word and leaves for work.

Nice talking to you, too, Mr. Rosey-sunshine. He's so angry all the time, and I don't know why. I thought he'd cheer up now that so much of the stress has relaxed. It was just non-stop stress for so long: me working long hours, his ugly divorce and custody fight with Melanie, my cancer, then fertility treatments... But now it is all behind us and life is settling down. I mean, we're still completely broke, but nobody is dying. I thought he'd relax! But he's just as stressed as ever. I try not to let it bother me, I try to be cheerful, I try to be supportive and all that shit, but it is pretty hard when he is so cold to me. He's been ignoring me for days. It is pretty clear that he's pissed about something, but I couldn't begin to guess what. Is it me? Is it work? Honestly I'd need to have "the patience of a saint" to not get pissed off with being completely shut out all of the time.

And, sadly, I use up all of my saintly patience spending ten hours a day with a pack of preschoolers.

I just can't help but wonder if this is just who he is. If the funny, happy guy that I fell in love with eight years ago while stranded in that airport by the fog was the anomaly, and the real Isaac is mood swings and pessimism.

I hear panicked screaming coming from downstairs. "I'm coming Hana!" I call out. Yes, I can tell which child is screaming from one floor away. This is my superpower. I'd rather be able to fly, but what can you do?

Down the stairs – ouch my pelvis – Ari is sitting on top of Hana, who is face down on the rug, and he's bouncing gleefully on her bum. Hana's face is the picture of devastation.

"Ari! Hana is not enjoying that game. Do you hear her crying? Do you see her face? She is very sad."

Ari clearly couldn't care less. Without missing a beat he's off his sister and running to the next thing. I feel my rage bubble up. He is only two I remind myself. Instead of enacting a satisfying revenge, I focus on Hana: she's curled up in my arms in tears, her soft little hands around my neck. She's feeling more and more like a big kid every day, but there's still some baby cuddles left yet.

But, of course, Ruby hates when I comfort the other children and she starts to push Hana's hands away, scratching my neck and pulling my hair in the process. Fuck this kid! I've never had a baby struggle so long to adapt to daycare. I can't imagine the effects of the trauma on her from being this anxiety-ridden all day. For three weeks she's been in constant fear! It is like she thinks I've kidnapped her. I guess as far as she's concerned I have. She doesn't know where her mom is or when she'll see her again. She doesn't know if I am trustworthy, or who these other kids are.

I have told her mom that Ruby's struggling, but I haven't told her exactly how much. I know that she has enough guilt already: she made it clear from the beginning that she didn't want to go back to work, that she'd rather stay home with Ruby, but they can't afford it. The last thing I want to do is make this transition harder for her by making her feel guilty about what it is doing to her baby.

The dads never seem to have any guilt about these decisions... or maybe they hide it better, I don't know.

I hate seeing the kids suffer as they transition to daycare. It is part of the reason I'm already growing tired of this work. I just can't give them what they need, and I feel a bit like I'm running a scam when I pretend that daycare is a great thing. As hard as I try, I'm no substitute for their family or their home. I mean, for most kids it hasn't been like this. Most kids grow to love it here: it becomes their second home, but always, those first few days, before they come to trust me, are horrible. I'm just too empathetic and all I can think about is how scared they must be....

And Ruby might be the straw that breaks this camel's back, figuratively and literally.

More and more I'm convinced that I have to close the daycare. I love it: it is possibly my favourite job that I've ever had, but it is killing me. Both physically and mentally. And I don't even make minimum wage. It just isn't worth it.

Hana has wearied of fighting Ruby for my affection, and has apparently forgiven her brother for the attack, because she leaps from my lap and chases after him pretending to be a hippo to his elephant.

In the meantime, I need to restock the daybag with diapers and spare clothes plus snacks for the park. I've got 30 minutes to get that together, fill their water bottles, change bums and dress the twins and then load it all into the van, wrestle five little butts into car seats. And Isaac didn't walk the dog so I'll have to bring her too.

You know, easy peasy. Maybe I'll bake a cake while I'm at it.

I read a book somewhere that if you plaster a fake smile on your face it sends a message to the brain to release endorphins and you actually feel better.

Fake smile plastered.

8:40 am

Andrea

It isn't even a month into the school year and already I feel like I've done this a million times. I didn't used to find any of these routines mundane, but suddenly it feels like I'm drowning in mediocrity: drive the kids around, work at a dull job, drive the kids around, make a half-assed dinner, go to bed, repeat.

Fuck.

It is only a ten minute drive from Alisha's house to Wallace's school. Wallace says "Goodbye mom. I love you," as if he's reciting lines from a script, and abandons the car without a second glance. He's so particular and specific, and he was always so clingy with me, that I thought school would be harder for him. But he seems to be doing just fine. I guess the routine, rules and order of an institution are predictable enough that he is able to stay balanced in the face of 30 unpredictable five-year-olds. I'm happy, of course, that he's doing well. But I'm also a little bit heartbroken that he doesn't need me the way he used to.

It's a twenty minute drive from Wallace's school to my

work at the Lifestyle:Wellness head office. It is a new building that we just moved into last year. It was inspired by Google and Twifagram's employee-centered philosophy. The idea is that you make work really inviting and fun so that your staff don't mind that they never get to go home. There's a napping room and a games room and lots of natural light and live plants. The cafeteria has TVs and couches, and a different gourmet food truck shows up every day for healthy lunches. It is all very cool and novel and completely wasted on me. The only perk I care about is the gym membership and being encouraged to work out during office hours. Now if they would just bring in an on-site chiropractor and massage therapist then I could spend the entire day away from my desk.

I hate my job.

But I didn't realize it until two weeks ago, after I was told that there was a cluster of cancer cells the size of a golf ball swallowing my left ovary. That this vicious lump had sent its murderous little cells through my lymph system and some of them had settled on my pelvic bone and my spine, eating away at the bone and pinching my spinal chord, which is what caused the strange numbness and made it hard to pee. I went to the doctor thinking I had a really nasty UTI, and instead found out that my bones were infected with a cancer that cannot be cured.

"Treatment might buy you a few more years" the doctor said.

But I will die from this.

And suddenly I realized I'm living the wrong life.

As I take off my coat, I look at the pictures on my desk of my wedding and my family. When I start my computer up the monitor's wallpaper is pictures of my boys.

It looks like the right life. My kids are amazing, my

husband is handsome, our condo is immaculate. This is what the perfect life looks like. And I've worked my ass off to get here from a childhood of poverty, raised by an immigrant mother.

But it is a lie. The perfect house + perfect husband + perfect kids + perfect job = happiness narrative? It is a lie.

And I'm fucking furious. Spending my whole life pushing myself to accomplish the next thing I was supposed to: school, university, job, marriage, kids. I'm furious I never did the things that I wanted to. It was always later. Later I'll travel, later I'll write children's books, later I'll love my husband.

But there is no later. There is only two years left.

"Uhhhhh.... Andrea? Are you in there?" Diane was standing over my desk laughing awkwardly.

"Oh, hey Diane." Ugh, people. The worst thing about work. "I'm just in a coffee coma. Don't mind me." I breathe. I wasn't breathing.

"Like, you've had too much coffee? Or not enough?"

"Both?" I shrug. Diane is a work friend. Simple as that. There was a time I considered we might be more: we used to take lunch time walks and we did a movie night once, but the truth is she just complains too much. She's a real downer. I feel bad, because I don't think she has any friends, her husband sounds like a real dud, and her kids are exhausting, so I know she could use a friend. But conversation with her is so heavy. So I avoid her now. Especially for the last two weeks. The last thing I need is one more thing bringing me down.

I turn my attention to my computer, opening the files that I should be working on today.

"Oh, I know how you feel. Theo climbed into my bed at five am today and wouldn't sleep, and I didn't get to bed until after midnight because Adara was out with God knows who doing God knows what. And when she finally came home she just locked her door and wouldn't talk to me. I think she's doing drugs. Or having s-e-x. I'm going to be raising my grandchild while still sharing a bed with my son."

"Maybe she's doing drugs AND having sex." I can't believe that I said that out loud.

Diane rolled her eyes at me and snorted, "You have the worst sense of humour."

"You are not the first person to tell me that." I'm still staring blankly at my screen, pretending to do work but honestly I can't even see the words anymore. My brain just got so overwhelmed that it gave up on me about a week ago and I've literally accomplished nothing since.

"Have you got that stuff for the new payroll program ready yet?" Diana shows no sign of leaving me alone.

I sigh. No, not even close. "Almost. Maybe tomorrow."

"Oh, good. Jeff was asking about it. I told him that I thought you were pretty much done."

Great.

I'm still staring at my monitor, looking busy, but Diane doesn't leave.

"Jack and I had a huge fight last night."

Oh, no. Here we go.

I mentally scold myself for my cruelty.

"He gets home from work and just sits on his ass, complaining about how hard his day was. But then he just watches TV and plays with his phone while I cook and clean and do the laundry and pack lunches and help with homework and get Theo and Andy to bed... And then, at ten pm when I'm finally done with all of that and sit down to hang out with him, suddenly he has work to do and he's out in the garage until two am. Like, what the hell? He doesn't contribute, he doesn't talk to me. Why am I even married to him?"

Why ARE you even married to him? "That is ridiculous. He sounds like a gorilla. Actually, I think even gorillas are more generous with their affection."

Diane keeps going as if I hadn't said anything: "And I'm starting to think he's cheating on me. I looked on his phone and he's got all these messages with this person from work. Jesse. Talking about her sexy behind and does she want to f-u-c-k. So I confronted him – he says Jesse is a man and it is all a big joke. A "fag joke" he said."

People still use that word?

"He forgets that I met Jesse. Last Christmas. We bumped into her in the mall. She's not exactly what I'd consider sexy. She's nothing special. Short and a bit fat. Not his type. So I don't know what to think. What do you think?"

I think he's cheating on you.

This time, thankfully, I have the self control to keep that thought to myself. But surely she's smarter than this?

"Is it a deal breaker? If he's cheating on you?"

She looks at me as if I've grown horns. "Of course it's a deal breaker."

"Oh, Diane," I can't help but laugh. I sometimes forget how squeaky-clean she is. Spelling out swear words and scandalized by moral ambiguities. "Please, don't think I'm going to judge you. I have a few friends in open relationships. Fidelity just isn't important to some people."

"Well, it is definitely important to me." She lowers her voice, "I feel betrayed when he masturbates, so it would certainly destroy me if he cheated."

I can't help but snort with laughter at the way she

mouths the word "masturbates" as if she were summoning Voldemort and her cheeks go bright red with embarrassment. I reply with my most blunt tone: "I don't like when they masturbate either. It's like they're strangling a tiny, naked weasel." Now it is Diane who snorts with laughter.

"You are shameless, Andrea. I should get to work. Do you feel like a lunch break walk today?"

Oh, God, please, no.

"Ah, I'm thinking of doing the noon spinning class.... Although I really should sit right here until I'm done this payroll shit."

"Andrea, I can help if you need it. I can find the time." Diane is one of those people who can be totally swamped by her own life but still find a way to help other people. And everyone walks all over her as a result.

Shit, I should really be nicer to her.

I should do a lot of things.

"That's really nice of you, Diane. I might take you up on that offer. Let me see how today goes."

Diane heads back toward her desk, but doesn't make it, stopping instead at Victoria's desk for another chat.

At least I'm not the only one who doesn't get anything done around here.

OK. Payroll. I should have done this a week ago. It isn't like anyone would be angry: all I have to do is tell them the truth and I'd be let off the hook completely. I'd likely be sent home for a paid week of family time.

So why do I keep sitting here staring at this fucking file, too paralyzed with anxiety to even begin?

Today is the day. Today I'm going to do this shit.

Right after I check Twifagram.

twifagram

Alisha

I personally know 3 women who have been raped...

My heart skips a beat, but of course she's not talking about me. She doesn't know. Nobody knows and nobody ever will know, #metoo or not.

Alisha

I personally know 3 women who have been raped. I know 2 men who are rapists. I know 3 women whose lives have been destroyed by rape. I don't know any men whose lives have been destroyed by a rape accusation. I #BelieveWomen

19 Likes   9 Comments

Alisha

I have no doubt that I know more victims of rape who haven't confided in me, and more perpetrators who've just continued to get away with it and live among us smug and dangerous

---

I love her for saying this sort of thing, for always speaking out on behalf of those of us too damaged to do so. But I also hate it, because no matter how many people agree with her, there's always going to be one asshole there to shit all over it....

René

It is so infuriating. I always knew that rape culture was a problem, but I can't believe how many men don't know it. How many actively deny it. It is terrifying.

Maria

Things are changing, but not fast enough!

Ellen

Well said!

Kristy

Well said! #BelieveWomen

Heather

I know 4 women who've been raped. I used to know 2 rapists. I've never known any men falsely accused of rape. I #BelieveWomen.

Jake

I know 3 men whove been falsely accused of rape. 1 of them lost his job. I dont know any women whove been raped and I dont know any men whove committed rape. So should I write #believemen?

And there he is. Jake. I've never even met the guy. I think he was one of Lish's classmates from her Master's program she did in Boston. I've seen him on Alisha's Twifagram enough to know that he pretends to be wise and enlightened, he's 'got friends who are Black' and he 'loves women', but he'll vote for the most right wing asshole politicians out there if he 'likes their economic policy.' He seems to have that 'how cool am I for not giving a fuck about anybody except myself' attitude.

Ellen

I'm sorry that your friend lost his job unjustly, but when weighed in the balance with a woman loosing her sense of safety, her trust of men, her ability to love and connect, and possibly also her job, friends, and family, also unjustly. Compared to that, your friend's misfortune seems like a fairly small price to pay, don't you think? I mean, he probably just went and got another one, didn't he?

Heather

Jake, if you know 4 women, then you know a woman who has been sexually assaulted. If you know 3 men, then you know a man willing to commit rape. Sexual assault is all around you, every day, and you don't see it because it doesn't affect you. That is called "privilege." But the time to open your eyes is now.

I'm glad there are women like these, with the patience to fight this fight. But I'm not touching it with a ten foot pole.

Scrolling through my Twifagram feed. Kitten pictures. Wedding pictures.

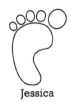

Jessica

35 Likes   41 Comments

Her baby was born the same day as Sofia's. This little boy is the same age that Grey would have been.

I'm crushed with sadness.

These should have been Sofia's baby pictures. This should have been her 35 likes and 41 comments gushing about how cute he is. Instead Sof is alone in a big empty house, no likes, no loves, no gushing, no baby, no husband. Completely alone.

Fuck this bullshit. Life is too hard. Nobody prepared us for this.

I close the browser and click on the payroll files.

And stare at the screen blankly.

9:30 am

Sofia

The best thing about the weed is that I don't dream. For the first few days after Grey died my mom and dad and my brother and sister and their spouses and kids, and my cousins, Colin's mom and step-dad, and Colin's dad and his silly little girlfriend, his grandpa and brothers and their wives and 700 kids, all of them were coming and going so we were never alone, not even at night. So I didn't really get a chance to toke. At the same time, I still couldn't really believe Grey was gone, and had it in my head it was unsafe to toke. But, also, I was in such shock, such a daze, that I didn't really need it yet: my brain was foggy enough.

But the dreams. Every dream was about Grey: in my womb, dead. A one-year-old baby dead in the crib. A happy five-year-old hit by a car and dying in my arms. A grown man, handsome and tall, disappearing in the breeze like he was made of sand. I awoke from every dream sweating and terrified.

But with the weed my sleep is empty. And when I wake up there is a brief moment where I forget everything that has happened. For a brief moment I am still pregnant, and Colin is sleeping in the bed beside me.

If I could just find a way to stay in that moment forever.

Instead, reality washes over me like an icy wave, and I relive the events of that terrible day all at once: the Doppler screaming with the absence of a baby's staccato heartbeat. The somber faces and brisk language of the doctors, nurses, and my midwife Jennifer as I push through the contractions. The silence in the room as the limp, purple body arrives. The rush of movement as he is swept away, the umbilical cord still pulsing.... The memories send my mind and body into a panic: my skin prickles and my hair stands on end. Then there's the sudden and familiar agonizing pain in my chest, as if a giant hand has punched through my rib cage and ripped my heart from my chest, leaving a gaping empty hole while my lungs collapse. For a moment I feel like I'm drowning, and I find myself welcoming the loss of consciousness that comes with death.

But that doesn't happen. The pain settles in like an unwanted house guest, but death does not come for me.

I desperately need to pee.

How long ago was Drae here? The cup of take-out coffee on my side table is still warm, but not warm enough to drink. The curtains are still open but it is overcast. I hope it rains. A gloomy day is far less offensive to me than a sunny one. It was so sunny when we buried Grey and it seemed like an unnecessarily cruel taunt on Mother Nature's part. People kept saying "At least we have a nice day for it," but I wanted the sky to be crying for him.

The sooner I go pee the sooner I can be back in bed.

I could just lie here forever. My arms and legs weigh a ton. Lifting them seems an impossible task.

If I peed the bed would I just lie in it all day?

If I lay in it all day would that mean I'm broken beyond all repair?

I don't need to pee in bed to know that I am.

The sooner I go to the bathroom the sooner I'll be back in bed.

When Colin and I bought this house it never occurred to me the downside of only one bathroom is that I have to walk past the nursery to use the toilet. As soon as we got home from the hospital Colin closed Grey's door so that we could no longer see the jungle walls and lion mobile.

But I still know they are there.

I kind of want to open the door. I suddenly realize I've wanted it open all along.

With Colin gone, I should.

I was out of bed without even thinking about it. As if, for a brief moment, I'd forgotten how heavy I was. I tricked my mind by distracting it. I immediately want to crawl back under the covers, but instead I summon all of my courage and walk forward.

Toward his door.

My heart is thumping in my throat. My hands are as cold as ice, and clammy.

I should pee first.

I flee for the bathroom.

Like our bedroom, the bathroom has been cleared of all baby-related paraphernalia. Unless you count the half empty box of adult diapers I used for the postpartum bleeding up until yesterday.

What do I do with a half box of unused adult diapers? Save them for next time?

Except there won't be a next time. That was it. My only

chance. My happy family was within reach, and now I'm alone again.

So completely alone.

I could wear the diapers and then I wouldn't have to leave my bed at all.

That is simultaneously the best and worst idea I've ever had.

I finished with the toilet ages ago, but I find getting off the toilet is nearly as daunting as getting out of bed was.

But I'm going to open his door. His room deserves to be seen. It deserves to be loved. Not locked away like some family shame.

That thought gets me off the toilet. I bring the adult diapers with me and toss them into my room (just in case) before turning to face Grey's door again.

Just a plain white door. We had put a sign on the door. It was black with pale blue letters spelling his name. Colin must have taken it down.

I take a deep breath. This is going to hurt.

Like a band-aid.

I open the door.

The first thing I notice is the smell. The overwhelming floral aroma is tainted by the sickly sweet odor of decomposing plants. The room is dark: the black-out curtains that we installed for optimal baby naps are pulled shut. But I can see the dozen or so floral arrangements and potted plants scattered about the floor, changing table, and dresser. In the crib and on the rocking chair are various items that Colin collected from around the house and deposited in here: stuffed animals, a diaper bag, a bottle warmer, the ultrasound pictures, cards from the baby shower and the funeral. Behind the door is the stroller, collapsed in a heap with the car seat balanced on top of it.

Everything. Every piece of evidence that we had a child is locked away in here.

I plod barefoot down the hall toward the kitchen and living room, searching everywhere for any item relating to the pregnancy.

Nothing. Not a single sign.

Colin couldn't stand any reminders.

Including me.

Well that is fucking bullshit.

I return to the nursery. I march in boldly this time. I open the curtains and daylight floods the room: these windows face south and the sun is just peeking out from between the clouds, and it feels good on my face now.

I don't want to pretend it never happened. I don't want to erase it. I don't want the pain, either, but I can't lock that up in a dark room. The pain will always be there, whether this door is open or closed.

Hanging over the back of the crib is the blanket my grandmother made for me as a baby. I took it to the hospital when I went into labour. We wrapped Grey in it when we held him, and when they took his pictures. I thought I would bury him with it, but at the last minute I realized it was the only thing I had that belonged to him. The only thing he ever used. Instead I buried him with a blanket my cousin crocheted for him and I kept this one for me.

I hug Grey's blanket, and, overwhelmed by the effort, curl up on the pale blue carpet, amid the flowers. I stare up at the mobile that he should be staring at, and weep for my baby boy for the millionth time.

9:40 am

Maja

Getting out of the house was a nightmare.

Eloise had a meltdown when I tried to get her dressed, and in the end I gave up so she's wearing her Spiderman costume for the third day (and night) in a row. Complete with syrup stains from breakfast today, grass stained knees from yesterday, and spaghetti sauce sleeves from the day before. She looks so trashy wearing it. People will think we're some poor immigrant family who neglect their kids. But I just can't keep fighting this fight.

Claire got herself dressed, which took forever, and then, as I was throwing some snacks in my bag, she had a poop explosion and I had to carefully peel off all of her poopy clothes, wipe her whole body with a cloth, and re-dress her.

Then Nate woke up. He was pissed off at how much noise we were making and pissed off that he was late for work and pissed off about the poopy clothes on the shower floor.

"God forbid you help out," I scowled at him as he

stomped out of the bathroom: because of course he'd rather skip his shower than deal with the mess himself.

He stopped and turned to give me a look of disgust, "Jesus, you have such an attitude problem. I only just woke up and already you are nagging me. I can't do anything right with you."

I was so filled with rage I couldn't even say anything. Yeah, this is WHY I'm angry at you! Because you stay up all night partying alone and making a mess, and in the morning I get to clean it all up while you sleep in!! I just let him walk away, though. Somehow he always finds a way to make himself the victim, so it would just be a waste of breath. But it's now a half hour later and I'm still carrying that rage. I can feel it in me, bubbling like a dormant volcano.

I got the poop cleaned up and Claire re-dressed (thank God she let me dress her this time) and then Elle refused to wear running shoes.

"I hate shoes! I want sandals." She has always been picky about what she wears – no tags, no seams, no rough fabrics, and her feet like to breathe.

"It's too cold for sandals, Elle. Summer is over. It sucks, I know, I wish it could be summer forever, but today you need to wear shoes." And then I heard behind me:

"Look mommy! I did it!" I turned to see a completely naked Claire triumphantly holding her arms above her head in celebration of undressing herself with no help at all.

Motherfucker.

"You did it!" That was the least believable celebration ever. I was so done by that point, but still holding my temper! "But Cee, we need to put it all right back on again because we need to get in the truck."

We climbed into the truck fifteen minutes late. Then I spent ten more minutes trying to reason with a five year old (what a futile effort that is) over seat belts. I was so far down the end of my rope by that point that it was a miracle – a miracle! – I didn't just pin Elle down and buckle the fucking thing myself. But I know if I do that, if I betrayed her like that, she would make me suffer for it for the rest of the day. So I had to reason with her. I had to get her to choose. In the end she did the seat belt up herself, but then it took six tries to get the truck to start. I hate this fucking piece of shit truck, but Nate traded in my car so he could get a new truck and I get the beater. I almost started crying. But I took a breath and stayed calm and got the truck going. As we pull out of the driveway I am patting myself on the back for having a really fucking hard morning and pulling it off without yelling.

Alisha

Today, 9:40 am
I'm late. Again.

Well, at least she's not cursing me, wondering where I am.

I'm always late. Lish takes five kids with her everywhere she goes and still manages to arrive before me. I'm such a flake.

I don't need to be so stressed. My fists are clenched, my shoulders are hunched, even the muscles stretched taut around my belly are twitching from how much I'm clenching. Relax, Maja. Breathe.

71

I put some calm music on the radio and try to let it all go.

"I don't like this song. Can we listen to *My Little Pony*?"

Ugh, fucking *My Little Pony*.

"No!" says Claire. "Raffi!"

"NO! *My Little Pony*!"

"NORAFFI!!!!!!!!"

"GIRLS!" I hate the screaming. Why do they have to scream everything? "I've got this new Halloween CD we got from the library, why don't we listen to that?"

"Yeah!" they agree. Thank God for the library.

The music hasn't even started when Elle starts up again: "Mom, my seatbelt hurts. I don't want to wear my seatbelt."

"I know, Peanut, I don't like mine either. They're not comfortable at all. But we have to wear them."

"It huuuuuuuuuuurts." She whines. I hate that sound even more than the screaming.

"Sorry baby, we're almost there and then you can take it off."

She starts to kick my seat, "but it huuuuuuuuuuuuuuuuuuuuuuuuurts. It huuuuuuuuuurts Mamma, it huuuuuuuurts."

"It's not going to kill you, Elle. It is only a few more minutes."

Silence. For a full minute there's silence. Well, there's the cheesy version of Monster Mash on the stereo, but the girls don't complain for a whole minute. Elle must be really pissed off at me to be silent for this long.

Then I hear the familiar click of a car-seat belt unbuckling.

You've got to be fucking kidding me.

I pull the truck over at the side of the road. We're in

a wealthy suburb: the kind with big garages, small lawns, and no sidewalks.

Deep breath. Deep breath. I am shaking with rage. I need to calm down before I deal with this.

I get out of the truck and open Elle's door sooner than I should.

"Elle. We talked about this."

"I don't like it. It hurts."

"I know it hurts. I wish that it didn't hurt. But it would hurt a lot more if we got in a crash and you went flying through the front window." That was definitely harsher than it should have been. But For Fuck Sake!

"NO! I won't wear it!"

"ELOISE PUT ON THE FUCKING SEAT BELT!" I scream so loudly that every person in every house and every car must have heard it. I'm standing in the street next to this beat up old piece of shit truck in a coat that doesn't even come close to hiding my belly bump, screaming at a kid who's covered in food and dirt – I must look like total trash. My body temperature is through the roof, my face red hot: I'm sweating in the cool fall air.

"NEVER!!!!" She screams right back in my face, in a rage equally matched.

"JUST DO WHAT YOU ARE TOLD!!!" I'm blind with fury now, and as I shout I imagine how good it would feel to just squeeze her so hard that she disappears, and then she's crying and I realize that I am squeezing her. I'm squeezing her little arms so hard, as if my rage has caused my muscles to spasm, and the harder I squeeze the more relief I feel. I just want to squeeze her into obedience, and I imagine her bones snapping in my hands....

I let go. I shut the door and walk away from the two girls crying in the back seat of the truck. I sit on the curb.

I'm shaking. I'm angry. I shouldn't have done that. But I'm still so angry. She's so fucking infuriating. All day all she's done is yell and scream and lose her shit with me. Everything I do is wrong. I have to walk on fucking eggshells for fear she'll explode! No human on earth could take that abuse all day!

I can't believe I did that.

My poor babies. I can hear them both crying through the glass. A car drives by slowly. I worry for a second they'll stop to offer help. Maybe I look like my car broke down. But no, they keep driving. Just a crazy pregnant woman falling apart. She doesn't need help.

I want to cry. How could I be so horrible?

God, I hate myself.

I can feel my anger dissipate and my heart soften. I take a few deep breaths and then stand up and return to the truck. I open Elle's door. Her face is streaked with tears and she's holding her arms where I squeezed them. On the other side of the truck Claire, in her rear-facing car seat, is crying too. Her face red, her eyes wide.

How messed up it is that the person they look to for comfort is the same person that terrorized them in the first place.

"Oh, my babies. I'm sorry, my babies." I manage to squeeze into the truck, past Elle's car seat, past her legs, and I sit on the seat in between them. I kiss them both. "I'm sorry for scaring you both. I'm sorry for hurting you Elle. That is not ok. It is never ok for me to hurt you, no matter how naughty you are. You didn't deserve that. I'm sorry baby. Will you be ok?"

I am painfully aware this is pretty much how Nate behaves when he's gone too far.

Well, that's not entirely true. He apologizes, but then adds: "But if you didn't...".

Elle sits forward in her seat and removes her coat to look at her arms. They are red where I squeezed her but probably not enough to bruise. That seems impossible when I think about how hard I squeezed. How hard I wanted to squeeze.

"Oh, my Peanut. My Eloise," I kiss the red marks, "I'm so sorry." Both girls are sobbing quietly now. They both look so devastatingly sad. I hold one hand in each of mine and I sing their favourite song from Robert Munsch: "I love you forever, I'll like you for always, as long as I'm living, my babies you'll be."

Silence.

"Can we go to the park?" Elle asks, as if nothing had happened.

"Yes, let's do it." I kiss them one more time, and this time I get smiles.

Eloise's seat belt is still unbuckled.

I get into the front of the truck and drive to the park.

10:00 am

Alisha

We're a full half hour late for the park but we still beat Maja.

It was a heck of a time getting here. I must have had four hot flashes before we even left the house. A hot flash packing our bags, a hot flash putting the kids into their splash pants, coats and boots, and a hot flash when, just as we were about to leave, Hana disappeared into the bathroom.

Hana is potty training herself. It sounds like every parent's dream, but it isn't. She doesn't include Isaac or I in the process. She lets herself into the bathroom, removes her own pants and poopy diaper, and puts herself on the toilet. And gets off. Then back on. Then plays with the toilet paper, dropping the whole roll in. Then climbs up to the sink to wash her hands, running the water for ages while she pumps out all of the soap. The end result is an overflowing sink, backed up toilet, and poop on the floor, poop on the toilet, poop on the sink, poop all over her legs and clothes, and, if we don't realize where she's gone in time, her poopy bum streaking across the living room.

Thankfully this time I caught her fairly early in the process and cleanup only took a minute. And I managed to do it without flipping my lid, which is a bonus because Hana is really sensitive to shouting.

When we finally headed out to the van, five tottering kids, a dog (fucking Isaac, as if I don't have my hands full enough), and my big daybag, I had another hot flash getting all five kids into their car seats. At the best of times buckling a kid into a car seat is a horrible ordeal, even when they cooperate, but now I'm doing it with a coat on. Ugh! I hate that summer is over!

Although today they didn't give me too much trouble with the car seats. Of course, Ruby clawed at me as if I was pushing her into a meat grinder, a look of pleading terror on her face as I fastened the straps across her chest while trying my best not to pinch her writhing hands in the clip. I could tell by her droopy eyes there was a good chance she'd cry herself to sleep on the ride. Zach never helps with his car seat. He just sits there like a heavy lump, staring at me while I dig the buckle out from under his butt. I even have to lift his arms into the straps for him. Chuck, the hero, always does his own belt. He even adjusted the chest clip to the right height. And the twins cooperated, which is great because they usually play the jellyfish game when it is time to get into their car seats. That is another one of my favourites.

By the time I got into the drivers' seat I was throwing off my coat and opening the windows to the cool morning air.

The hot flashes are new. My hysterectomy was just over two years ago, during my c-section, but I didn't really have any menopause symptoms until about a month ago, when the weather started to get cooler. At first they came every other day or so, but now they are happening about three times an hour! It is fucking intolerable.

Not only are they happening more often, but they are

stronger than they were in the beginning. And the term 'hot flash' itself is misleading. It is so much more than that. For me it starts with a panicked feeling. Like, this sudden sense that something isn't right but I don't know what it is. I get very uncomfortable and suddenly need to move around. Then it is like someone flipped a switch at the cellular level in my body and all at once every single cell gets hot. The heat builds and builds, beginning on the inside and rising to the surface, until my skin begins to tingle and sweat seeps from every skin pore. The only relief is to create an outlet for the heat. Lose the socks, lift the shirt, expose my arms: the more skin that I expose the sooner the panic will recede.

And then suddenly my whole body goes back to normal. As if the switch is flipped to 'off' once again. And I am left shivering: a sweaty, exposed, mess.

I mentioned it to my doctor when I was there last week. "Yes, hot flashes are an inconvenient part of menopause."

I hate my doctor.

"Yes, but why now, two years later, am I suddenly having such intense symptoms. Could it mean that my thyroid is acting up? Or could the cancer be back?"

"I can't give you hormones. It will just increase your cancer risk."

She never listens to me. Just like the time I told her I had postpartum depression and she gave me an online quiz and told me I was fine. So much for all that new mom literature that tells you to "ask for help".

I was there to get some codeine for my migraines. Maja, bless her, covered the daycare so I could go to the doctor's office. I once took all of the daycare kids to that doctor's office, when the twins needed their vaccinations. I've always wondered if that is why my doctor talks to me like

I'm ignorant white trash. My previous doctor, at the university, always spoke to me like an equal. This doctor acts like I'm barely literate. I can't figure out if she's like that to everyone or just people she thinks are lesser than her.

Jerk or bigot?

Anyway, I was thankful I didn't have to take the kids on an outing like that when I was five days into a migraine.

"Why do you need codeine for migraines?" She asked me suspiciously, "Why not rizatriptan or naproxen?"

"Because codeine works?" and the stuff for migraines costs twenty five dollars for one pill and codeine is only about twenty five cents for one pill so it is a no brainer, really.

"How often do you take codeine?"

Well, you haven't written me a prescription in so long you forget we've already had this conversation, so clearly not that often...

Anyway, the point is, I'm in menopause overdrive. So, I'm sweaty and I smell like BO and toddler poop and I'm getting another migraine and I'm a half hour late for the park.

All this plus my anxiety still being high after yesterday, and I was feeling pretty shaky when we pulled out of the driveway. I plastered on my best fake smile and geared up to give myself a pep talk. And that is when Zach started singing.

The radio in my van broke about a month ago, so I've been encouraging the kids to sing in its absence. Zach is the only one who has taken up the offer, and today he jumped in with lots of enthusiasm.

"I've got a great big cock, cock, cockapoo!"

I almost died. I have no idea where this song came from

79

or what it means but it is amazing. That shit would go viral if I had it on tape.

Don't let him see you laughing!

Shortly after that the knock-knock jokes started.

"Knock Knock!" Zach shouted.

"Who's there?" Chuck knows the drill.

"Poopy-face farts in your mouth!!" the boys burst into laughter. The twins laugh too – not because they liked the joke but just because laughter makes them laugh.

I love the twins together. It is just the most amazing thing, to see their relationship. They just laugh at each other all the time, without anything happening: they just look at each other and laugh. Or spontaneously start dancing. And they understood each other long before I could understand them. They just babbled back and forth with each other, giggle, and then they'd go get into some sort of trouble as if they'd been hatching a plan. I love imagining them staying this close as they grow up. It is a beautiful thing, creating two little people and them loving each other so much. It almost makes me want to reach out to my brother, but of course my relationship with my brother is basically the complete opposite to the twins, so I know better.

My mood is much improved as I pull the van into the park.

There are no other cars in the parking lot, and no other people in the playground. I unbuckle everyone and open both van doors and set them loose. Four tiny people run to the playground like a line of drunk ants. I open the trunk to let out Sheba and she runs after the kids, sniffing every tree and bush on the way. I grab her leash, the picnic blanket, and the day bag. Ruby is still sleeping so I opt to leave her in her car seat for now. I can let her sleep for a half hour before it will interfere with her afternoon nap. If I leave one of the doors open I'll be able to hear her if she wakes up.

The whole park will.

The whole city will.

Maja's beaten up old pickup truck pulls into the parking lot as I'm making my way toward the playground. I can tell as soon as Maja gets out of the truck she's having a bad morning. Her anger is like a dark cloud hanging over her. I feel tired just looking at her: I remember how uncomfortable it was in the third trimester as if it were yesterday. How little sleep you get and how everything hurts. And she's juggling Eloise and Claire on top of that. They are not the easiest kids I know. Well, Claire isn't so difficult, although she does pick up some terrible habits from her sister, but Elle is short-tempered, highly-sensitive, painfully perfectionist and has extreme anxiety. As hard as Maja works to help Elle cope with her peculiarities, she never seems to get a break.

It is easy for me, on the outside, to diagnose the issues: Maja herself is sensitive, perfectionist, and short-tempered with anxiety, and the two of them are trapped in a feedback loop. The only solution I have is that Maja needs to take care of herself and her own health, so she has more patience for Elle, but that would mean that Nate would have to help out with the kids more, and that is never going to happen in a million years. He thinks parenting is women's work, like some sort of caveman. He actually said as much, way back when Maja started dating him in university, but we all thought he was joking.

Lesson learned.

Oh, I heard a great quote about that recently. I think it

was Maya Angelou: "When someone shows you who they are, believe them the first time."

Smart woman.

I think we all need more of that.

So, I just have to watch Maja and Elle and Claire struggle and suffer and feel like failures and there's not much that I can do to help.

I mean, I offer help all the time, but she's too proud to take it.

Which reminds me, I must prep some freezer meals for Maja for when the baby comes.

Maja's girls are on the climber with my kids now. Elle and Zach and Chuck play well together, even though Elle is two years older. She mostly tells the boys what to do and where to go and what to say and they go along with it. Claire and my twins get along fantastically. They just toddle around like the three stooges, falling off things and giggling. Of all six kids, Ari is certainly the most unpredictable, so I stick closest to him, making sure Ruby in the van is within earshot.

As Maja approaches I can see she's been crying. I wonder if that is Nate's doing or Elle's? Or both.

"Sorry I'm late." She sighs.

"Oh, no. I was only here about two minutes before you. Are you ok?" Her eyes are puffy but she doesn't look like she's been beaten or anything. I know Nate has hit her, but I don't think it is a regular thing. Years ago I would have insisted that if a man hits you even once you should leave him, but I'm more realistic now, and I realize most of us would be single if we were that obstinate.

"No, but, whatever." Maja is like Drae that way: a very private person. As opposed to me: I never stop talking about myself and couldn't keep a secret if it was my job.

Maja is different than Drae, in that her face is an open book so she's not quite able to hide her struggles. Whereas Drae is full of secrets. I often think I don't really know her at all. She just gives us tiny hints at her true self.

"Do you want to talk about it?" I know that she won't.

"No." She smiles at me. A forced smile. A 'tough it out, champ' smile. But she looks like she might cry. My heart breaks for her. Maja puts up with a lot of shit from the people who are supposed to love her. Nate, Elle, her parents, her brother... they all disrespect her and take advantage of her. They've fooled her into thinking she's weak, when actually she's stronger than all of them, because she keeps on going despite all of their attempts to crush her.

"Do you want me to distract you?"

"Yes, please." Maja sighed.

"Well did I tell you about the paint night I went to?" As I speak I lay my picnic blanket on the grass, a few feet away from the playground, and in the sun to ward off the chill. I drop the day bag and, just as I'm about to continue the story, I notice that Ari is considering a slide that is way above his skill level. Hana or Claire, or even Zach, would think twice about that slide and back away slowly, but not Ari. He will step off that platform without a moment's hesitation, so I move fast.

He does, of course. He doesn't think about it, doesn't even sit down, just steps off the edge and plummets down the sheer drop, one leg behind and one in front so his whole body twists in the air and nearly flips over the rimmed edge of the slide. My outstretched hand reaches him at just this moment and, grabbing his shirt, I'm able to straighten his aim and slow his fall just enough to keep him from crashing to the ground.

He comes to a stop at the bottom of the slide and pauses, laying on his back and staring up at me. His face a mixture of shock and fear.

My heart is beating a million miles an hour.

Ari laughs maniacally and rushes back to the stairs.

Jesus hell that kid has a death-wish.

"Well, that certainly distracted me!" Maja shouts from her seat on the blanket.

"I think this kid is going to give me a heart condition." He's at the top already and this time he pauses and sits down carefully before launching himself down the steep slope. He falls cleanly this time and stops at the bottom like a pro.

At least there's some reason to hope: he learns quickly.

Hana and Claire are playing safely on the baby slide. Elle and Zach and Chuck are all trying to balance together on the giant round swing, giggling away. They're all good for now, so I peek in on Ruby, who is still sleeping soundly, and then join Maja on the picnic blanket.

"What was I saying?" Really, I was in the middle of something...

Maja looks up from her phone.

"Drae says you're supposed to talk to me about something?"

Ari is getting cocky on the slide again, and he goes flying off the end and crashes into the dirt, laughing all the way. Jesus Christ.

"Yes! About Sofia!" I'd almost forgotten, and feel a sudden sadness and a dark frown creeps across Maja's face. We're all heartbroken over Grey's death, but I imagine that Maja must also be terrified, with only a few weeks left before her baby comes. Of course the risk was always there, but now we actually feel how real it is. Feel a fraction of the pain that Sof must be feeling. My chest hurts just imagining.... "Drae says that Sof is a mess and we need to take care of her for a bit. She wants us all to go over there tonight."

Maja frowns, "I thought she might be really bad. She hasn't been replying to my messages. But she looked so together at the funeral, I had hoped...." Maja's voice trails off.

"Yeah, she did look remarkably together. I wondered if maybe she was in shock. She was so social – she greeted everyone and made small talk... it wasn't like her at all."

"I wonder if it all overwhelmed her once the funeral was over and everyone went home?" Maja says this in a way that makes me wonder if she struggles with depression. Heck, I assume everyone struggles with depression. How couldn't you? Life is too hard.

"I guess it must have. But apparently now she's alone and doesn't have any food. And Colin left her." Poor Sofia. She should be falling in love with little fingers and toes but instead she's alone in the dark.

"Colin what?!"

The three babies are playing in the sand now, and the big kids are walking single-file, balancing on the big wooden railway ties that encircle the playground, arms outstretched. "He left! Two days ago, Drae said."

"No, he didn't! He seems so nice! He always tries so hard!" Maja is rubbing her belly and wincing. Baby is probably trampling some vital organ, as babies do.

"Yeah, he does always seem to legitimately want to do his best, but Sof said he is not a good communicator. And do you remember at the wedding? His family were total hicks. I doubt anybody showed him how to cope with heartache or depression. I imagine he just pushes it down and gets eaten from the inside out."

"That's Nate. The only emotion he knows is rage. Do you think he'd leave me if I lost the baby?" Maja grumbled, looking at the grass.

I wish he would leave you. I don't say it with my mouth but I'm sure my face says it for me.

"No," she answers the question herself, "he'd just drink more and yell more and make everything worse."

I wonder if she would leave him then? I constantly wonder how bad it would have to get for her to finally give up on him. I had hoped that when he got drunk at her home-birth with Claire that she might leave him then, but nope. She's still holding out hope for him.

Elle runs up to us, "Chuckie is hurt!"

I can't see Chuck – the three of them had balanced their way all around the perimeter of the playground and are on the opposite side, obscured by the playground equipment.

Chuck never gets hurt – he's like that comic book character who's made out of rock – so I'm worried immediately and I'm up and dashing across the sand before Elle adds, for dramatic flair: "It's really bad! There's blood!"

Chuck is sitting on the wooden retaining wall, curled around his right knee. He has hurt himself badly enough that his jeans have ripped open and there's a tiny trickle of blood. But he is not crying. He is not making any noise at all, not even breathing, in an effort not to cry. I suddenly remember the only time I've seen Chuck cry and his father said 'You can smack him if he doesn't stop' and laughed at himself. I must have given him a proper dirty look because he stopped laughing pretty quickly.

"Oh, buddy, oh Chuckie. That is a nasty one." The gash

in his knee is almost an inch long, but thin and jagged. Nothing to worry about but it's a big wound when you are three. His face is red and he's literally biting his lip to hold back the tears.

I scoop him up in my arms, "It's ok to cry, Chuck, you can let it out." And he did. He opened his mouth and out came the most heartbreaking wail, his face contorted with pain and sadness. "Oh, buddy, I'll bet that helped." He leans his head into my chest for comfort and I kiss him on the head. It's been almost two years I've been taking care of this little guy and I could probably count on two hands the number of times he's come to me for affection. The other kids come for cuddles that many times in a day! So it feels really nice to have him needing me after all this time.

We settle down on the picnic blanket, a sobbing Chuck on my lap. "Should we put a band-aid on it?" he nods his head and I reach for the day bag.

The babies can smell excitement and they come waddling over. "Band-aid, mamma, band-aid!" they squeal excitedly. Band-aids are the most universally loved object in my daycare and I'm soon surrounded by reaching hands. Even Sheba comes to see what is going on.

I fish out my first aid kit and distribute the small bandages to the uninjured kids and I reserve one big one for Chuck's knee. I add some antiseptic cream and he doesn't even flinch when I press on it.

"There you go, all fixed." I love bandaids with preschoolers. They are like magic. I suspect things will get more difficult when they get older and that magic wears off.

"Yeh." He says in the coolest tone that he can muster. But the smile on his face betrays him and then he gives me a hug.

"Mmmm, thank you, Chuckie. I'm glad you feel better."

And without a word he runs off to play, with Elle and Zach hot on his heels. They make a beeline toward the grove of trees where they usually like to build a pretend fire pit and roast imaginary marshmallows. The dog trails behind them.

The little ones are still fiddling with their band-aids when suddenly Hana screams with frustration. Her little bottom lip is jutting out. She's gotten her band-aid stuck to itself on both sides. Luckily I only buy the really cheap shitty band-aids, so I am easily able to unstick them and I return it to her. Meanwhile Claire has opened her bandage effortlessly and placed it perfectly across her knee and Ari's band-aid is... where?

Oh. My. God. He shoved the whole thing, wrapper and all, in his mouth.

"Dude! It isn't food!" I laugh at him. "Can I have that band-aid please? I don't want you to choke on it." I put my hand below his mouth and, with his elfish grin, he spits the mangled scrap into my hand. "Thank you, buddy. Now go play!"

As Ari and Claire run off, Hana screams in fury again. This time she throws the bandage on the ground and pouts twice as dramatically. It has completely lost its stickiness. I can't help but laugh, although I try to hide it from her, but she is so cute when she is furious.

"So, what is the plan with Sofia?" Maja is picking up the abandoned scraps of band-aids and wrappers (they are so wasteful and I feel guilty, but they're also a great fine motor developer, so...). I give Hana a fresh bandage and her face lights up.

"We're going there around seven? Drae is going to do a grocery shop, we'll all clean and just generally shower her with love so she doesn't give up on life completely." Sofia is a hell of a tough woman, but I don't know how anyone picks themselves up after something like this.

Hana is happy with her new bandage and runs off to play.

"I don't know if I can do it." Maja's face is twisted into a frown again. It seems like it has been there all morning. "I can't leave the kids with Nate if he's drinking, and it is Friday, so he will definitely be drinking."

The last time I visited Maja I watched Nate walk across the living room so drunk he could barely keep his eyes open, yet he was balancing Claire on his shoulders. My heart was in my throat just watching it. A few minutes later he disappeared and then I saw his truck pulling away. 'Did I just see Nate driving his truck? Isn't he pretty drunk?' and Maja sighed: 'He's going to lose his licence again. He never fucking learns.' I had wanted to call the police, but I knew it would just mean more pain and suffering for Maja. Thank God he didn't kill anyone because I never would have forgiven myself. I still feel sick about it.

But it is clear his judgment can't be trusted when he's drinking.

"I'll ask Isaac. I bet he'd be ok to babysit if Nate is too wasted." Isaac will be wasted too, but he's good with the kids when he smokes weed. He actually puts down his phone and pays attention to them. They make a mess and nobody goes to bed and they eat chocolate at eleven pm, but they have fun and everyone is safe, so I don't mind it once in a while.

I dig my phone from the diaper bag and text him:

Alisha

Today, 10:29 am
Hey Honey. Would you be willing to watch
Maja's girls for a couple of hours tonight
while we go take care of Sofia? Maja doesn't
want to leave them with Nate.

I don't have to tell him why, he knows what a dick Nate is.

"I just hope he replies," I say to Maja, "he's pissed off at me and I don't know why."

"How do you know he's pissed off at you if he doesn't tell you why?"

"He doesn't talk to me or look at me. And when I ask him what is wrong he snaps at me that 'nothing is wrong' but not even the dog believes him. I think he's angry because I told him I want to close the daycare, and he's worried about money."

"You do? I thought you loved doing daycare!" Maja sounds genuinely shocked, which surprises me since I feel like I complain about the daycare non-stop.

"I do, it is a wonderful job. I love the kids and it's a lot of fun, but it's killing me. My anxiety keeps getting worse and my body is falling apart. That migraine last week? I can't keep doing this to myself." If I'm honest, I'm on the road to a complete mental breakdown, but I don't want to sound over-dramatic.

"Surely when Ruby settles in things will be easier?"

"Ah, shit. Ruby...." I look at my watch: 10:30. I should wake her up. Ugh. Life is so much easier when she is sleeping.

I return to the van and gather Ruby's bottle and blankie and the baby carrier. "Ruby, darling, wake up baby girl."

She is crying before she even opens her eyes.

Of course, right at that moment another car pulls into the parking lot. Our big kids are still in the woods, I can hear Elle commanding Zach and Chuck who are both "hup, two, three, four"ing, and the babies are on the spinny-thing, so they're good, but I need to get the dog on her leash.

"Come on, Ruby baby. I need to get you out, darling." Now she's crying with her eyes open, and we head toward the playground.

"Sheba!" I call for the dog. I hate putting her on the leash. And she hates when I put her on the leash. She wouldn't hurt a flea, and usually when people see her with all of these kids they know that she's not dangerous, but I guess some people don't know dogs, and they can't tell the difference between a happy dog and an attacking dog. For them, yeah, I can see how Sheba would be scary. She looks a bit like a cross between a German Shepherd and a wolf, and she is bigger than all five of my kids together. So I put her on a leash when there are other people around. Of course, she's supposed to be on a leash all the time, but then none of us would have any fun at all, so forget that.

She comes straight to me. Sweet! I look like I'm in control for once! The last time I took Sheba to the park I had treats in my pocket, so she must be expecting a repeat of that. "Sorry, girl, I'm not that organized today." I say over the sounds of Ruby wailing in my ear, and I clip the leash onto Sheba and then to the nearby tree.

I sit on the blanket with Maja to my right and Sheba to my left, and Ruby in my lap. Thankfully Ruby loves the dog so she actually STOPS CRYING and crawls toward her to play with her furry ears. And everything is calm.

Phew.

The new car that pulled up has three adults and a kid who is likely about two and a half. 3:1 is never a good ratio, in my experience. No kid needs that many eyes on them.

"Actually," settled in, I remember that we were talking about how stressful the daycare is, "yesterday it was Zach who made me want to quit."

"Oh, no! What is up with Zach?"

"Mommy, can we have snack?" Elle yells from amid the bushes.

"Five minutes." Maja holds up her open hand to illustrate the number five. Elle pops back into the woods.

"Ah, Zach is having some anger issues. His temper tantrums have been getting progressively worse, and yesterday he was an absolute menace. In the first hour he strangled Chuck with a blanket, suffocated Ari with a pillow, pushed Hana off the couch and punched me in the face."

"Holy crap! But Zach has always been such a little sweetheart! What happened?"

"I don't know. I'm pretty sure he's getting anxiety from Ruby crying all the time. I know I am, and it makes me want to strangle, suffocate and punch other people, so I guess I can understand his feelings. But I'm also wondering if it is related to Sof? It's gotta mess him up, learning that a baby can die? Or maybe there's something going on at home. Has Drae said anything to you? She doesn't really get personal with me."

"No, nothing to me. Do you think something is up with her and Damien?"

"Who knows. She never complains about him the way

the rest of us complain about our partners, does she? But they've always seemed like such a strange match. I would never have imagined her ending up with someone like Damien. He's so...." What is the word? Awkward? Dull? Predictable? Dweeby?

"Missionary Position." Maja for the win.

I laugh out loud. "That is exactly it. She's such a firecracker and he's such a dud."

"I have talked to Drae about this." Maja nods, "She's about as desperate for a good f-u-c-k as I am."

I put on an exaggerated shocked and scandalized smile, but I do legitimately blush when she says this. It isn't that I'm a prudish pearl-clutcher, but rather I just never think about sex. I went from cancer to IVF to chemo to pregnant to breastfeeding to menopause. I haven't been interested in sex for so long, I've kind of forgotten it even exists.

"Nate isn't taking care of you?" I manage to ask.

"Oh, I don't know. He just always seems to have better things to do. And I'm not really into angry drunk sex."

"Excuse me?!" the grandma across the playground calls out to us, "is this one yours?" she points at Ari. "He's eating the sand."

Immediately I'm blushing, embarrassed and feeling confronted, which I never handle well. I reply with "Yeah, sometimes he does that." Not my best comeback, but I feel panicky, especially since we were sitting here talking about sex and not hovering over our kids' every movements to keep them safe.

And now of course I'm having a hot flash and I'm pulling my clothes off like a pedophile.

That whole family is looking at me like I've got a demon on my shoulders, so I add: "He'll realize it is gross and stop.

Or maybe he won't, and then we'll know to enroll him in the special school." Do they like a joke?

No. No they don't.

"I'm pretty sure he's going to need a special school anyway. That kid is crazy," Maja laughs, loudly enough for the grandma to hear, filling the awkward space between us and giving grandma an opportunity to laugh.

But she doesn't take the out.

"He could get worms from eating that."

"He could. That is a risk, yes." She thinks I'm some ignorant neglectful mom. We must look a sight – three two year olds, a one year old, and Maja pregnant to bursting... and they haven't even seen the other three kids in the bushes. But I'm not just sitting here because I'm lazy. I've done the research. I know what I'm doing.

And I don't need to explain myself to anyone. Well, except Zach, Chuck and Ruby's parents. Their opinions are the only ones that count.

Not this random helicopter family.

I know this, but I still feel shame in the shadow of this lady's glare. And self doubt begins to kick in... maybe I should...

"Mommy? Is it five minutes yet?" Elle and Zach and Chuck emerge from the forest and run toward us. The babies know the drill and abandon their play, sand streaming off their clothes as they run our way. All seven kids converge on our picnic blanket and the feeding frenzy begins.

Requests come at me from seven directions at once as I reach for the day bag. Maja pulls out avocados and rice crackers and home made peanut butter with veggie sticks, but I've got crackers and cheese and pepperoni slices, so all the kids dive into my supplies first, making little mini sandwiches. With all of these kids in close proximity Ruby starts clawing at me protectively again, trying to scale me like a tree, and Sheba is inching her way onto the picnic blanket, making a move on Ari's mini-sandwich at the same time my phone buzzes with a new message...

I don't even notice the hover family leaving.

10:40 am

Andrea

I've only been here for two hours. It feels like at least eight.

Eight years.

I wonder what my kids are doing now. I grab my phone and text Lish:

Andrea

Today, 10:40 am
How's my funny boy?

I stare at my computer screen. I have actually accomplished some work. Not nearly enough, but it is something.

But I had a bit of a light bulb moment: Since I can't seem to bring myself to talk to the people I love about my diagnosis, maybe I should talk with strangers about it. The counselor at the cancer clinic told me there was a support group that meets once a month but that sounds terrible to me.

But maybe Twifagram?

I've already been on Twifagram a dozen times this

morning. Basically any time the payroll files get too boring or difficult I find myself on Twifagram without even realizing I've done it. I did have to block Jessica Hammond's post about her cute baby because my broken heart can't handle it. And I had to block Alisha's post about rape because it makes me feel like a victim, and I fucking hate that. So now my newsfeed is mostly sarcastic memes, just the way I like it.

There's Mike from high school posting about his Trans daughter. He's fighting the Ontario government for repealing the sex ed curriculum that taught that Transgender is a real thing. Good for him! Mike was a bit of a bully in high school (but so many of the guys were, it was the only way to be one of the cool kids) and often mocked my gay friend, so I love seeing that he's changed and grown for his kids. Good for him.

My phone buzzes

Andrea

Today, 10:40 am
How's my funny boy?

Alisha

Today, 10:42 am

HA! Of course he's holding a butterfly hostage. So Zach.

I love that I was able to send my kids to Lish for daycare. She is like family. And the twins are like family. Watching that new baby cry for her mom while she adjusts to daycare, Zach didn't have that. He was just going to Lish's. I didn't have any mom guilt at all! I only wish she'd been open three years earlier, so Wallace could have gone to her for more than just a few months.

Leaving Zach with Lish is actually better than leaving him with family because Lish is obsessed with it. She might have left academia but she will always be an academic, and she approached daycare like it was a second PhD. I think she's read every book on child development ever written. Any time I ask her a simple question, she gives me a twenty minute answer and a reading list for homework!

I never read any of them though. I hate parenting books. They make me feel like a bad mom.

Lish took the same approach to cancer: reading everything she could get her hands on. I'm sure she would have loads of information she could share with me about my diagnosis and treatment options.

If I told her.

But every time I think about telling her I remember

taking her to chemotherapy. I remember her hair falling out in chunks.

And then I try to think of something else. Anything else.

So, what was I doing?

Payroll.

Fuck.

NO! I was going to join a Twifagram group for people with cancer.

I search Cancer. There are loads of them. I search Ovarian Cancer, again there are loads. I pick the Canadian one and click "Join". Then I search Metastatic Cancer and join the first one on the list. Now I have to wait to be approved.

I re-open the payroll files. I fucking hate this. I want to go to the gym but it's too early. That is my big time-waster: my ace, I can't use it too soon.

Just one more file. Just one more. I can do one.

My phone buzzes

MOM

Today, 10:44 am
What is wrong with you? Why are you avoiding
me?

OMG I really want to ignore that text. The anxiety I get from that woman. Just simple words on my phone but they stir up all the guilt and shame that I carry thanks to my dear, crazy mother.

'But she gave up everything to give you a better life in Canada' people always say. Bullshit. She came here to give herself a better life – I was supposed to marry a rich lawyer so she could live out her life in our granny suite.

But I showed her. I married a man who makes literally $0 a year. No granny suite. My kids don't even have separate rooms.

I am such a disappointment. And so selfish, making my own choices and living my own life for me.

And now I'm skipping Friday night dinner. And not answering her calls to listen to her complain about how selfish I am.

Wait until she hears I'm dying. Most selfish thing I could do to her. She created me, therefore she owns me, and I'm certain she will forbid me from dying.

I just can't reply to her right now.

I really want to go to the gym. I could just run all afternoon. Maybe do some stairs to really punish myself.

My phone buzzes with a Twifagram notification:

twifagram

Your request to join Living with Metastatic Cancer has been approved.

I go to the group and I scroll through the posts. I read post after post of amazingly strong women dealing with cancer, hospitals, doctors, symptoms, treatments, surgery, side effects, ignorant comments, plus the usual family, household shit and mom struggles. There are plenty of inspirational quotes: "Life doesn't always get better. But you do. You get stronger, you get wiser, you get softer. With tattered wings you rise, and the world watches in wonder at the breathless beauty of a human who survived this. L. R. Knost."

Wow. That is a hell of a quote. These people understand.

And then there is a picture of a woman in a hospital bed with her two young sons on either side of her. The post says that she is Sandra Walden, the founder of this group, and that she died last night. There are over 1000 comments from all of the women in the group remembering her, this woman most of them have never met, sending love and condolences to her two boys.

And that is what breaks me. Those two boys growing up without their mother. I just break into a million pieces.

The pain rises through me like a train running me over. I want to cry like a baby, just wail with self-pity, but I can't. Not here. Not in the middle of my office with Chad and Richard talking about Marvel vs DC and the pussification of society.

So, like I haven't done since I was seventeen, I run to the bathroom to cry.

Thankfully the bathroom is only a few paces down the hall. I don't even check that I'm alone, a rookie mistake, before I shut the stall door behind me and the mournful wail escapes my throat. It reminds me of the sounds I made while giving birth. It is primal and agonizing.

How can this be real? How can this be my life? I finally started to feel like I had purpose in my life, raising these two amazing little boys, and now I die?

And what will happen to my boys? How will Damien ever manage? He doesn't even know where the band-aids are! How the hell would he ever manage meals and schedules and bedtime and play dates and birthday parties and Christmas and picture day? They will be forever scarred, forever wondering who their mom was, forever wondering if she would be proud of them...

I'm shaking on the floor of the bathroom cubicle. I'm crying so hard that I'm no longer making any sound because I'm not really breathing. A couple of times I retch, as if to vomit, but nothing comes out.

My boys. How much will this damage them? How much sadness will they bear when they should really be carefree, catching frogs and reading books?

"Andrea? Are you ok?"

Motherfucker!

It's Diane.

Motherfucker.

"Yeah, I'm just... just... having one of those moments." Of course she is in the bathroom when I'm having a mental fucking breakdown. Of course she is.

"Yeah, I know those moments. Can I do anything to help? Do you need anything?"

Bless her, but seriously, fuck my life. "No, I'm ok. I just need a minute."

"When you are up for it, I could walk you to the napping room. You might be more comfortable in there?"

Oh my fucking God the napping room. Why didn't I think of that in the first place? I completely forgot that I work in a daycare for adults. That would have been so much better than crying on this filthy floor, under these neon lights while Diane pees.

My hands are shaking violently as I unlatch the door. "Let's do it." I can't believe how well I've pulled myself together there. "How shitty do I look?"

"Actually, not bad. Just a little puffy." But as I wash my

hands I can see in the mirror that she is lying through her teeth. The circles around my eyes are so big I look like a troll doll from the eighties. But whatever. The napping rooms are in the quieter wing of the building so hopefully nobody I know will see me.

As we walk Diane chats loudly and animatedly about I-don't-know-what. It is possible that she's really trying to have a conversation with me but I'm pretty sure that she's actually trying to draw any potential attention away from my blotchy face. I'm thankful.

The napping rooms are small and windowless but have real beds and real bedding and are actually very comfortable. Diane turns on the bedside lamp and offers to bring a coffee. "Yes, black, thanks a lot." And then I'm alone.

I can't stop shaking. My whole body is shivering. I crawl under the covers with all of my clothes on and pull them over my head to warm myself. Every muscle in my body is clenched.

I think I'm having a panic attack.

This is how my body should react if I'm being chased by a bear.

Except the bear is cancer. It is going to play with me first, and then eat me really slowly from the inside, one organ at a time.

What am I going to do?

Wallace will take care of Zach. He is so mature, so thoughtful. Wallace has always been mommy's helper. He'll feel such pressure to live up to my expectations. I must make sure he knows he is good enough, that I am proud.

How will I prepare them for a life without me? Where do I even begin?

When I was in my third year at university I rented a house with Sofia and a couple of other girls, one of whom was a Palestinian immigrant. She'd lost her father to cancer when she was six. She didn't remember him, the only picture that she had of him was of the two of them at a swimming pool, shortly before he died, her sitting on his shoulders. She meditated on that photo every day, mourning the loss of her father as if it were yesterday. Her arms were a mess of scars from years of cutting herself, because the physical pain ameliorated the emotional pain.

I can't leave my boys like that.

And I can't leave them with Damien. He is completely unequipped to raise two boys. He'll move back to Montreal and have his fucking neurotic mother raise them. And my mom will never get to see the boys. They'll be complete strangers.

I wish I could give them to Sofia. She loves them like they are her own. I know she would give them the best life. She understands loss, and she would be good to them. And she'd keep my mother in their life.

How do I make that happen?

Just then there is a knock on the door. "Yeah, come in" I mumble from under the blanket, and the door opens. I peek out from under the covers, expecting it to be Diane with my coffee, but it is Jeff. My supervisor.

Fuck. Thanks Diane. Fucking rat.

"Hey Drae. I brought you a coffee. Is it safe for you to drink coffee?"

Is it safe? I don't know. I mean, I'm going to die anyways... but how does he know?

He places the coffee on the little bedside table and takes a seat on the little chair in the far corner. It is a small room, and he is a tall man, so his legs stretch almost all the way to my face. I sit up in bed and he looks at me with a sad smile. Jeff is a nice boss, kind and a good listener and always with his door open, both literally and metaphorically. So it isn't that I don't trust him with this information, I have no doubt he'll be empathetic and caring and all that. I'm just filled with terror by the idea of speaking it out loud. I can pretend it is only a figment of my imagination, some over-dramatic fantasy, until I speak it out loud.

"I must say, I've been worried about you lately. I've noticed how much your productivity has dropped. It is kind of a relief to have an explanation."

A relief?

"So when do we lose you?"

"Excuse me?" I'm really confused now. How does he know? And how is he so nonchalant about my death?

"Your mat-leave? When will you take it?"

Holy fuck he thinks I'm pregnant.

I laugh out loud. A loud rude laugh that sounds like a boisterous goose.

"Have I got the wrong end of the stick? Diane said..."

"Yeah, Diane would. No, Jeff, I'm not pregnant." I take a deep sigh. I really do have to tell him. "You are going to wish that I was, though."

He leans forward wearing his most kind and empathetic face.

"Jeff." Sigh. "I have cancer." But I don't actually say cancer. I whisper "can" and then the words catch in my throat as it closes and my eyes well up with tears and I can't breath.

Fucking fuck, Drae. Pull yourself together.

Deep breath. Deep breath.

I don't think Jeff understood what I said because he's

still wearing his kind and empathetic face, not his "someone just dropped a bomb" face.

I wipe my eyes and say the worst part, which for some reason is easier to speak, "The doctor says it is untreatable. Terminal. He gave me two years."

"Holy shit, Drae." There's the "someone just dropped a bomb" face that I was looking for.

I smile through my tears at his swearing. I've never heard Jeff swear before.

"Yeah, that was pretty much my reaction."

"When did... how long have you known this?"

"Two weeks?" it seems crazy to say it out loud, that I've been keeping this secret for two weeks.

"Drae, you should have told me. You don't have to be here. You should be in bed. You should be with your family!"

"Probably. I don't think I'm very good at being sick."

"Will you have treatment? Is there no hope at all?" he's leaning forward in his chair now, his face pursed and serious.

"I don't know. The doctor said that treatment could give me a few more years. He wanted me to start right away, but I haven't."

"Yeah, I get that. My aunt had some really terrible type of cancer and the treatment for it was so brutal. It made her feel worse than the cancer, and she died within a few months anyway, so maybe it isn't worth it."

Thanks for the uplifting story, Jeff.

"And my cousin's wife. She had surgery to remove half of her internal organs and she still died."

Jesus Christ.

He looks at me and then backpedals: "But yours could be different. You never know. The doctors are wrong all the time. I saw a documentary about a woman who cured her cancer with marijuana." He smiles at me, "Don't tell anyone your boss suggested you take up pot."

Somehow I don't feel like laughing. I force a smile but nobody is buying it.

"Drae, seriously, whatever you need. I'll pass the payroll files over to Diane, you can take medical leave for as long as you need it, or you can come to work if it helps you. Whatever you need, ok? You just say the word."

Lucky Diane. "Thanks Jeff. I appreciate it. When I figure out what the hell it is that I need, I'll let you know. I might leave early today."

"Yeah, good. Yes. Definitely." He nods enthusiastically. He seems relieved to have some way to be the good guy in this situation.

"And maybe.... I haven't really told anyone yet, so..."

"Of course. Lips are sealed. Absolutely. Although the whole office is going to think you are pregnant if I don't stop Diane. I won't tell her about this, though. You have my word."

Jeff stood to leave. Thank God. I feel so empty. I just want to hide alone in the dark and hug myself.

"Anything else that I can get you?"

"No thanks, Jeff. I'm perfect." Fake smile.

He hesitates one moment more, and then slips out, carefully closing the door behind him.

I curl into a ball and pull the covers back over my head.

10:55 am

Maja

"Twenty minutes more, guys, and then we head home for lunch!" Alisha yells. The kids show no sign that they've heard her. They are all concentrating deeply. We've moved away from the playground, thankfully, since there are now three other families playing there, and toward the little forest. There's a huge willow tree that fell in the spring and it makes a fantastic jungle gym, with something for all difficulty levels. The big kids are scrambling on the main trunk, a good six feet off the ground, and the babies are on a small branch nearer the ground, riding it like a giant horse for three.

"So your mom is opposed to you homeschooling Elle?" Alisha returns to the conversation that we were having before she had to rescue Ari from another tight spot.

I sigh, "Everyone is opposed to me homeschooling Elle. Nate said she'll be retarded if I'm her teacher."

"Because he's so smart that he actually still uses that word?"

"Ha, yeah, no kidding. And Mom and Dad are horrified. They think that doctor or lawyer are the only acceptable careers and a homeschooled kid would be shut out of those jobs. They are still getting over the disappointment of me becoming a computer programmer. I might as well have worked at McDonald's as far as they're concerned." Not that any of it matters now, since I haven't worked in so long I probably don't even remember how to do my job and nobody would ever hire me.

Alisha has that look on her face: the incredulous angry feminist look she gets right before she goes on a rant.

"Oh, eff those dinosaurs." She censors herself for the sake of Ruby, the most miserable baby in the world, who is surprisingly not crying in the carrier on her back. "First off, you'd be a great homeschooler. You were one of the smartest people I knew at university. In fact, I'm pretty sure Nate started dating you so you'd do his homework. So he knows you are smarter than him, he just won't admit it because then he'd have to respect your opinion. Secondly, I was at your graduation ceremony, and I saw your parents cheer louder than all of the other parents in that room. They are just pretending to be disappointed in you. And, finally, Nate is a sexist prick. I want to see him stay home with the kids and you go back to work, because you'd be running the company in no time."

"HA! Nobody wants to see that. Can you imagine? The mess? The kids would starve." He'd be drunk all the time. The girls would be taught to play online poker....

"Yeah, nobody wants that. You're right. But you managed to convince them that Elle should stay home this year at least?" Lish is really invested in homeschooling the twins. She's so sure of herself, and that this is the right thing for her to do, but I'm not so convinced. I don't know if I'm smart enough. I don't know if I'm patient enough. I know the school system is flawed, and I know how easy it is for kids to fall through the cracks, but the people there have training to deal with kids like Elle. I think. I hope. But putting her in a room with 30 other kids and only one adult? I can't see her handling that well. And Lish has been the one person who has always been in my corner for this. She'll be disappointed in me if I cave...

"No. They all tell me I'm wrong. But I'm the one who would enroll her and I'm the one who would take her, and I'm not doing it. If it is so important to them, they can do it." And they won't, because they are all just talk and no action. Back-seat drivers, the lot of them.

"Good for you!" Alisha beams at me. And then runs off to save Ari again.

Except I could actually picture them reporting me to Children's Aid. My own family. They are that mean. All of them. And Nate's family too. They just want me to stay in my lane: the lane where I do all of the work and do whatever they tell me to and don't do any thinking of my own.

Zach suddenly screams at the top of his lungs (actually it is more like the roar of a wild animal) and Elle wails like a siren. She is on the branch above him and she's got a big stick and is hitting him on the head and he's yanking her leg, trying to pull her out of the tree. All of this is happening five feet in the air.

Lish and I both move.

"ELLE! PUT THAT STICK DOWN!!!" I yell. I feel the anger wash through me and I am immediately back up to full alert.

"Zach, breathe," Lish says, calmly but with authority. She is much closer to the tree and is beside the fighting children in an instant. "Elle, breathe. I know you are angry but you don't have to hurt your friend. You can just let it go. You know if you hurt your friend you will feel bad later."

Both kids look like they are paused while they ponder Alisha's words and consider what to do next. Both faces are frozen expressions of rage. Elle's arm is raised, preparing to bring the stick down one more time, and Zach's hands are clenched like cat's claws just inches from Elle's leg. Lish waits so patiently while they think, whereas all I want to do is swoop in there yelling, take the stick, and send them both in opposite directions to play alone.

Why can't I stay cool under pressure like that? Why do I just fly off the handle so quickly, and want to hurt everyone?

When the kids have their moment to think, and still haven't lashed out, Lish changes their focus: "Zach, where do you want to climb to?" with his bottom lip jutting out he points to the branch that Elle is on and grunts unhappily. "OK, and Elle, where do you want to climb to?" she points to where Zach is sitting. "Well, that's perfect! You just need to swap!" Lish talks them through the complex maneuver, providing some extra balance but mostly they manage it themselves. The whole time Ruby is watching the action intently from over Lish's shoulder from the baby carrier. In no time the kids are all back to their focused work like nothing ever happened.

"We're leaving in TEN MINUTES!" Lish calls as she steps back toward me.

"OMG Lish, you stayed so calm! I just wanted to take the stick out of Elle's hands and beat her with it. I don't know how you have so much self-control."

"I was more tempted to clobber Zach with it, but I've been dealing with a lot of this from him lately, so I've had lots of practice at ignoring my baser desires." Lish jokes.

"This is his new thing – he pretends to be a lion which he thinks gives him permission to bite and scratch and roar because that is what lions do."

"Wow. That is so not like him."

"He's driving me nuts. He does it as a defense mechanism, but he gets defensive about everything. If I say anything he doesn't like, even: "Hey, Zach, Hana is upset that you punched her in the face" he flies into a rage and starts roaring and throwing things around the room. Like I'm the asshole for telling him that he can't be an asshole."

I laugh ironically. "Sounds like Nate." So much. If he feels even the tiniest bit criticized he'll start shouting 'You're never happy. I can't do anything right' and I just keep thinking, how is that my fault? That you can't do anything right? I've never actually said that, though, because he'd almost certainly lose his shit if I did.

"Ugh, Isaac too. And every man on the internet: How dare you call me a bad person for saying something blatantly bad? You are so intolerant! Shut your mouth and let me be a dick already."

"Yup. I'm a bitch for not letting him trample all over me."

"The girls were never like that. Remember the two little girls I took care of last summer? They fought too, lost their tempers and raged, but you could always talk them down from it. You could use empathy to reason with them, and they'd do the right thing in the end. But with the boys it is like they lose their ability to communicate when they are emotional. And they seem to get so lost in their anger that they can't see anyone else. Which, now that I think about it, also sounds like Isaac. He just shuts down and shuts me out as soon as life gets tough. What about Elle? Can she still communicate when she's emotional?"

"HAHA! Honestly, I don't think Elle ever stops talking. She even talks in her sleep." It is both my favourite and least favourite thing about her. I love that she's an open book, but my ears get tired by noon most days and I just crave an hour of silence so much.

Lish continues to talk about her gender stuff. She is always trying to find patterns and meaning in everything. I don't quite get it. Sometimes things are just things, and you can't find meaning to it. She may have quit her job as a Gender Studies Professor but she certainly didn't abandon her passion.

But my mind wanders back to the way Lish handled that fight so calmly, and how I was ready to cause actual physical harm to my child – for the second time today – because I was just so angry.

"So how do you do it?" I ask when she pauses for a breath. "How do you stay so calm when he's being so angry?"

"Ugh, it is a struggle. I've been working on it for a long time. Do you remember Amy? She was three, and she had the worst temper tantrums. She was so cruel and manipulative and she never did anything that I asked. I kept losing my temper with her, and one day I was so angry I whipped a bowl across the room and it smashed into a dozen pieces and frightened the kids so much they all cried. That was my rock bottom."

That was your rock bottom? I've done much worse than that.

"I put myself into therapy, I read books, I kept a daycare diary with all the challenges and how I could tackle them, I gave myself a sticker chart and the kids got to decide if I'd earned a sticker for not yelling. I had to learn about my triggers and where they came from. It has been a LOT of work. And whenever I think I'm getting better at it, it gets harder again. I'm handling things better than I was, but with Ruby's constant crying and now Zach turning into Satan as soon as he turned three, my skills are really being tested."

"I hate to rain on your parade, but five-year-olds are no picnic either." The kids have now begun to abandon the tree and move back toward the playground, stopping at a patch of grass under a tree to play with a caterpillar that Elle spotted.

"You and Elle had a fight this morning?" Alisha asks quietly enough that Elle can't hear her.

I sigh. I know I can tell Lish this. I know she won't judge me. But saying it out loud will just sound so terrible... "Elle unbuckled her car seat and I lost my temper and... I really hurt her."

"She unbuckled her car seat? Oh, hell no!"

"Yeah, but I shouldn't...." What? I shouldn't what? I shouldn't lose my temper? Shouldn't be violent? Shouldn't be a mother? Shouldn't be having a third? "I really lost my shit." I feel like I'm losing my mind. I'm working so hard but I'm still failing.

Alisha's face turns sour. "Maja, you are seven months pregnant with your third child. You are exhausted and overworked. Your kids are on you, yelling at you, all day and night, and your husband has no respect for you and doesn't lift a finger to help. You are doing the impossible, and all on your own. You are allowed to eff up now and then."

But I'm fucking up my kids. Alisha doesn't know the half of it. If she only knew how terrible Nate and I are. I feel like I might cry again.

"Maja," she turns to look me in the eye, "Did you tell her you were sorry?"

"Yeah..."

"Did you promise to keep trying your best?"

"Yeah, but..."

"Then you are being an amazing mom. You are teaching her that life is hard and everyone stumbles but that we pick ourselves up, try to fix it and try to do better. What better lesson in life is there than that?"

But I'm out of control. I'm abusive.

I'm abusive.

"Can't I teach her about making mistakes by, like, burning dinner or spilling the milk?" rather than giving her bruises.

"You could, sure, but that seems so 1950s housewife. You are more committed than that."

I know that Alisha means well, and I do appreciate her trying to pep me up, but I'm not really sold. Between Nate's drinking and swearing and bullying, and my losing my shit on them every single day, these kids will be in therapy for life.

Eloise will anyway. I've already broken her.

I feel so shitty.

"Can we talk about something else?"

"Yeah, for sure. Although, we should really head out soon. I need to get these guys home and fed and down for nap by one because Chuck's dad picks him up at three and wakes up all of the kids every time, no matter how many times I've asked him to stay in the car and just send a text so I can bring Chuck out."

"That's really rude!" I don't know how Lish can put up with all this, and for other people's kids. The only reason I put up with it from my own is because I love them.

Someone else's kids I'm pretty sure I'd be tempted to just lock them in a closet all day. "These kids are more hassle than they're worth. You need to ask for more money."

"Guys, FIVE MINUTES!" Lish calls out. "Yeah, five bucks an hour isn't really a comfort. And most people think that is too much to pay for childcare." We start gathering up our things.

"Doesn't that piss you off? I mean, it's like THE hardest job, and people expect you to do it for the joy of it?"

"Yeah, it does." Lish sighs, "It infuriates me. Not just for me but there are hundreds of thousands of women who do this for less than minimum wage. Nobody is ever going to pay us what we deserve, no matter how good we might be at it, no matter how hard it is, because we're supposed to want to do it for free because it is so fulfilling. Which is sexist bullshit. I'll bet the President finds his job fulfilling, but we pay him shitloads."

"Yeah. Some people say he should get more."

"Exactly. Women are supposed to work for emotional fulfillment and men are supposed to work for money. That is how it is."

"This is one of the reasons that I'm scared to send Elle to school. Who would put this much effort into a kid who isn't their own? I mean, I want to give up on her a dozen times a day, so how the hell is some poor overworked, underpaid teacher who doesn't even love her going to find the patience to deal with her?"

"Exactly. And once a kid is labeled "problem child" that is all anyone will see. Including the kid."

I might have already labeled her that.

"Alright my little chickens! It is time to get into the van!" Lish makes it look so easy. She just starts putting her stuff, Ruby, and the dog into the van and the other four kids trickle over and get into their seats, without any of the threats and blackmail that I have to use to get my kids to leave. My kids, who are now in Lish's van kicking up a stink because they want to go home with Lish. Again, I just want to yell. To scream them into the truck with the sheer force of my anger. But Lish gets close, holds their hands, and promises them a sleepover soon. Only then do they begrudgingly come to me.

Maybe I should send Elle to school. It would be a hell of a lot easier to let someone else deal with her. And maybe I'd be less beaten down and wouldn't fail so much.

I buckle Claire into her seat and kiss her sweet rosy cheeks. Then I come around to Elle's side. I'm dreading this. I'm so tense. I'm bracing for a fight. No doubt she is too. "Hey Peanut. Up into your seat so I can buckle you in."

Without a word she gets into her seat and helps me clip her in.

What. The. Fuck.

I wave goodbye to Alisha, who is still buckling kids in (what a pain in the ass that must be, five car seats. Ugh. Imagine those people with, like, seven kids...) and off we go.

It was nice to get out. When the weather is warm we're in the park or the woods every day, at least once a week with Alisha's gang. We have such fun. But now it is starting to feel like winter is just around the corner and that bums me out. And next summer I'll have a five month old, so we won't have nearly as much freedom.

At least I hope I'll have a five month old.

Poor Sofia. I can't even imagine. A few weeks ago I didn't even know if I wanted this baby. It was Nate's idea. Like, completely. He lied about wearing a condom because he wanted a son but I didn't want another pregnancy. He thought it was funny – still does. I was furious for so long, but then Grey died and suddenly I am terrified that I might lose the baby. Nate said, 'See, I knew you'd be happy to have a baby. Women love babies. It is what you are here for.' Alisha would have a fit about that one. But he's right, isn't he? I hate when he's right....

As we drive, Elle and Claire are laughing. Elle is making fart sounds and it is just cracking her sister up. I love how much they make each other laugh. Elle can be so mean sometimes – she just needs to be in control of everything and Claire is just so uncontrollable. Claire is like the match to Elle's powder keg.

But right now they are giggling themselves to tears.

It is because they can't reach each other. Then things would be different.

I'm so tense. I'm just totally on edge. I'll never get this day back on track if I don't relax.

I see the flashing lights before I hear the siren. They come from the SUV that is doing a u-turn behind me.

And then I see that Elle is out of her car seat, rubbing her butt on the window. She was pretending to poop out the window. That is what Claire was laughing at. That was the farting noise.

I am so angry I actually feel like murdering her. I want to slam on the brakes so hard that she'll go flying out, past my head and through the window. My compulsion to do it is so strong that it terrifies me even more than the sirens bleep-bleeping behind me.

With exaggerated care I brake and pull over.

"What is that sound, Mommy?" Elle straightens up in her seat. I can see her face in my mirror and it looks terrified. Three things Elle doesn't like: bright lights, loud noises, and getting caught.

"We're being pulled over by the police because you weren't wearing your fucking seatbelt."

She bursts into tears. Fuck. That was unnecessary Maja.

It seems like forever that we are at the side of the road waiting for the cop to get out of his car. Both girls are screaming their heads off. Elle is frantically trying to re-buckle her seatbelt, screaming, "Mama I can't do it! I can't do it!" and tears are streaming down her cheeks. It is as if she believes the police officer himself is going to crash the car.

Maybe she does think that. I don't know what her little head understands about this world.

I know you are supposed to stay in your seat when you get pulled over, but the girls are terrified, Claire can hardly breathe she's crying so hard, and neither of them can hear any of my calming words. I go for it – rolling down the window and opening the door while shouting "I just need to get them to calm down!" but who knows if he heard me over the screaming. I can't help but think it is a good thing that I'm a cute, tiny, pregnant Filipino woman, not a Black man (or even a pregnant Black woman for that matter), and the police officer, who is finally getting out of his car now, doesn't see me as the least bit of a threat. He nods at me as I climb into the back seat and calm the girls down.

"Ssshshhhhh, my babies. It is ok. Breathe nice and deep with me, calm down." But Elle is still hyperventilating. I sing the song that calms them, and when they can hear me speaking I say: "Elle, Claire, listen to me. The police officer isn't a bad man, he's just making sure that everyone follows the rules, and since we weren't following the rules he'll give us a ticket and we'll have to pay money, but that is all. Once he gives us the ticket we'll go home, ok?" Elle nods, her sad little face red and streaked with tears. While I speak I buckle her car seat: "OK, I'm going to get out of the truck now and talk to him." Panic sweeps across her face at the thought of me getting out and she grabs my arm desperately. "Baby, I promise you, he's a nice man. I'll bet he even has little kids at home. Should we ask him?" Elle nods yes.

I get out of the truck.

"Thank you, officer." I say to his amused face. He's in his 30s. White. He looks like he's about to give me a scolding, like I'm a naughty child.

"I'll need your license and registration, ma'am."

"Of course." I crawl into the front and grab my purse.

"Little ones were pretty upset."

"Yeah, we had an argument on the way to the park because she unbuckled her seat. I told her that I have to buckle her in or the police will take me away for being a bad mom." That isn't totally a lie. I did say that once.

"Oh, no, ma'am." He spoke loudly and slowly and winked at Elle through her window, "I won't take you away. I won't take anybody away. But this young lady here needs to promise to keep her seat buckled. I've seen what can happen when children don't buckle up, and I don't want that to happen to a pretty little girl like you."

So, if she was ugly...?

He smiles and tips his hat at Elle, as if he's been watching too many American westerns. He even speaks with a drawl. I would roll my eyes if I wasn't a nervous wreck.

He turns his attention to me.

"Are you alright ma'am? You look like you are about to have a baby any minute."

"Oh, I have a little bit to go still." Just two months, but I won't tell you that because then you'll feel like an idiot. "But, yes, I'm ok." I hand him my license and registration.

"OK, you hold tight." He takes the paperwork and heads back to the cruiser.

"Mom?" Elle whispers, even though the officer is nowhere near us.

"Yeah, baby?"

"You didn't ask him."

"Ask him what?"

"If he has kids."

"Oh, right. Remind me when he comes back."

I shut my door and buckle my seat belt, but keep the window open, while I wait for him to return. It seems like he's gone forever. I have time to notice how tense I am, how cold and clammy my hands are. And the baby is wriggling inside me, putting pressure on my ribs and bladder at the same time. It feels so tight, so stretched, I dread to think how big I'll be at nine months.

"I won't give you a ticket this time, ma'am. But in the future, if you see her remove her seatbelt, pull over as soon as it is safe to do so and get her back in there."

"Yes, of course." Duh.

"But hopefully just talking to me will scare some sense into them. If I see you again though...." He winks at me. I'm not sure what that is supposed to mean, so I just smile awkwardly.

He hands me my paperwork and pats the roof of my truck paternally. "You have a good day then, girls. Best of luck with baby number three there." He smiles.

"Mom!" Elle whispers again.

"Sorry, officer, my daughter wants to know if you have children."

"I do, ma'am. Five sons." He holds up his hand with all five fingers splayed.

"Five?" Jesus Christ, his poor wife.

"Yes, Ma'am."

"Did you hear that, Elle? He has five boys."

"Five?!" she yells. "Wow!"

"Maybe you'll be lucky enough to have a little brother too." He smiles, clearly pretty proud of himself.

"Yeah, that is what my husband thinks too." I never told Nate the results of the ultrasound: it is a girl. And I'm not about to tell this cop.

"Every man ought to have a son." He winks, as if it was my decision and he had just handed me the winning argument. "Alright, well you all have a good day now, you hear? And you be safe, little lady." He points at Elle as he steps away from the car, and then he stands there and watches as I start the engine, put the truck in drive, and pull away, my hands still shaking like a leaf.

As we turn the corner I can see him still standing there, hands on his hips like some cheesy cowboy cop.

Damn I could use a drink.

11:36 am

Sofia

I wake up on the floor in Grey's room. My eyes are so puffy they hardly open.

And I'm actually really hungry.

Drae brought food. Was that today?

What time is it?

Daylight.

I climb up off the floor. I think about putting Grey's blanket back on the crib but then I remember I don't need to.

No more locking him away.

I also grab a vase of white carnations from the changing table. They need some water, but they look good. I leave Grey's door open.

I put the vase on the dresser in my room and survey the mess I've been living in.

What a fucking disaster.

I'm going to clean this up. I'm going to eat some food and clean this up and have a shower.

But I'm not doing the laundry. That is going too far.

The food Drae brought me is on the bedside table. Beside it is my phone on the charger. It is fully charged but turned off. I grab the phone and the food and, with

Grey's blanket, take them to the living room couch where it doesn't smell like rotting breast milk and despair.

I'm hungry enough that the cold breakfast sandwich tastes good. My phone boots up and beeps about fifteen times with all of the messages.

Andrea

Thursday, 9:45 am
How are you two?

Thursday, 1:21 pm
Do you need anything? I can bring food, run errands?

Thursday, 5:35 pm
Are you OK? You aren't answering my messages. Which is ok, I just need to know that you are still alive.

Thursday, 9:48 pm
Answer?

Today, 7:18 am
OK, I'm on the way over and I'm bringing coffee.

Oh, Drae. You are the best.

Alisha

Thursday, 10:55 am
Hugs. Thinking of you.

Today, 9:18 am
Thinking of you. Sending hugs. Drae told me
about Colin. Want me to drag him home by his
ear like Maja's mom used to do? I will do that
for you. I can do it with or without the
obscenities. Your choice. HUGS.

Yeah, Maja's mom totally fulfills the Tiger Mom
stereotype. I appreciate the joke, but I can't laugh.

Maja

Thursday, 8:48 pm
How are you holding up? Can I bring you
anything?

Today, 10:48 am
So, Drae and Lish are coming over tonight to
pamper you. Should I come? Or will I make it
worse? I'm like one giant, walking trigger...

Oh, poor Maja. As if her pregnancy hasn't been stressful

enough, now she's probably terrified and feeling guilty on top of that. But I have no idea how I can be happy for her when her baby comes.

MOM

Thursday, 9:22 pm
Your father and I think you should go back to work. It would take your mind off of things

Jesus, Mom. That is the last thing I need. How can she possibly think that hanging out with pregnant ladies and delivering babies would take my mind off things?

Stephany

Thursday, 9:48 am
When do you think you'll be ready to come back to work? I need someone to cover a weekend... Hugs!

Fucking oblivious Stephany. Worst midwife ever. Well, no, she'd be ok at the job if babies were only born Monday to Friday, nine to five.

Jennifer

Today, 8:28 am
Hey sweetheart. It is time for us to schedule
your 1 week postpartum visit. I'll come to
you, of course. Is tomorrow good?

Oh, Jennifer. She was such a rock for me on that day, and I love her for that. But I don't know if I'll ever be able to talk to her without the whole day flooding back over me.

Nick

Thursday, 9:23 pm
Dude, avoid mom at all costs. That woman is
heartless. Love you. Sorry life is shitty.

I love my brother. He is the only member of my family who hasn't been constantly telling me what I need to do or how I should be feeling. How is everyone so terrible at emotional labour except the self-professed neanderthal?

I guess because he completely ignored every lesson about human behaviour that my mother tried to pass on to him? I don't know. I don't know how he got through our childhood so unscathed. Nothing sticks to him.

My sister, on the other hand...

VIOLA

Thursday, 8:55 pm
Hey, this is totally an inappropriate
question, but if you don't want to go back to
work, our nanny just quit. It might get mom
off your back.

My sister is just a taller, English-language version of mom,
I swear.

And I've seen how she talks to her nannies. Not if it was
the last job on earth.

YAYA

Thursday, 8:08 pm
Dearest Sofia. Abue and I are thinking of you.
Just remember, Everything happens for a
reason. God has a plan for you. We're praying
for you and Colin and Greyson. Love, Yaya.

God wanted me to carry a baby for nine months and then
for him to die and my husband to leave me? Nice guy, your
God.

I know Grandma means well, but I don't find the God
narrative comforting.

Fuck, that was too much. I feel completely overwhelmed. I'm not replying to these now.

And I'm not going back to work. Ever. I can never go back to work again. It is just not even a question. I'll burst into tears every time I deliver a baby. I'll recommend every mom have a c-section at 30 weeks. I can never be a midwife again. It is just preposterous.

I fucking loved that job.

Lost my child, and my husband, and my job. All in one week.

Fucking bullshit.

I take the last bite of the breakfast that Drae brought me. I don't even remember eating it.

All of those texts and nothing from Colin. Or his family.

That his family wouldn't reach out isn't really surprising. They never liked me. Heck, I don't think they even like Colin. They tell him he's lazy, he doesn't care about anything or anyone except himself... but then when he gets interested in something they make fun of him for it.

Like this baby. He was so excited but they kept saying shit like, 'You'll be a terrible dad. You'll be so wrapped up in yourself you'll leave him in the grocery store parking lot and drive off!' When he said he was going to be at the birth – something he was really looking forward to after hearing me talk about all of the amazing births I've witnessed – they laughed at him. 'You'll be scarred for life! No man should see that! You'll run like a scared little puppy and turn into a faggot!'

Maybe they never liked me because I never liked them. Bunch of rednecks.

Colin does try. He was raised in a home where a man

was defined by his ability to disrespect women, and he works in construction, where objectifying women is a competitive sport, and sexism, racism and homophobia are as natural as gravity. But none of it ever sat well with him, and the result is that he hardly speaks. He is shy and quiet and full of shame that he's not man enough, not smart enough, not strong enough, not in control.

Then he married me. A highly educated, well traveled, strong woman with a successful and demanding career. His family have called him my wife, a cuck, asked him if he's on his period... really they are disgusting people. His mom is just as cruel. She's always using their narrow definition of masculinity to control her sons: 'be a man and get the job done and quit your whining' is pretty much the gyst of everything she's ever said.

Even at Grey's funeral she scolded him when he let me carry a huge vase of flowers across the funeral home. 'The girl is in mourning, she shouldn't be lifting a finger to work, get your ass over there.'

I mean, I did want him to carry it for me, but not because I was in mourning – he was in mourning too! – but because I'd just given birth three days ago.

Everyone seems to forget that you still give birth when your baby dies. I still had 2nd degree tearing and six stitches. I'm still healing!

I'll never really heal.

Ugh.

I liked it better when my phone was turned off.

I toss the phone aside and reach for the remote and my 420 box.

Netflix.

Queer Eye.

Roll a joint.

Roll another joint for later.

And a third for emergencies.

This episode is about a mother trying to mend her relationship with her gay son. She'd pushed him away out of shame.

I would never have done that to my son. I would have loved Grey if he was gay. I would have loved him if he was blind or deaf or had ADHD or SPD or ASD or if he was tall or fat. I would have loved him if he was terrible at sports or had a short temper or said that he wanted to be a girl.

I would have loved him unconditionally.

I do love him unconditionally, and I don't know anything about him.

I turn off the TV and pick up my phone again.

Twifagram: Food pictures. News items about the politician accused of rape. Dog pictures.

Oh, Lish has been talking politics on Twifagram again. She always knows how to stir the pot... A couple of years ago she had a discussion about abortion that got so heated she lost several friends over it.

Probably not good friends...

---

twifagram

Alisha

I personally know 3 women who have been raped. I know 2 men who are rapists. I know 3

women whose lives have been destroyed by rape.
I don't know any men whose lives have been
destroyed by a rape accusation. I
#BelieveWomen

22 Likes 11 Comments

Alisha

I have no doubt that I know more victims of
rape who haven't confided in me, and more
perpetrators who've just continued to get
away with it and live among us smug and
dangerous

René

It is so infuriating. I always knew that rape
culture was a problem, but I can't believe how
many men don't know it. How many actively
deny it. It is terrifying.

Maria

Things are changing, but not fast enough!

Ellen

Well said!

Kristy

Well said! #BelieveWomen

Heather

I know 4 women who've been raped. I used to
know 2 rapists. I've never known any men
falsely accused of rape. I #BelieveWomen.

Jake

I know 3 men whove been falsely accused of
rape. 1 of them lost his job. I dont know any
women whove been raped and I dont know any
men whove committed rape. So should I write
#believemen?

Ellen

I'm sorry that your friend lost his job
unjustly, but when weighed in the balance
with a woman loosing her sense of safety, her
trust of men, her ability to love and connect,
and possibly also her job, friends, and
family, also unjustly. Compared to that, your
friend's misfortune seems like a fairly small
price to pay, don't you think? I mean, he
probably just went and got another one,
didn't he?

Heather

Jake, if you know 4 women, then you know a woman who has been sexually assaulted. If you know 3 men, then you know a man willing to commit rape. Sexual assault is all around you, every day, and you don't see it because it doesn't affect you. That is called "privilege." But the time to open your eyes is now.

Jake

@Heather no he didnt just get a new job he was unemployed for 5 years because everyone is afraid of the PC police not even mcdonalds would hire him and his wife left him

Jake

@Ellen that 1 in 3 stat is bullshit your fake
news totally twisted that study the real stat
is 13%

I wonder how many women Jake has sexually harassed. And then told her she's "too sensitive" when she tried to call him on it. He's clearly one of those guys who thinks it is his right to make other people uncomfortable.

I know at least one girl who has been raped. My sister. By her college boyfriend. And I've been groped and stalked and catcalled and men have exposed themselves to me, rubbed themselves on me, and insulted me more times than I can count. I have always just assumed that all women have those experiences, and I can't believe how many men don't know this.

But not my Colin. He's a gentleman. A woke gentleman. A woke gentleman raised by cavemen.

I check again to see if he sent me a message. But there's nothing since eight days ago:

Sofia

One Week Ago
I don't think these are Braxton-Hicks honey!
I think this might be the real thing!

COLIN

Sweet Jesus! I just dropped rebar on Jack's toe. I'll be home in 30 seconds!

Sofia

DON'T SPEED!

Baby will wait! They're still, like, 5 minutes apart!

Bring home some snacks for the midwives.

Snacks. We ate those when we came home from the hospital without a baby.

He was so excited. He must be hurting so much.

But he shut me out. Shut himself down and shut me out.

When we needed each other the most he just pushed all that pain down inside and went back to work. He's probably being a total dick with a temper when he should be here crying with me.

Ugh.

Back to Twifagram for a distraction.

Jessica

56 Likes   47 Comments

I drop the phone like it is on fire.

My throat tightens and I can't breathe. The blood rushes to my head and I feel hot and red, like I might explode. Is this a panic attack?

Oh, my baby. My baby. That should have been my baby photo shoot. And I don't even believe in baby photo shoots. Cramming a naked little newborn into a teacup. How humiliating.

But the only pictures I have of my boy were the ones the hospital took. They did a great job, he almost looks like a sweet little sleeping newborn. But his colour is a bit too grey, his skin is dry and caked with vernix. It is as though he's permanently frozen in that moment of birth before he could take a breath and inflate his lungs.

Omg this hurts too much.

I pick up one of my newly rolled joints and retreat to the bedroom. The mess can wait. Showering can wait. Right now I must curl up in bed and hug my own chest so tight that it won't hurt so much.

12:10 pm

Alisha

It was going well when we left the park. Everyone got in the van without incident and we left two minutes before I'd hoped to!

But Ruby cried the whole drive home. By the time I pulled the van into the driveway my nerves were shot. Nothing triggers my anxiety like crying (nice career choice, Lish).

Crying sets off everyone else's anxiety too: the twins were getting irritable and, when I unbuckled everyone's car seats and opened the van door, Zach went rogue.

Usually Zach would happily lead the other children from the van to the back gate and into the yard. He learned how to unlatch the gate a few weeks ago and he's happy to have been assigned the job of official gate opener. But for some reason this time he didn't head up the driveway, but ran down the sidewalk of my quiet suburb.

I've had some experience with kids who run. When I first opened the daycare I had this three-year-old boy for only a month. He was quiet and angry and anti-social. I often wondered if he might be on the spectrum, but I had so little personal experience with autism that I didn't dare tell his parents my suspicions. He hated daycare, me, and the other children and in that one month he ran away four times. The first time he figured out how to open the gate, and he just bolted. I ran after him but he was fast and had a head start. He made it all the way to the main road before I caught him. Then I had to carry him, writhing and screaming, all the way home.

That night I added another latch to the gate. It was so complicated that even the parents had a hard time with it.

The next time he ran away he climbed the fence into our neighbours' yard and ran off through their gate. I was in the house making lunch and, through my front window, I saw him emerge on her sidewalk. I almost rushed out the front door to grab him and drag him back in, but then I saw him stop. He looked around. He just stared into space for a few minutes and then he sat down under a tree.

He didn't know where to go.

That's when I realized one of my most valuable parenting lessons: kids know they need us. In that moment this kid realized he was helpless without me. He didn't know which way was home. He didn't know where his parents were. He realized he couldn't run away.

I could see how much more relaxed he was out there, thinking he'd escaped. He was free to run away if he wanted to, but he was choosing not to. It seemed empowering for him. I kept my eyes on him the whole time, listening to the playful screams of the other four kids in the backyard, and after a few minutes he made his way back through the neighbour's yard, and over my fence.

I stopped taking the kids outside on the days he came, but he still got out two more times – once by unlocking the baby-gate AND the deadbolt of the back door. Another time by stacking a chair on top of a table and crawling out through the fucking basement window. I could never get over how quickly he worked. I think he must have spent all morning hatching his plan and waiting until I stepped away to change a diaper or make food and poof! Off he went.

I terminated care after the 4th breakout. I really wanted to help him, but I just wasn't equipped to deal with that.

I remembered that boy in the moment when Zach ran off. I resisted the urge to chase Zach, resisted the urge to lose my temper. I just shouted, "OK, Zach, we're going inside. Come in when you are ready for lunch!" He was now five houses down the street, but he'd stopped running and was clearly near the limit of his comfort zone.

Ruby was still crying, the twins were starting to sob, and Chuck clearly wanted to run with Zach but was too scared to try. I had to get them inside where they were relatively safe and contained, but I couldn't take my eyes off Zach in case there were cars.

Fucking fuck I don't need this. I just want to feed them and put them to bed. Fucking Zach and his fucking temper. What is he even angry about?

I wanted to scream so hard.

But I talked myself down, got the screaming babies and a bitter but obedient Chuck inside the front door, where they could watch me through the living room window – not ideal, but it would have to do, and I took the dog out of the van's trunk space and latched her leash to the front porch, and then, as nonchalantly as I could, made my way down the street to Zach.

Zach was now sitting under a tree beside the street. We were seven houses away from mine and I could still hear Ruby and the twins screaming.

I can't believe that nobody has ever called Children's

Aid on me. There must be screaming coming from my house all day.

Zach didn't look at me. I wanted to shout at him: Do you know how dangerous this is?! Running away? You could get hit by a car. You could get kidnapped! I'm leaving the babies alone in the house screaming because you are a selfish little asshole! I wanted to grab him by the arm and drag him back.

But instead I said, "You must be pretty angry, eh buddy?"

"Me no like you, Lish. Me nunning away."

"Yeah, that's fair. It sucks that I'm always telling you what to do." Validate his feelings, let him be heard, then he'll chill out and come back. This can be quick and painless if I don't blow it.

"I wanna do to Odonnels."

"Ooooooh. That is why you are angry." Jesus fucking McDonalds. We drove past the cursed golden arches on the drive home and he yelled out that we should go there and I just laughed. I'm not taking five kids to McDonalds. First, I'm not crazy, and second, I'm not blowing almost my entire day's earnings on happy meals that nobody is going to eat. Well apparently Zach was so furious about that unforgivable sleight he was trying to walk there himself. "Yeah, I get that. It is pretty cool at McDonalds. What food would you have gotten if we could have gone there?"

The babies were still screaming. They're going to get fucking brain damage.

"Teesebuger!"

"Oh, sweet. That sounds yummy. What toy would you have gotten, do you think?"

"Tatboy!"

"Batboy?"

"No, Tatboy!"

"Catboy?"

"Yeah, Tatboy!"

"Oh, awesome. I wish we could have done that today. Although we did have lots of fun in the park. And I was thinking of maybe making pasta with meatballs for lunch."

"Meatballs?"

I've got him now.

"Yeah, but maybe not. I mean, there's no point in making your favourite if you are running away. I guess I could just make dog food with ketchup? I think the babies would eat that."

"Eeeeeeewwwww!" he laughed.

"Or cat poop with strawberries?

He laughed again, "Are you dust doking?"

"Unless... do you want to come in with me for some meatballs?"

"Otay." He got up to his feet and took my hand and turned me back toward the house.

Yes! Awesome. Just get everyone downstairs, I can unload the stuff in the van later. Today is leftover lunch day so Zach can have the pasta and everyone else can have sweet potato with sausage and rice with chickpeas, and if that isn't enough there's yogurt and ...

Of course that was when Zach pulled away. We were almost home. Close enough that I could see the tear tracks on Ari, Hana, and Ruby's cheeks through the window. But Zach got his mischievous look on his face and bolted around the bush on my front yard, begging for a chase.

I was aware, in that moment, that Zach had anxiety about entering that house full of screaming babies, and this was his way of saying he wanted to play with me instead. But I was also going crazy from the screaming that was never going to stop until I went into the house or the babies all slipped into comas from trauma. I was also aware that wasn't a real thing but it definitely felt like a life or death situation. I was just fucking done with this fucking shit.

I grabbed Zach roughly, slung him under my arm like a sack of potatoes, and carried him kicking and screaming into the house.

There were four kids screaming as I took them all downstairs. Four kids screaming as I buckled them into their chairs. Four kids screaming as I put on their bibs and put plates of cold leftovers in front of them (thank fuck I didn't have to cook!). Poor Chuckie just sat there with his hands over his ears. He's such a sensitive little soul. My mind jumps to his father joking about smacking him: why would anyone ever need to hit such a sweet, agreeable child?

And then only Ruby was screaming. I sat on the floor beside her and, with a little affection, some calm breathing and skin contact, even she stopped crying and ate.

OMG blessed silence.

I am now lying on the floor right beside the table while the kids eat. I take a few deep breaths. I am shaking. I want to cry. I want to barf. My heart is in my throat.

Jesus this day is going to kill me. It might even be worse than yesterday.

No, yesterday was still worse.

I need to quit this job. Before it kills me.

I don't feel much calmer, but there is work to do. I get up, put some relaxing music on my computer and put my own lunch – leftovers from last night – in the microwave.

And now Ruby is starting to get upset again.

What is most astounding about Ruby getting upset is

just the level of panic she reaches. Within seconds she is blind with terror. She is clawing at her bib, scratching herself all around the neck. She pushes her chair frantically away from the table, tipping it backward and I catch it before she hits the ground, but the fall frightens her and she screams all the louder. She's knocking chunks of food on the floor with her flailing arms and chunks of rice are clinging to her skin and clothes and hair. I try to clean her off but she's clawing me like a terrified cat and I just let her climb into my arms covered in food.

She whimpers miserably and I try to brush off as much rice as I can. This can't be good for her. To be this unhappy here, and for three weeks now, this kind of long-term anxiety has got to be doing her permanent damage.

"I done!" shouts Zach. "Det me a coth!"

"I done! I done!" shout the twins.

"Guys, you've hardly eaten anything. I don't want you complaining you are hungry in twenty minutes."

"I not hungry! I pomise!" Zach whines.

Sure you're not. "I'm hoping you can just take a couple more bites, to make sure your tummy is full to the top."

"No! Det me a coth!"

"Zach, buddy, it hurts my feelings when you talk to me like that. How would you say it kindly?" Breathe. I mustn't shout at him. But every atom in my body wants to.

I am in control of me. If I'm in control of me he'll get control of him.

As I get him the cloth, Ruby in tow, he cheerfully says, "Pease Lish." and the twin's parrot him, "Pease Lish."

"Thank you guys. I enjoy doing things for you when you are nice to me. I feel appreciated."

Five faces wiped, five bibs off, five plates cleared, all

while Ruby whimpered away in my arms. Because of course the baby carrier is still in the van.

And I'm definitely getting a migraine. I need to drink some water and eat some food.

And not be carrying this kid around everywhere.

"ROAAAAAAARRRRRRRR!!!!" Zach is screaming in frustration, holding a plum-sized rock over his head, preparing to launch it at Chuck, who is crouched under the kiddie picnic table looking terrified.

Where the fuck did he get a rock?

"Zach!" I say it very loudly, to catch his attention.

"I very angry!!"

"I see that. That must feel terrible, Zach. But I know you don't really want to hurt your friend."

"I do want to urt him!"

"Oh, I know it feels like you do! Sometimes I feel that way too!" I'm right beside him now, but I don't take the rock. If I take it he'll go on a rampage, but if I convince him to give it up we can move on. "But I always regret it when I hurt my friends, don't you?"

"No! I want to urt him! He not my fend! He not pay wi me!"

Maybe he doesn't want to play with you because you are threatening to throw a fucking rock at his head?

"Zach, do you see Chuck's face? Do you see how scared he is?"

Zach softens for a moment, and then hardens again. "Roaaarrr!" he screams again. He's just so overwhelmed with emotion and he doesn't know what to do with it. He just wants to hurt everyone else as much as he's hurting. I feel so sad for him, but I also want to yank the rock from his hands and throw him out of the daycare altogether.

Ruby starts to cry again. The twins are watching the

standoff from across the room, out of the line of fire. Chuck looks like he wants to cry, his hands cupped over his ears again.

"Zach, what can we do to help get your angry out? Can we take some deep breaths together?"

"Nufing! I too angry!"

"Do you want to throw the rock at the pillows?"

"NO!"

Fuck this shit. I'm done with this.

I take the rock.

Zach roars again. He hits my legs with both fists. He grabs the plastic picnic table that Chuck is trying to hide under and flips it. He looks around for more things to throw and break. I'm furious. I want to roar back at him and throw the rock at his defiant little fucking little face.

I plop the screaming Ruby down on the floor and grab Zach just as he reaches for the calm down bottle. Fucking calm down bottle has never once calmed him down, only provided him a weapon. I don't know why I thought it would help. Again I sling him under my arm, again I'm too rough with him, but it is tame compared to what I want to do, and I practically throw him into the bathroom.

"I love you Zach, but you're going to have to stay in the bathroom until I know you won't hurt anybody."

I slam the door behind him.

Fuck fuck fuck I did that all wrong. Fuck.

I survey the room. Chuck is still frozen to the floor where the picnic table used to be. The twins have forgotten all about it already and are digging through the dress up box. Ruby is frantically crawling toward me and clawing at my legs.

I pick her up. My head explodes in pain when I bend

over. I've been waiting all day for this migraine to break, and there it is. Fuck.

"Are you ok Chuck?"

He nods his head emphatically, but by the look on his face I can see he's lying and he is actually really upset. I kiss him on the head and ruffle his sandy hair. "I love you Chuckie. I'm sorry for all of the yelling."

I enter the bathroom.

There's toilet paper all over the floor. Zach roars at me again as I enter, but I can see he's moved through anger and into shame.

He lets me cuddle him. We sit on the floor together, Zach, Ruby and I, and I give Zach a squeeze and some kisses.

"Zach, you know I love you even when you are angry?"

"I no love you."

"That's ok. Zach. You know it is ok to be angry? I get angry too. It's just not ok to hurt people."

"But Chuck wouldn't pay wi me."

"Oh, I'll bet that made you really sad."

"Yeah."

"But you know, you can't make someone want to play with you. And if he is afraid that you will hurt him, then he definitely won't want to play with you. But if he sees that you are having fun, then he'll want to play."

"I want to go home."

"Oh, buddy." I give him another hug. Ruby tries to push him away, so I wedge myself between them.

"I thought maybe we'd have a dance party?"

"Yeah!" his face lights up.

Oh, thank fuck.

A minute later four kids are dancing and jumping and giggling to Pharrell's *Happy*.

Jesus Fucking Christ this day.

I need a joint. I'll have to settle for a codeine for this migraine. I just need to get some food in my tummy first.

I run the microwave for another minute because my food is cold. The dog is barking. Oh, shit, she's still tied to the front porch!

I lug Ruby upstairs to let Sheba in, and while I'm there I go out to the van. The side door is still wide open. Nice one, Lish. It is so quiet outside. I stop for a moment, there on my front lawn. I close my eyes and take a deep breath. The sun is trying to shine through the clouds and the wind is gently rustling the leaves. So quiet. I wish I could just stay out here. I almost feel like a real human being out here.

If I can just get to nap time I'm home free.

"Alisha! I was about to call the police about that dog!" the sound of my neighbour's voice startles me so much that I jump, and Ruby starts to cry again. "He's been barking for hours. That is disturbing the peace, you know." She scolds me like I'm a naughty child, and the look on her face as she watches me over the fence is one I'm certain her children and grandchildren know well.

I stare at her dumbfounded. I'm not sure what to say. Sorry my dog barked? Thank you for not calling the police? Why the fuck didn't you just knock on my door or bring her in yourself since it is pretty fucking obvious to anyone with half a brain that I've got my hands full and could use the help? No, no, you'd rather just call the cops on me?

"Sorry, Alice. I couldn't hear him over all of the screaming." I shout over Ruby's wails as I walk away. I close the van's side door, and open the trunk to retrieve the carrier.

Fucking Alice. She's always complaining about all the many ways that I'm dropping the ball. My lawn full of dandelions, my hedges that need trimming, the fucking rain that comes off my roof and runs into her basement, as if I had control over the weather.... Last spring Isaac actually said to her that if she didn't like the hedges she could trim them herself, and ever since then she's just taken every opportunity to talk about how useless Isaac is.

Fuck her.

I drag myself back into the daycare where the kids are dancing wildly, and I strap Ruby back into the carrier on my back. The four kids are giggling wildly as if everything was perfect today.

Meanwhile my anxiety is so high I feel like I've been in a car crash. I'm hot and sweaty and cold and clammy and shaking like a leaf. I feel sick to my stomach but I'm also starving. And my head. The slamming pain is ramping up.

I step over the little baby gate that keeps the kids out of my daycare kitchen. It is really just a wet bar but I've added a microwave, mini-fridge, toaster oven and hot plate so I can cook pretty much anything down here. I much prefer my kitchen upstairs, but this one serves its purpose.

My lunch in the microwave is cold. Again. I'm about to give it another minute when there's a huge crash beside me. Ruby has reached out from her perch on my back and grabbed a stack of dirty dishes and dumped them on the floor.

Rice, meatballs, tomato sauce, corn and peas, sausage, sweet potatoes, yogurt, all over the carpet.

I'm screaming at the top of my lungs. It is a primal scream, full of rage and fury and frustration. My fists and eyes are clenched. My whole body is clenched. It is all I can do not to whip the first thing that I can find as hard as I can.

I can't do this! I can't take this anymore! I can't stand another minute of this fucking shit!

Ruby is reaching for the toaster oven now. I want to break her fucking arm off.

Jesus Christ, Alisha, pull it together.

Out of the little kitchen. I take Ruby off my back again and put her on the floor to scream. I drown her wails out with the little handheld vacuum. While I clean up the mess I feel the tears filling my eyes. My head hurts so much. So much. And my throat.

I microwave my lunch again while Ruby scratches and shrieks at the gate. To get out of the kitchen with my plate I have to climb over the kitchen gate again, but she won't get out of the way. She's just screaming and clawing at my leg and I can't put my foot down and I feel so compelled to fucking kick her fucking little body GETOUTOFTHEFUCKINGWAY!!!!!!! I scream inside my mind, rage pulsing through me and all of my muscles clenched, while somehow still managing to appear perfectly calm on the outside.

And I'm out. I sit on the floor with my back against the wall so that screaming Ruby can sit in my lap and calm down. Within seconds Zach and the twins are in my face.

"What you eating Lisha? Can I hab some? I huuuuuuuuungy."

Mother fucking Jesus fucking Christ you fucking asshole.

"No, Zach, this is my lunch. You already had yours."

"But I huuuuuuungy."

I am so full of rage it takes every bit of strength I have to just do nothing. It is a miracle I am strong enough to resist this anger, it is so thick and wild and fierce.

All four of them. All four are screaming RIGHT IN MY FUCKING FACE. Their anger and sorrow is washing over me in waves. I am drowning in it. Like, my body is an empty tub and sadness and pain are filling me up until I contain nothing else.

I close my eyes and eat. I breathe.

I breathe.

Dear God. The tears are streaming down my face. I can't do this. I want to run away and never come back. I can't do this.

I breathe.

1:45 pm

Andrea

It was about an hour before I felt calm enough to leave the napping room. When I did I was sure everyone was staring at me as I walked down the hall to my office. I had checked my face with my phone's camera and it wasn't too puffy, and there's no way Diane told EVERYONE already, so I chalked it up to paranoia.

And I was only at my desk for two minutes when Diane came to ask if I was ok.

"Yeah, I'll be alright. Thanks Diane."

"I found that if I ate saltine crackers throughout the day I didn't feel so sick."

"I'm not pregnant, Diane. I'm just dealing with some personal stuff and it is stressing me out." I guess Jeff didn't talk to her...

"OH! Ok. Silly me. It isn't your husband is it? Are the kids OK?"

"Yes, everyone is ok. But I'd love some time alone to get my head together."

"Yeah, sure. Of course... He isn't cheating on you is he?"

"Diane..." I sighed.

"Yes, sorry."

And only two minutes later Jeff was checking on me: "I'd really feel better if you went home, Drae."

Because your feelings are the ones that matter, "I will. I'm just going to do a few things first."

But the truth is, I don't want to go home. I'd be alone with Damien and he'd want to know why I wasn't at work and I don't know what I'd say.

OR he might not even come out of his room. Which would probably make me feel even worse.

I went to the gym and pushed myself so hard I thought I might faint. And now here I am at my desk eating leftover salmon and quinoa wishing it was a big greasy pizza.

I'm not sure if terminal cancer means I should eat more pizza or less pizza.

But apparently I should smoke more weed.

My phone buzzes.

It's from Damien. I asked him to pick up the boys tonight and he's finally replying, two hours later.

DAMIEN

Today, 1:46 pm
Damien: I'd really rather not.I'm confident that you can find a way.

Jesus fucking Christ. You've got to be kidding me.

As it is, the whole situation is ridiculous. Wallace's school is a three minute drive from our house. All Damien has to do is sacrifice ten minutes of his day to go get him, but nope. That's too big of an ask. Instead I pay $30 a day for before and after school care so that I can drop him off before I go to work and pick him up on the way home. That is almost as much as I pay for Zach's entire day at Lish's daycare. That is $600/month of the money I work my ass off to make so Damien can chase his dream job.

Right now that dream job is a website designer. He has no experience designing websites but he is smart and good with tech so about a year ago he started to teach himself website design. He's currently working on a pro-bono project for a friend's business, "for my portfolio" he says. Before that he was a photographer. He took gorgeous photos, he's a real artist, but he found that there's no money in photography unless you do weddings and baby pictures, and he felt like that was beneath him. Before that he was a writer. When I met him he was working on the Great American Novel. It was really good, he's a wonderful writer, and it was published and everything, but it only sold a couple of thousand copies and he didn't see any money because the publisher went bankrupt.

He is a talented man, and full of passion. He throws himself into whatever project he's working on, and it has always resulted in some fantastic work.

Just, never any income.

And, really, I could be ok with that except his projects take priority over everything. Over the boys, over me, over the bills, over the chores, even over his own sleep and diet. He just completely loses himself down the rabbit hole and the rest of the world ceases to exist.

So when I ask him if he can pick up Wallace tonight so I can do some grocery shopping for Sof, he says he's too busy. Because his time is more valuable than mine.

And I can't help but wonder how this will work when I'm gone.

The thought terrifies me, actually. How many times will he forget to pick the boys up from something? How many activities will they miss because he has lost himself in another project?

But I've already had a mental breakdown today so maybe I'll think about this another time.

I feel like the only time I'm not risking a mental breakdown is when I'm dreaming.

Ever since the diagnosis I've been having the sexiest dreams. Dreams where I'm having the wildest, raunchiest sex with faceless, nameless men. Men of all different skin colours with bulging biceps and thick necks, and they find me so desirable they can hardly control themselves. And when I wake up I feel like I'm about to have an orgasm.

And it occurs to me that these men have come closer to giving me an orgasm than any real man ever has.

How sad is that?

Will I die without knowing good sex?

Am I ok with that?

No. No I am not.

Just then my desk phone rings. It is reception.

"Hi Andrea? I have your mother here."

"My mother?" Damn. I guess when I don't answer my cell phone she just calls the office. "Ugh, can you just tell her I'm not at my desk and I'll call her back later?"

"No, I mean, physically standing here in front of me."

Oh. My. Fucking. God. "She is not!" I stand up to look. The front of the HR department is one giant glass wall, stretching from the roof to the ground two floors below, overlooking the bright and open atrium. I can easily see down to the front entrance and, there, on the other side of the glass sliding doors, is my mother. She is dressed in immaculate business attire and, although she's only just five feet tall, she's standing as large and confident as if she were six foot six.

"She says you won't answer her calls so she needed to check you hadn't been kidnapped." Janet is only just managing to stifle a laugh.

"Jesus Christ. I'll be right down. Don't you dare let her in! She'll tell everyone they aren't working hard enough!"

"OK, Andrea. I'll be sure to let her know you said that." Janet is using her most proper receptionist voice so I know that she is joking but I still say,

"Don't you dare!" before I hang up the phone.

Christ, Mother. Why can't you just let me avoid you for a couple of days?

I shut down my computer, grab my things and head for the elevator.

Well, Jeff will be pleased I left early.

And Diane will be crazy with worry. She'll ask everyone in the building where I am until Janet finally fills her in.

"Oh, there she is!" Mom's face lights up when she sees me. To the outsider she appears to be just a sweet little old lady who is happy to see her kid, but I know it is all a part of her act where she pours on the love and then hits you with the guilt and control and manipulation. "I've been so worried about you, darling."

"Hi Mom." I give her a hug and then to Janet I smile awkwardly, "Thanks Janet. Do you mind telling Jeff I've gone. He already knows I'm leaving early today."

"Yeah, for su..." Janet starts but my mother interrupts.

"Is it this woman's job to be your go-between? If you want to skip out on work early you should face the music yourself, not pass the buck to this kind lady." She smiles sweetly, "Janet has been so helpful, haven't you dear?"

I must get my mother out of here before she tries to talk someone into firing me.

"Mom, I'm not skipping out." As I usher my mom to the door I mouth the words "Thank you" to Janet. "I have errands to run but I can drive you home on the way."

"Oh, no, I can take the bus home. You should get back to your important job. You must be very busy if you don't even have time to reply to my texts." She says as she makes a beeline toward my car in the parking lot: she clearly has no intention of getting the bus.

"It is fine, Mom. I was leaving early today anyway."

"I phoned your house but nobody answered. I wondered if maybe Damien was at work."

I don't respond. She knows perfectly well that Damien does not have a job, and this is just one more passive-aggressive dig. I just open the passenger side door for my mom to get in and then move around to my door. She's already talking when I get inside.

"I really just wanted to know what Zach and Wallace would like for dinner tonight. Do they still like my Ugali or should I make spaghetti with meatballs? I know when some little children grow up it isn't cool to eat those weird foods of their heritage anymore. Before you know it they'll be so embarrassed by their Bibi that they won't even want to come for dinner." Again I know this is just part of her game. She knows how much the boys love her Ugali. It is their favourite Kenyan food.

"Mom, I've already told you, we won't be able to come for dinner tonight." I pull out of the parking lot and head east toward mom's seniors' condo building.

"It is happening already. Nobody loves Bibi. When I was...."

"Mom!" I interrupt her. Interrupting my mom is often the only way to get a word in, and even then she sometimes only pauses to take a breath and then starts right back up again without hearing a word I say. "I can't come because I need to take care of Sofia tonight."

I said the only thing that would distract her from the guilt trip. "Oh, that darling girl." Mom is instantly on the verge of tears. Mom has cried every time I've mentioned Sofia for the past week. Mom lost a baby before I was born. Back in Nairobi. I don't know any of the details except the hospital was responsible for his death. She told me once this is the reason she wanted to come to Canada, and why she stayed when my dad went back: she blames Kenya for his death. Although most of the time she tells people she stays because Kenya is too hot. Which is clearly a lie, because the humidity in the summers here is way worse than the weather in Kenya.

Mom has never really talked about that boy. Until last week I sort of thought it was behind her, but since I told her about Grey she's been mourning the loss of my brother as if it were yesterday. At the funeral she held Sofia and they wept together for what seemed like forever. I never really thought about how much losing a child must have eaten away at my mother until Sofia lost Grey. Of course she must have been destroyed. You never put that behind you. And suddenly I'm revisiting all of these childhood memories of my mother crying for no apparent reason and spending days at a time in bed. When I was young this was embarrassing and inconvenient, but now I realize she must have had depression.

Which is why I can't tell my mom about my cancer.

Which is why I'm avoiding her.

Mom grabs my hand and squeezes it firmly. "She is lucky to have a friend in this dark time. You tell her that she is in my prayers."

"I will Mama." I won't tell her Sofia is an atheist.

"Now, what is wrong with you?" she switches gears like a race car driver: from heartbroken to accusatory in 0.3 seconds. But she doesn't give me a chance to answer before she jumps to her own conclusions: "It is that useless husband of yours, who won't get a job. My father had four wives and provided for each of them better than your husband."

My grandfather only had three wives. My mother likes to embellish. She told me once that you have to exaggerate because people always assume you are exaggerating anyway. So, if she said her dad only had three wives people would round it down to two. So she has to lie. My mother's mind is a really special place.

"You should leave that man and marry a doctor so you can stay at home with the children instead of having strangers raise them."

"Mom, you went to college and worked two jobs when I was little, what are you talking about?"

"Yes, and look how you turned out! Your children deserve better. They deserve their mother."

I'm always amazed at the way my mother can be so terribly cruel while complimenting me. It is a skill she has practiced a lot.

"Mom, I can't just leave my husband and marry a doctor."

"You've never been one to aim high, have you?"

"Mother, please remember that you thought Damien

was the perfect husband for me. You used to tell people you had matched us yourself."

"I did no such thing. But that was before I knew he was a loser."

"Mother, he is my husband."

"I just don't want you ending up alone and poor like I am. I was supposed to be giving you a better future in Canada, but you are still paying the bills and raising the kids alone like I did. You know, your father and his dirty girlfriend..."

"His wife."

"... and their dirty kids have a better life in Kenya than we have here. They have a maid! Maybe I should go live with them."

You might end up doing just that, Mama.

Thank God we pull into mom's building at that moment because I'm really just about done listening to her belittle and insult me while also making me feel terribly, painfully guilty about absolutely everything, including my own death. I'm barely holding myself together as it is, she is the last thing I needed.

"Mom, I have to drop you and run. I'm doing grocery shopping for Sofia and then I've got to pick up the boys."

"Too busy for your old mom. I know how it is."

"Mom, I'll visit on the weekend, ok? And we'll all come for Friday dinner next week."

"Yes, if you want. I don't want to be a burden."

The woman makes me crazy.

She's out of the car and into the lobby and I drive off.

Grocery store. I'll just get Sofia a bunch of prepared food, some fresh fruit, things that take zero effort and will still provide some basic nutrients.

Of course after a talk with my mother the conversation

rolls around in my mind like a piece of debris in the ocean, over and over, around and around, trying to understand what she said and what she meant, what is true and what is hyperbole.

Is Damien a loser?

I certainly didn't think so when I married him. He is everything a woman is supposed to look for in a man: well educated, well spoken, and well presented, from a family that is well educated, well spoken, and well presented. He is confident and handsome.

And white, that was important to mom. She always says, loudly and unabashedly, that Black men don't stick around – which infuriates me because it just isn't true. All of the Black men we know are committed and present husbands and fathers. Yeah, my dad left, but he didn't leave us, he left Canada and we stayed. Heck, my grandfather was committed to three wives, and he stuck around for all of them. So I don't know why she believes that nonsense. She watches too much TV.

That a man like Damien would even talk to a poor, immigrant girl like me was more than I could have dreamed of. So when he wanted to date me, and then he asked me to marry him.... Well, I was over the moon.

But did I love him?

Do I love him?

I don't even think I know what love is. How can I be a 34-year-old married mother of two and not know if I've ever been in love?

Did I fall in love with him? Or did I fall in love with the life he represented? The Canadian success story. Because I was never going to find someone better than this?

Is Mom right? Do I sell myself short?

He is a good guy. He respects me. He doesn't drink or

gamble or do drugs. I know that he isn't cheating because he never leaves his office. He does love the boys and is great with them when he is able to forget about work for a minute. I mean, when I get together with other women they all complain about their husbands' drinking, how much mess they make, how they never help out, how they say such rude and cruel things. Damien is a dream by comparison.

On paper, yeah, he is perfect.

Except he's so completely wrapped up in himself I might as well not even exist.

And I can't even remember the last time we had sex. And when we did it was robotic and routine.

It is a life without passion.

And I am invisible to him.

I don't think he'll even miss me when I'm gone. Except that nobody would buy groceries or do his laundry.

Is that how I want to spend the rest of my life? Being invisible, without knowing love, without feeling passion?

As I pull into the grocery store parking lot I feel like I'm going to be sick again.

Oh dear god this day.

I can't keep doing this to myself. My mind can't handle it.

Alisha

I don't remember what movie it was, but there was a scene where all of these WWII Allied military vehicles were rumbling over this little stone bridge, and the bridge just creaked and groaned and shuddered. What the soldiers don't know was that the retreating German army planted a huge bomb beneath the bridge, and every creak and groan and rumble threatened to trigger the bomb which was capable of exploding the bridge and every person within a quarter mile in one giant bloody conflagration.

That bridge is my mind. Every day there is another convoy. It is a miracle that it hasn't blown everyone to smithereens.

The house is still and quiet now but my head is buzzing and my body twitches. I'm lying on the living room couch. The kids are all downstairs, asleep at last, and I have about 25 minutes to calm myself down before Chuck's dad comes and wakes them all up and it starts all over again.

My back aches, my pelvis aches, my head aches.... I was

able to finally take a pill for the migraine about an hour and a half ago, so I'm feeling some relief in my neck, shoulders and head, but geez.

This day.

After my tear-filled lunch, things didn't get much better. I was able to get the four older kids distracted with "Going on a Lion Hunt" playing on my computer, but Ruby was having none of it. She screamed through diaper change and clung to me like a drowning rat as I gave her a bottle.

I still haven't figured out how to juggle nap time with Ruby. At her interview Ruby's mom swore she was an easy napper, but I have never once seen that child fall asleep without a fight. I started with everyone napping together in the same room, but Ruby screamed so loudly, both when going to sleep and when waking up, I had to put her in a separate room.

But unfortunately I can't be in two places at once.

Ruby's mom's instructions were to just put her in a dark room with some white noise and she'd fall asleep on her own with no crying. Sounds nice, but every time I've tried this Ruby has cried so hard she starts to choke. I can't just listen to that: it tears my heart out, hearing a child panic like that. A couple of times I've been able to get her to fall asleep in about ten minutes by rubbing her back while singing to her. Not today. I swear I tried for 45 minutes and got nowhere. Singing didn't work, not rocking, not rubbing that spot at the base of the head, not stroking my fingers down her nose. Nothing. She was clearly tired, and fell asleep a few times, but if I tried to leave the room she'd wake and panic.

Meanwhile the other four kids were alone with nothing but my playlist to keep them out of trouble. I was able to peek in on them a few times – when I was so triggered by Ruby's crying I had to leave the room – and thank goodness they were all playing wonderfully. At one point I just sat on the stairs between the two rooms, listening to the bigger kids playing and Ruby screaming with terror and I cried. I was just so spent, so done, so strung thin, crying was literally the only thing I could do.

Finally at two o'clock I gave up on Ruby to put the others to bed. I could hear her crying two rooms away while I set up the beds: two mats on the floor for Chuck and Zach and the pull-out couch for the twins and me. I could hear her crying while I read four bedtime stories, and I could hear her crying while I kissed everyone goodnight. And then I curled up in bed with Ari and Hana, their soft warm little hands on my neck and face. And it broke my heart for Ruby, alone in the dark in my laundry room, scared and feeling abandoned, while my kids were cuddled safe and secure with their mommy.

She did, eventually, cry herself to sleep around the same time that I was sure the twins were both sleeping. I wiggled my way out of Ari and Hana's grasps and, shaking like a leaf, sneaked upstairs to put myself back together again.

I've been thinking about all of these movies and TV shows that tell the protagonist's sob story: 'When I was only eight years old my mother just up and walked out one day and never came back.' These shows always leave you thinking, What kind of shitty mom does that?

But now I'm like, oh, yeah, I feel you shitty mom. I totally get the mom who runs away. Because I fantasize about doing it every day.

I'm running on empty all the time. Constantly pushed to my limit. Five times a day I think I can't possibly survive another minute of this madness, but then somehow I do. I am much stronger than I ever thought I was, but I'm seriously worried I'm doing permanent, irreparable, psychological damage.

I can't keep doing this.

I mean, I've loved the daycare. It was a great job to take on after my cancer. It was fun and inspiring and life affirming, and has afternoon nap and dance parties. It has been a really good learning ground to help me be a better mom.

But it isn't any of those things anymore. The damage that was done to my body just can't heal when I'm always carrying kids. And then there's the lack of sleep, the lack of personal space... there is no time for me anymore. And of course having kids seems to rewire your brain so the sound of crying children sends you into an irrational rage, and my hormones are so messed up pretty much everything makes me cry... and the result is anxiety so severe I find myself shaking like a leaf several times a day.

I've been working so hard to deal with the anxiety. I've made such progress in not reacting with violence or yelling, but the anxiety itself is not getting better. In fact, it is getting worse. I know the daycare is the reason.

I don't regret opening the daycare, but I'll regret it if I don't close very soon.

Of course Isaac is worried about money. Isaac is always worried about money. Me wanting to close the daycare to help my mental health means he suddenly has a greater mental strain because he worries about money more than I do.

I'm guessing that is why he is angry at me. Which is fair, but if I have a total mental breakdown I won't be able to make money either, so I'm not about to try to ignore this problem and hope it goes away.

Why don't I go back to academia? Well, if I could get

a job in the current climate, where something like 75% of classes are being taught by adjunct professors, who have no job security, no benefits, and no respect, there is still the fact that I just wasn't happy in academia. It is the sort of career where you really have to be obsessive about what you do – you have to live, eat and breathe your area of interest with little recognition and no guarantee of a job. I just wasn't obsessed. I wanted to have outside interests. I wanted a life. And my cancer diagnosis was the kick in the pants I needed to prioritize my life over my career.

I get a notification on my phone that there's been a comment on my Twifagram post. Oh, right. I forgot about that. But when I open my phone I see the text that Maja sent me a half hour ago:

Maja

Today, 2:07 pm
Of course they aren't going to nap. Why would they nap? The chances of getting a solid hour to myself are the same as the chances of a flying unicorn that poops candy.

HA! It is true.

I have Ari's socks in my pocket. He refuses to wear socks, and I'm always picking them up wherever I go.

And I cut my finger while doing the dishes and it hurts like a bitch. Tiniest cuts always hurt the most. And it needs a new bandage because this one is all over the place.

With much regret I get my ass off the couch. I grab a

bandage and my laptop, and head back to my spot on the couch.

Jessica

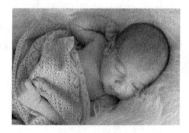

67 Likes   51 Comments

Instantly I'm crying. I cry for the boy I'll never know. Grey was lined up to take Zach's spot in the daycare when Zach starts school next year. Sof had planned to visit weekly while on her Mat leave. We were so looking forward to this. We were all so excited that she was finally joining us on this motherhood adventure, and now the loss feels so monumental. She should be coming to us for advice about sore nipples and trouble peeing but instead she's all alone in her house with nobody to comfort her. Nobody to hold.

Alisha

I personally know 3 women who have been
raped. I know 2 men who are rapists. I know 3
women whose lives have been destroyed by
rape. I don't know any men whose lives have
been destroyed by a rape accusation. I
#BelieveWomen

22 Likes 11 Comments

Alisha

I have no doubt that I know more victims of
rape who haven't confided in me, and more
perpetrators who've just continued to get
away with it and live among us smug and
dangerous

René

It is so infuriating. I always knew that rape
culture was a problem, but I can't believe how
many men don't know it. How many actively
deny it. It is terrifying.

Maria

Things are changing, but not fast enough!

Ellen

Well said!

Kristy

Well said! #BelieveWomen

Heather

I know 4 women who've been raped. I used to

know 2 rapists. I've never known any men
falsely accused of rape. I #BelieveWomen.

Jake

I know 3 men whove been falsely accused of
rape. 1 of them lost his job. I dont know any
women whove been raped and I dont know any
men whove committed rape. So should I write
#believemen?

Ellen

I'm sorry that your friend lost his job
unjustly, but when weighed in the balance
with a woman loosing her sense of safety, her
trust of men, her ability to love and connect,
and possibly also her job, friends, and
family, also unjustly. Compared to that, your
friend's misfortune seems like a fairly small
price to pay, don't you think? I mean, he
probably just went and got another one,
didn't he?

Heather

Jake, if you know 4 women, then you know a woman who has been sexually assaulted. If you know 3 men, then you know a man willing to commit rape. Sexual assault is all around you, every day, and you don't see it because it doesn't affect you. That is called "privilege." But the time to open your eyes is now.

Jake

@Heather no he didnt just get a new job he was unemployed for 5 years because everyone is afraid of the PC police not even mcdonalds would hire him and his wife left him

Jake

@Ellen that 1 in 3 stat is bullshit your fake news totally twisted that study the real stat is 13%

Heather

@Jake - Is it possible that his wife left him because he actually was a rapist? I mean, did you talk to her about it? Or did you just take his word on the matter?

Ellen

@Jake - Oh, only 13% of men want to rape me. That is ok then. I don't know what I was complaining about.

Just changing the subject for a second, did you know that only .00009% of Muslims are Terrorists? I wonder what your opinion is on bringing in Syrian refugees?

Maybe I don't need to enter this discussion after all. It seems like Heather and Ellen have it covered! Damn, girls!

Ellen's message reminds me that I need to reply to the email from Mitchell about his Refugee paperwork. Mitchell is someone I know from my university days, and I have been helping him and a group of his co-workers with their refugee sponsorship application, since I did one two years ago and we successfully brought in a family from Yemen.

Unfortunately, Mitchell turns out to be a real pain in the ass. He is a terrible communicator, I never know what he's trying to say, he'll forget what we've agreed upon and just do whatever he feels like. I'm really regretting this whole thing.

But once I start to learn the stories of these families, I find it really hard to just walk away. What is a little suffering on my end compared to what they've been through?

The Middle East holds a special place in my heart. I took a trip to Syria once, when I was 21. At the time it was a vibrant country with all of the modern conveniences set amid castles and open air markets and the call to prayer wafting on the air. I loved it, and had hoped to go back one day, but I doubt that will happen now.

Not long ago my British hairdresser (you know, a real expert on the subject) asked me 'How do you know they are who they say?' I was really proud of my reply: 'I know that they live in Syria. And that Syria is at war right now. And that there are guns and bombs and chemical weapons being used. And that every day hundreds of innocent civilians die. And that this family don't want to be in the middle of that. Isn't that enough?' The woman was speechless for a moment. And then, 'But what if they are terrorists?' 'Well,' I replied, 'the group I'm bringing in right now is a widow with four children.' She shook her head,

'Terrorists were children once.' I could feel my face getting hot, and I said: 'Well, if those kids grow up to be terrorists it will be because their dad was killed by an American bomb while he was operating to save a Canadian journalist, and then Canada refused to rescue them because white people can't tell the difference between a good brown person and a bad brown person.'

No, just kidding. Of course I didn't say that. Instead I catered to her white fragility and went with: 'You are British, you might know that during WWII something like 7,000 British children were brought to Canada to keep them safe during the bombings. Canadian families took care of these British children like they were their own for up to six years. I wonder if anybody asked 'how do you know if they are who they say'?' Of course, I really wanted to tack on the end, 'or is that different because the children were white?' but I suspect her mind had already gone there, because she looked down at my hair and changed the subject.

This is why it is probably better to have political discussions in person: we are all generally too polite to let it get heated. But when there's a screen to hide behind we end up saying something way more vicious than we would in person.

I press send on my reply to Mitchell. I check my watch: five minutes until Chuck's dad gets here. Jesus. Maybe if I get him up now and sneak him out quietly we can be waiting on the front lawn when his dad comes, and the dog won't bark and wake the kids up?

Ugh. I sigh and get off the couch. My back and hips and legs all groan in protest. At least the drugs have kicked in and my headache is just a weak shadow in the back of my head.

177

Only two and a half more hours. Two and a half hours and they'll all be gone.

Except my crazy children. Unfortunately nobody comes to get them.

3:40 pm

Maja

At least he's in a good mood.

It is because he's three beers in.

The good mood won't last long.

Sober, he's a grump. Drunk, he's an asshole. But from beer #2 until beer #4 he's the happiest man alive. And he's just opened beer #3. So for now it is all laughter and smiles. I should try to enjoy it while it lasts.

When we got home from the park both girls were exhausted from the traumatic experience with the police officer. There was a meltdown getting in the house, a meltdown getting off shoes, a meltdown getting lunch.... Clearly Elle needed a nap. Most kids her age don't nap anymore, but she needs it more days than not. So there was another meltdown when I said "no TV, it's time for nap."

Of course, the more they need a nap the more they fight it, and it took an hour and a half to get them to finally wind down enough to sleep.

Twenty minutes later Nate crashed in the door, arms full of beer and shopping bags, his voice booming. He announced that he'd quit his job and decided to be a professional gambler. He won $2000 last night, "A week's salary in one night!" and it was time to celebrate. I was not feeling celebratory, and I was ready to kill him when he charged into Elle's room singing and dragged her out of bed, then got Claire.

I bit my tongue. So hard. He'll do it anyways, if I like it or not, so I might as well not fight it.

They've been playing and giggling ever since. He'd bought them a fort building kit and they set it up in the living room. Then they got dressed up and had a tea party inside, and now they're having a dance party in the living room – the girls in their fanciest party dresses and Nate in my sarong and sun hat.

I'm watching them from the kitchen while I prepare lasagne, Nate's favourite (of course it is, because it is the most work). My back is hurting too much to stand at the counter so I'm sitting at the table awkwardly layering cheese and noodles and meat and sauce, dripping it all over my belly that always seems to be in the way.

It is lovely seeing them play together. The sound of them laughing makes me feel such joy.

This is the Nate that I fell in love with. The man that had me laughing all night until my stomach hurt.

We used to have such fun.

Nate comes into the kitchen to fetch beer #4.

He's only been home for a half hour and he's already four beers in. He's definitely not watching the girls tonight. I hope Isaac can do it. Otherwise I'll be spending the night at home listening to Nate rant about everything that is wrong with the world while he stumbles around making a mess and hurting the girls' feelings.

Gotta love Friday night.

I used to enjoy Friday nights with Nate. Before we had

kids we'd go clubbing and dance for hours and then go home and fuck four times in a row. We'd go to beautiful beaches around the world to parties that lasted for days. We used to train for runs together and push each other to be stronger and faster. We were a great couple. I don't know how we got here.

We met in our second year "Introduction to Discrete Mathematics" course. I started a study group and the eight people that joined all became great friends. During reading week they all planned a trip to Costa Rica, but of course I couldn't afford to go. Then Nate bought me a ticket! I couldn't believe it. That was when I knew that he was the one. Of course, I didn't even have a passport and it was too short notice to get one (although I've learned since that I actually could have gotten a rush passport), so he gave the ticket to his friend Frank instead. When they came back Nate took me to that fancy hotel in Niagara Falls that has the water slide, and we went to Marineland and the butterfly conservatory – he said "This is basically exactly what it was like in Costa Rica. You didn't miss anything." And then we had lots of wild sex.

We don't really have much sex anymore.

We dated casually for those first two years. He didn't want to get too serious: "it would be a distraction from school" he said. We both dated other people, but nobody made me feel special like Nate did.

I don't feel special anymore.

In fourth year he turned his attention fully to me. He introduced me to his family, he started talking about the future, and after our last exam our whole computer science class went out to the student bar and he asked if I'd marry him. It wasn't romantic or showy, but I don't really like to be the centre of attention, so that was ok with me.

He never did give me an engagement ring, but I was over the moon anyways.

I never imagined how much things would change.

Now Nate is flying the girls around the living room like airplanes. The girls are so wound-up – they didn't get enough sleep and it is clear that they are quickly spiraling out of control.

This is probably going to get ugly.

Nate's family paid for much of the wedding. My father doesn't know that. Nate's mother really wanted it to be a big deal: she explained the Portuguese love big weddings, and "since I don't have a daughter, I want to spoil you as if you were my own" she said. She is a lovely woman, but pushy in a way that I'm not used to – my mom is a silent manipulator, whereas Nate's mom is a bulldozer, and she'll roll right over me if I let her (and most of the time I do).

So, we had a big flashy wedding and we bought a big house in a good school district and Nate and I went to work with the same company.

Then everyone waited for me to start having babies.

And like a good girl I did.

Of course, I didn't go back to work after my maternity leave. Nate insisted that the kids needed me. So he climbed up the chain of command and I withered away into professional obscurity.

I don't really regret it. I do like being home with the girls, as lonely and frustrating as it is. What I regret is how dependent it makes me. My career will never recover. I started as his superior but now I'd be lucky to get an entry-level position.

I wonder if Nate really quit his job...

"Nate, were you joking when you said you quit your job?" Nate has told the girls that he needs a break – he's hunched over and it looks like he's hurt his back – but both girls are hanging from his legs begging for more. I suddenly notice that beer #4 is empty and he's heading toward the fridge.

Oh, shit. I didn't realize that he was already done #4. I shouldn't have asked that question. Maybe he didn't hear me.

"Yeah, bitches!" he poses like a rapper. Yes, he's drunk now. "Fuck that place. I went in this morning and Mandy pulled the same old shit and I said, 'Fuck this place. I don't need this job.' and I left." He didn't really. He couldn't have. He's worked too hard to just burn bridges like that. It is all talk.

I really hope it is all talk.

I never know what to believe from him anymore. There are so many things he says, so many promises he makes, so many conversations we have, and then the next day it is like it never happened. Last weekend we had an entire conversation about inviting both of our parents for Thanksgiving, but the next day he had no idea what I was talking about. Or when he got that $3000 bonus and we talked about all of us going to the Dominican, but then he bought his stupid truck.

I can't even remember how many times he's promised to quit drinking. It never pans out. Oh, sure he'll quit for a little while. The first few weeks are hell as he suffers withdrawal and he's even angrier than usual. Then he falls into a depression, wandering about the house, lost and aimless. After a couple of months there will be a reason to celebrate and that's it, he's a drinker again. He's miserable without it, but he's miserable with it. But it is the only hobby he has. There's nothing he's passionate about.

Except possibly gambling. And I'm pretty sure that isn't going to work out well for any of us.

The girls are still hanging from his legs. They are getting desperate and two massive meltdowns are just seconds away.

He always does this. He winds them all up and then he just walks away. Then he gets angry at them when they are all wound up.

I need to take control of the situation before it gets ugly. Awkwardly rising from the table I call out, "Girls, daddy needs a break. Can you show me your awesome fort?"

"NO! We want to fly!"

"Me wanna fly!!"

There are tears forming as he pries their fingers from his pants.

"Girls, come on. Come with me!"

"DADDY!"

"Daddy!"

"Get the FUCK OFF ME!" he roars, kicking his legs roughly to knock them off. Both girls fall to the floor and burst into tears. They run to me.

As I comfort them Nate pours beer #5. "This is why I never want to play with you. You're too much. You never know when to quit." He swallows half the glass in one gulp. "You're just like your mother," he grins and then stumbles out of the room to his office mumbling, "three needy bitches..."

He's right about that. If I knew when to quit I would have left him two years ago.

4:10 pm

Sofia

I'm walking on the beach. The waves are big and loud. Their roar fills my ears. The gulls cry desperately over head, as if they have all lost their children on the wind. I'm searching the rocks along the shore. Searching frantically for something. I don't remember what. The wind swirls my hair and clothes up around me, and throws mist in my eyes. I can feel the panic rising in my chest. I've done something terribly wrong. I've made some terrible mistake, but I can't think what it was. If I can just find this lost thing among the rocks... The waves are getting bigger. They are crashing further and further up the beach. The thing that I am looking for will be washed away! I run. My foot connects with something large and hard. I lose my balance, fly through the air, and splash into the icy water. I'm tossing and turning in the waves. The water is so deep and the shore is so far I can hardly see it. My clothes are like lead weights, pulling me down under the surface. It is dark. It is cold.

I'm on a boat. It is a huge boat. Like, a yacht. And there is a dinner party. I'm in my coat and boots and dripping wet. This guy is talking to me. He is tall and blond and handsome and he is wearing a suit and holding a glass of champagne and he is talking about himself. He doesn't seem to notice that I'm not dressed for a party, or that I'm dripping water all over the deck. I need to change my clothes. I run from him. I run inside the boat, into a hallway filled with nameless doors. I open one into a cabin. It is the cabin of the boat that I took in China, up the Yangtze river. It is small, the walls have water stains and the carpet is worn. I find dry clothes and get dressed.

The door opens. It is Colin. He smiles.

He has the most handsome smile. It is playful. Sparkling.

I can't believe how lucky I am to have found him.

I didn't date anyone for years before Colin. That isn't true, I dated but I wasn't present. I didn't open up at all with anyone, and I certainly never allowed anyone the chance to connect with me. I built a wall and I liked it. In the years that I traveled it was easy, because everyone was transient and casual flings were the norm. When I went to University it was a bit harder: I kept getting "girlfriend-zoned" and very cool guys that I just wanted to hang out with weren't interested in being around me if I didn't want to grant them exclusive access to my vagina.

Jack Waterstone. He had the best taste in music. He always had great tickets to concerts. He invited me once, but I said it wasn't a date, so he asked someone else.

Jorge Garcia. He would have all-night World of Warcraft binges with the guys, but I turned him down for dinner and a movie, so he wouldn't let me join their WOW games.

Jermaine... I don't know what the fuck his last name was. He was always bragging about what a great goalie he was in soccer. I knew that I could play as well as him, but nope. "Only if you'll go on a date with me" he kept saying. "I'll let you score against me if you let me score with you" he laughed. I didn't need him to "let" me score, I just needed him to let me play.

Girlfriendzoned.

I'm awake now. I will not open my eyes. I will not get up. I will lie here in a desperate hope that I can slip back into that dream, where Colin's dimples light up my heart.

I generally didn't like University. I wasn't a big drinker. I wasn't a big partier. I didn't date. I didn't giggle with the girls when the boys took their tops off. I was too old for that shit. I'd already spent three years traveling, while all of the other kids were on their own for the first time and incapable of acting like adults. I felt old. I felt boring.

I was sure I'd made a mistake deciding to live in residence, but it turned out to be the best thing about university. I was in a unit with Lish and Drae and Maja and two other girls who thought we were nerds. I guess we were. We protested the Iraq War and attended feminist rallies. We would get high and have bake-offs. Or we would watch The Bachelor and drink every time someone said or did something misogynist. We had to revise the game because none of us had that high of an alcohol tolerance.

Maja was the most serious of us. She was on the track and field team, which meant training four days a week and treating her body like a temple, and she got top grades in all of her classes. She never smoked weed with us, and only drank on rare occasions, but she didn't judge us when we got wasted and she seemed to enjoy our company anyway. Drae was the least serious. She was trying to assert her independence from her overbearing mother.

She grew a 'fro and got a tattoo on her arm that said "Mine" and took acid and went to Korn concerts, thrashing about in the mosh pit. Lish started out a bit like the girl next door – she had a boyfriend back home who she dutifully called every evening... until he slept with some sixteen year old and broke her heart.

We went out that night. It is one of the most memorable nights from that first year: drunk as skunks screaming the lyrics to Eamon's *I Don't Want You Back* at the top of our lungs. Stumbling home from the bar, getting pizza at Stubies, Drae almost punching that guy who whistled at her and told her to "take it off, baby."

Jesus, that seems like a lifetime ago.

I studied Anthropology, like Lish, but it was too theoretical and I found it really irritating. The way that they invent complex and inaccessible language to describe the simplest and most natural phenomenon. It is really patronizing. In my third year I took a summer work placement with a professor who was studying rural midwifery in Laos. I attended six births that summer, and as soon as I came home I dropped out of Anthro and applied to the Midwifery program at Laurentian.

Ten years later I have attended over 500 births.

I love being a midwife. The unpredictable hours are a problem, but I have met so many amazing, kick ass women. Lish is a feminist via academia, and has all sorts of theory and evidence behind her beliefs. I am a feminist from experience, as one-by-one all of my misconceptions about femininity have been totally dismantled by the strongest, fiercest, most powerful women doing the awe-inspiring and mind-blowing act of creation.

Creation is a word that is so intricately linked to God. Being raised Catholic, it was always God is the creator, woman is the vessel. That's it. A vessel. The Abrahamic God steals creation from women and gives it to a man and makes women into man's servant. The men who created God committed the greatest act of misogyny in history. It opened the door for female servitude for millennia.

But I never say that sort of shit out loud. I don't want to look like a radical.

Even though it is true.

I think one of my favourite things about a birth is seeing the awe in the father's face when he witnesses what his wife is capable of. Some men, when faced with their wife's power, feel small and it pushes them to behave in unhealthy ways. But other men – most men, I'm glad to say – rise to the occasion, and vow to become a bigger man in the greatness of the moment.

And then there are the men who think birth is disgusting and refuse to be there. Which is just the ultimate way to take power away from women: recasting her glorious deed as something repulsive. Like people who compare breastfeeding to having a bowel movement. Jesus.

I wonder which kind of man Colin would be?

I was certain that he'd be the man who rose to the occasion. But now I'm not so sure.

We met online. These days it would be weird if you didn't. I had been on the dating app for two years and never went on a single date. I'd chatted with quite a few guys, but I always found some reason not to go meet them. They replied with single word answers. They make too many grammatical mistakes. They don't get my jokes. I was at a birth all night and now I just want to go to bed... I never lacked excuses.

Colin's sister-in-law created his dating profile. It was his first time on the app when he connected with me. My profile picture was of myself with a goat when I was in Laos, and he had a picture of himself with a goat at his brother's farm, so he had the clever idea of inviting me to Goat Yoga. It was so original that I didn't even try to come up with an excuse to bail. Neither of us cared for the yoga, but the goats had us both in stitches. It was a great start. I loved his calm energy, and he loved the way I spoke to him like an equal, patiently drawing conversation out of him like I was coaxing out a breached baby. I don't think anyone ever asked him so many questions about himself before, and they probably didn't wait for him to answer.

He is so soft and sweet. He has such a gentle heart. I think it is his best quality.

The girls were very surprised when Colin and I got serious. I think they all assumed I was a closeted lesbian. Not that I blame them. He is literally the first guy I've dated since they've known me.

And I don't think he's ever said more than five words in a row to any of them.

And now he's run off.

Was I wrong about him? I thought he was so kind. I thought he cared about me. That he understood me. I thought we were partners. Equals. Us against the world.

Maybe I was just a fool.

I wish I was still dreaming.

4:20 pm

Alisha

Thank goodness for the sun. The weather was all over the place this morning, but now the sky is clear and the wind has died off and it has turned into one of those beautiful autumn days where you just want to go apple picking or walk in the woods. The air smells like crisp leaves and there are still some cicadas buzzing away. The sun feels good on my face, and the codeine has kicked in fully so I'm relaxed and the migraine and pelvis pain are easy to ignore.

Zach and the twins are playing in the sandbox. Ruby is still asleep but the others woke up when Chuck's dad came to get him. I actually managed to wake Chuck and sneak him upstairs and we were playing on the front lawn when his dad arrived. I was patting myself on the back for managing this without waking the kids when Chuck's dad said he needed Chuck's blanket – the one that has been here for a year straight and they never once asked to take it home – and it was very important that I go get it. So I went inside, crept downstairs and into the dark room where Zach was sleeping on the floor and the twins were sleeping on the pull-out. I was blinded from having gone from bright sunshine to dark basement and felt my way along carefully. I was nearly at Chuck's bed when my toe hit something hard, and that hard thing (Zach's stupid rock that I told him he couldn't sleep with yet somehow there it was) shot across the carpet and "thunk" right into Zach's head. He woke up screaming. The twins woke up ready to play.

And now we are all here in the backyard.

Sigh.

I still don't know how he got that rock back.

Fingers crossed Ruby sleeps for three hours today. That means I'll only have to hold her for a half hour before her dad comes.

I'm usually very respectful of the requests parents make of me, but not today. Ruby's mother has asked that I only let her nap for an hour because they want to put her to bed at 6:30, but there is no way in hell that is happening today. First of all, I am generally of the opinion that if a child is sleeping it is because they need to sleep, and I don't like to mess with that (and I've already woken four kids before they were ready today). Secondly, Ruby is here from 7:30 until 5:30, five days a week, and they want to put her to bed at 6:30? When does this poor child get to spend time with her parents? And, thirdly, no. Just no. Not today. Today has been a hard day, at the end of a hard week, and I just don't have anything left. They are just going to have to give me a break today.

But Zach and the twins have been playing so peacefully for a half hour that I've been able to just lay back in my patio chair with the sun on my face and listen to the birds and the rustling leaves and I feel much calmer than I have all day.

I am so tired though. Hopefully I sleep tonight. My

insomnia doesn't usually last for more than four or five days, and today is day four, so maybe...

My phone that I'm trying to ignore buzzes for the third time in five minutes.

Sigh.

Twifagram is being needy today.

But only two messages are from Twifagram. One message is from Isaac.

ISAAC

Today, 4:24 pm
Are they going to get a divorce?

What? What the hell does that mean? I asked if he could watch Elle and Claire tonight and now, five hours later he replies with that?

This must have something to do with why he's not talking to me. He's always communicating in code and I have to collect the clues and piece them together. It is stupid.

He must think I'm going to divorce him?

Well, at least that puts me in familiar territory. He often thinks I'm going to leave him. And I spend a lot of time reassuring him I won't. Maybe I'm not that convincing, though, because nothing makes me want to leave him like constantly validating him.

I reply carefully, beginning with the Maori term for "my

darling", which we pull out when we are being really affectionate:

Alisha

Today, 4:26 pm
E ipo. What is going on that has you thinking of divorce? I don't want a divorce. I love you. I want to grow old with you.

When I was reading all of my child development books, in the early days of doing daycare, I learned there are two different belief systems that people internalize about intelligence: we either believe that we are born smart or dumb, good or bad, and there's nothing anyone can do about it (called a fixed mindset) or we believe anyone can be smart with enough effort (called a growth mindset). And although study after study has shown the latter to be true, the majority of us still have a fixed mindset. It is reflected in our language: 'you are so smart', 'what a good boy,' 'I'm not good with numbers,' 'he's the brains in the family'....

I know with certainty that Isaac has a fixed mindset. He believes that he could never be more than he is. Whenever he makes a mistake he scolds himself with "you're such a fucking idiot" and he quits anything that proves to be too difficult. And in eight years together, every time we fight, every time he feels like he's let me down, EVERY time, he gives up without a fight and assumes I'm going to walk. He even says it: "why don't you just leave me then?" any time I say anything the least bit critical.

It really isn't fair. He's basically saying he will never grow, he will never evolve. Either I accommodate for his inadequacies or I leave.

Which is fucking bullshit.

Life has changed a lot in the past eight years. Mostly it has gotten significantly harder. Him refusing to grow and evolve means I have to change enough for the both of us: I have to get faster, stronger, I have to push myself further every day, every week, and every year while he stays exactly the same as he was when we met. I often wonder, at what point should I start worrying about myself? Like, how much of myself am I supposed to sacrifice here?

For example:

This not talking to me bullshit. It was fine when we didn't have the twins, and only short visits with Kai. We could go for days, for weeks, and not have to talk until he was ready. Eventually, he would be in a place where he could speak his mind and feel heard and we'd work through it and then we could be a team again.

But now we have Kai two days a week, the twins, the dog, a house, two full-time jobs... I need our conflicts to be resolved quickly – because when he's not speaking to me it means I'm doing it all on my own: he works late, he hides in the garage, he smokes more weed, he stays up late and sleeps in late, and then he doesn't have time to walk the dog. Until he is ready to talk he will not spend time in the same room with me. Yeah, if I can catch him passing through and ask for his help he will do it, begrudgingly and half-assed, but he'll do it. It is like this for days. It has been almost a week this time.

There is a part of me that says, "It is who he is, you can't expect him to change if he's not capable."

Except that means I have to change. I have to be OK with being a single mom while he just checks out. I do almost all of the childcare, the house work, the errands, all in total isolation because the only adult I see with any regularity is too emotionally constipated to talk about his feelings! It is bullshit. This is an unhealthy behaviour that puts a strain on the whole family. I shouldn't need to accept it and accommodate for it. He should grow the fuck up and tell me why he is pissed off in the first place and stop wasting everyone's time.

So much for feeling relaxed.

My phone buzzes.

ISAAC

Today, 4:29 pm
I just don't see how this relationship can survive if we're not having sex.

Ooooooooohhhhhhh. Lightbulb. That is what this is about.

Fucking hell, that conversation was ages ago. We were making plans for our anniversary and I told him that it would be nice to rent a hotel, sure, but I didn't want to have sex. He's been stewing about this for over a week?

God, what a waste of energy.

Isaac and I have only had sex once since the twins were

born, and that was a pity fuck and I hated every second of it. Like, I felt like I was being raped. I feel uncomfortable thinking that because I don't want to make light of rape, but it really did feel horrible. Every fibre, every molecule of my being was screaming no to sex, and my separated pelvis was in agony. I felt like crying and vomiting. I felt so alone and used, that he could enjoy doing this thing to me that I hated so thoroughly.

I never told Isaac exactly how much I hated it, because I didn't want to hurt his feelings. I did make it clear I don't want to have sex again. Ever. I am no longer willing to give him pleasure at my expense. If that means he sleeps with other women, I will have to be ok with that. It isn't fair to make him give up something he enjoys: to make him choose between sex and me. I won't do that. But I won't have sex anymore.

I have explained this to him more times than I can count. He seems to understand my perspective, but then a few days or weeks later I find myself explaining it all again.

On that day when I said no to anniversary sex he went out to the garage to smoke a joint and then came back again. He asked: "So, what if I'm hooking up with some woman just to fuck but I end up falling in love with her. What then?"

I didn't really know what he wanted me to say. Thinking back now he probably wanted me to talk about how heartbroken I'd be, but I didn't. I just said, "Well, there's not much I can do about that."

So, basically, he's been ruminating on that for days. Avoiding me, avoiding the kids, and avoiding the housework, getting more and more upset every day and feeling more and more detached from me.

I really wish he'd just talked to me instead.

But it is true. There isn't much I can do about it. I don't want to have sex anymore, but I don't believe I can forbid him from ever having sex again for the rest of his life: that seems selfish and cruel. If he falls in love with someone else, well, I'm not going to stomp my feet and forbid that he see her. I don't own him. I can't force him to love only me. Sure, I would be sad, of course I would, but I know he'll always be in my life because he will always be the twins' father. I know we'll always be friends. So, really, I'm not worried or stressed – whatever will be, will be. I don't have any power to change it.

I suppose from his perspective it might seem like I'm saying I'd rather divorce than let him touch me. That I'm not willing to make this one little compromise to save our marriage. Even though I've explained to him all of the reasons why I don't want sex, I suppose he still doesn't realize how repulsed I am by it. I suppose he doesn't understand how much I have changed.

Because I have changed so much. My body has changed through all of the surgeries, my hormones have changed from pregnancy and menopause, my mind has changed after cancer and motherhood shifted my priorities... everything about my life has changed. Hell, I'm not even blonde anymore! At some point my hair just faded to the colour of dirt.

Whereas for Isaac, he still goes to the same job, he still has the same friends, the same body, the same life, more or less, except with two crazy kids thrown into the mix. To me, not wanting sex seems pretty minor amid all of those other things, but to him it is a major transition.

My phone buzzes again.

ISAAC

Today, 4:31 pm
I just don't know why were even together
anymore

Hmmmmmm.... I don't know. Because we love each other?
Like, is a regular fuck really all you married me for?

I should not reply to that one. No good will come of it.

Alisha

Today, 4:32 pm
I think we should talk about this tonight
when I get home from Sof's. Smoke a j together
and work through this.

Zach and the twins are building a trench in the sandbox.
They are working together really well and adding bridges
and trees made from sticks and houses made from rocks.

Man this job would be easier if I didn't have Ruby.

But then Zach would be my problem child, and I'd be
thinking, 'Man, this job would be easier if I didn't have
Zach.'

And then Ari would be my problem child. Where
would that leave me? Ha!

ISAAC

Today, 4:33 pm
Yea, I'd like that. I love you Lish. I'm sorry
I've been such a jerk.

Holy shit, an apology! That is rare.

Alisha

Today, 4:34 pm
I love you, Isaac. Thank you for talking to me
about this.

"Lish, can we have some water for our canal?" Zach asks. Of course it is a canal: last week we took a walk along the canal in town and Zach had loads of questions. Then we watched a bunch of videos about canals and we learned about canal locks, and then we watched a bunch of videos about locks. Now Zach builds canals every chance he gets.

"For sure, Zach. Let me put some water in a bucket and you can fill the canal yourself." I can't believe I got to sit down for almost a solid half hour! That was great. And Isaac is talking to me... I feel much calmer now.

ISAAC

Today, 4:36 pm
Thanks for being awesome.

Yeah, but you still haven't told me if you'll watch Elle and Claire tonight.

I'm filling up the bucket from the hose when the screaming begins: "Aaaaaaahhh!! Ari you broke my bridge!" Zach screams. Then Ari starts to cry.

Sheba starts to bark. Someone is here.

Then a wail rises from the basement. Ruby is awake.

Here we go again.

4:55 pm

Andrea

Behind our building is the nicest little park. There is no playground, so it isn't busy with children, but there is a lovely climbing tree where Wallace likes to sit and watch the world from above, where nobody can see him. There's a frog pond where Zach can practice his technique – he's trying to learn how to catch frogs without a net.

Obviously we had to go up to our condo to change into his frog-catching clothes first. He gets so unbelievably muddy. I'll probably have to strip him naked before we go up the elevator.

There's also a gazebo with a big wicker swing chair where I usually sit and work. I can see both boys and watch the couples and dog walkers strolling along the path that connects the complex to the shopping centre via the manicured woods. It is a lovely spot, and I feel more relaxed now than I have in days.

I brought my sketch book and pencils thinking that I'd be too distracted to get any real work done, but I'm still too distracted to sketch.

What will I do?

It would be nice if I could just do this. Just hang out with the boys and stare at them all day. I mean, they say it is important for parents to maintain routine and predictability for their kids when there are big changes happening, but it also seems so absurd to keep plugging along with work and school as if everything were normal when the most horrible tragedy of their lives is on the horizon.

How do I prepare them for this?

I stare blankly at the sketchbook in front of me for a solid three minutes before the obvious occurs to me.

I must write them a book.

A book about what? About cancer? About dying? About what to do when I'm gone? About what kind of men they could grow up to be? About all of those conversations I'd like to have with them but never will?

I have so much to say, I could write a whole series.

I feel the blood rush to my cheeks.

I really love this idea.

This could be my legacy to them. A series of books. Some they get now, some they get as they grow older. I could give them to Sofia to deliver as they grow up. Maybe on their birthdays?

This is the first good idea I've had in two weeks.

No, that's not true. The fantasy where I leave Damien and have wild sex with Hot Spin Instructor from Lifestyle:Wellness was also a great idea.

He was definitely flirting with me at the grocery store today.

I begin to sketch Zach, crouched over a frog, surrounded by tall green reeds. I love drawing my kids. I love that to notice so many details about them that I probably wouldn't otherwise. Like Zach's little cowlick. It would be a great way to spend my last couple of years on earth, illustrating a book about them. As I shade-in his hair my mind wanders back to the grocery store...

I was in the freezer aisle, filling my cart with frozen pizzas for Sofia. I didn't even know he was there until I heard his smoky voice behind me: "I hope this means you'll be coming to spin class every day this week."

I almost jumped out of my skin.

"Oh, shit, I'm so sorry. I didn't mean to scare you!" he looked legitimately concerned.

He was still wearing his workout clothes. Or maybe he's one of those people who always wears workout clothes, because he smelled great. He is tall and muscular, but not bulky, and his curly black hair and dimpled cheeky grin make him look a bit like a kid who is up to no good. But with green eyes and olive skin he could be on a magazine. The other ladies in my spin class and I call him Hot Spin Instructor. He does have a name, I think it is Ed? But Hot Spin Instructor suits him better. We have all taken bets on whether he is single or married, straight or gay. I put my claim on gay and single.

I tried hard to regain my composure and play it cool. "Oh, it's just my guilty conscience. You caught me. I was planning on eating all of these tonight."

"Not all by yourself, I hope." He leaned toward me ever so slightly and spoke conspiratorially, "that would be a shame."

Ok, so maybe Hot Spin Instructor isn't gay after all.

"Sadly, yes, they're all for me. I thought about inviting Martin from spin class, but I figured he'd just make a lot of noise about how much he was eating and how great it tasted while not actually eating anything." I was hoping that Hot Spin Instructor got the joke. Generally people who are sexy as fuck are too slow to get my jokes.

He laughed. Good sign. "He'd also spend a half hour telling you the right way to eat pizza, and that he knows all about pizza because he watched a bunch of videos. You are definitely better off without him."

Bam. Sexy and funny. And straight.

I wanted to say something really daring, like "Besides, I'm such a messy eater, I usually end up naked," but I froze and my laugh turned awkward.

I was saved then: we were interrupted by a shopper. "Excuse me," she smiled at me, an Asian woman with thick glasses and wildly unkempt hair, "Could you tell me where I can find the ketchup?"

"Uh, I'm not sure. I think it is back that way, by the salad dressing." I smiled. Thanks for saving me from saying something stupid, I thought as she wandered off.

"So, seriously, what are you doing tonight that you need so much pizza?" He eyed me sideways with a look that he undoubtedly knew was incredibly charming. "Husband's poker party? Kids' soccer party?"

Fishing for personal information.... I couldn't let him have it that easily.

"Oh, no, nothing like that. I'm having a lesbian orgy."

He laughed so loudly – a deep baritone that was more vibration than sound. Oh my god. A laugh like that, he could just stick his head between my legs and laugh and I'd probably orgasm.

"Ah, yes, that would certainly work up an appetite."

"You'd better believe it!" I smiled slyly.

"And lesbians love pizza. Everyone knows that."

"Really? I thought they just loved vaginas."

That laugh again. People started staring at us.

"I've always suspected that you were a bit of a wild one."
His smile was out of control. Those dimples.

"Why? Because I said vagina in a grocery store? Man,
you should have been there when I said 'cock ring' in a
church. That was really provocative."

He laughed again.

Oh my god I wanted to tear his clothes off.

I felt like a teenager.

"So, you've clearly got your hands full tonight, what
about tomorrow? Will you be too exhausted for spin
class?"

My heart skipped a beat. I wanted him to ask me out so
badly, but I was also terrified because I couldn't possibly
say yes. "Welllll...."

"Excuse me?" interrupted a white girl in her 30s with an
empty basket in one hand and a list in the other, "Where
did you move the coconut milk to?"

"I'm sorry, I don't work here." I smiled out of habit,
but I'm sure she could tell I was a bit peeved because she
stammered, "Oh, shit, sorry. I can never find any staff in
this place," and walked off.

As she walked away, Hot Spin Instructor gave me the
craziest look and mouthed "What the fuck was that?"

I just rolled my eyes and shrugged.

"You don't even look like you work here. You're wearing
a business suit." He whispered as she went out of earshot.

"I don't know. I've seen lots of shelf-stockers wearing a
Chanel blouse."

He ignored my joke that time, "Does that happen to you
a lot?"

"Oh, it happens to everyone." I suddenly felt really self-
conscious: my cheeks grew hot with embarrassment.

"Not once in my life has someone assumed I was an

employee of a grocery store." He leaned in close, his eyebrows raised, and whispered, "is it because you are black?" I'm not sure what my face looked like in that moment, but he instantly backpedaled: "I just... it's just... I once dated this girl and every time we went out, people asked her for directions. I never get asked when I'm alone, but when I was with her people asked every single day. She explained to me it was because she's a woman. People think women are kinder and helpful where they think men have more important things to do than help. I just wondered if this is one of those things where people are being biased without even knowing it."

This might have been one of the sexiest things a man has ever said to me.

I was so taken by surprise that I was at a loss for words.

Thinking back, I wonder why that turned me on so much. I guess I'm just not used to it. Any time someone does something that I feel is racism, Damien always shuts me down and defends them: "I'm sure that's not what happened" and then I start to feel like I'm paranoid.

But here was a sexy man who respected my perspective? I just don't even know what to do with that.

Except maybe go to spin class tomorrow.

Zach has caught the same frog three times in a row now, and Wallace has come down from his tree to take a look, but absolutely refuses to touch it, to Zach's dismay. Then the frog jumps for its life and both boys shout in alarm and then start laughing as they chase the poor little creature back to the pond.

I look down at my sketch pad – I did actually manage to draw a fairly good likeness of Zach by the pond, even with my mind so distracted. I feel calmer and more optimistic than I have in a while. I'm still a mess, but, like, two percent hopeful.

We'll have to head up to the condo soon. It is getting chilly as the sun sinks. I have to do dinner early so I can get to Sofia's by 7:00. I don't know why I picked 7:00. We're usually having dinner at that time, but I know Lish and Maja eat earlier, so it seemed like a good idea at the time.

Lish looked super tired when I picked Zach up today. I'm not surprised, carrying around that screaming baby all day. Plus the twins. To call Ari a handful is an understatement. I don't think that kid ever stops moving. When Maja and Nate hired a pony for Elle's birthday in the summer there were, like, 30 other kids and their parents there, and Ari was easily the craziest. Lish couldn't take her eyes off him for a second. He was running for the pony, running for the road, breaking into the house, falling down stairs, stealing food from other kids, climbing into random cars, stuck in a bush, falling off a picnic table, back to the pony again.

And on top of that, Zach running away on her today.

The little shit.

So, I can believe she's tired.

At least Isaac is a hands-on dad. He's done a great job with Kai, and you can see that he is confident with the twins. He takes the initiative and doesn't always have to be told what to do. He's a stoner, sure, but at least he's not a drunk.

Fucking Nate, on the other hand. I hated that Maja married him. At university he slept with every woman who would let him. He was shameless. He would do anything to get a fuck. He was one of those guys who saw sex as a game. As soon as he got his dick wet he'd won and she'd lost. And he is a competitive guy. I am certain that he cheats on Maja, and I hate him for it.

"Boys, it is getting dark. Time to go up now. I've got to make dinner." They completely ignore me, of course.

I don't want to be that person. As exhilarating as it is, flirting with Hot Spin Instructor, I can't cheat on my husband. I don't want that on my conscience. I don't want that to be my legacy.

I can't bear the thought of Damien being the only man I ever know.

I have to leave him.

I have to.

I can't die trapped in this cage.

5:24 pm

Sofia

I can hear my phone ringing in the living room.

Fucking phone. Fucking harbinger of pain and misery.

I check the time. Damn I just slept the whole afternoon.

Unless that was Colin calling. He should be finished work now. Maybe he's realized what a terrible mistake he's made and he is calling to beg me to forgive him.

There's nothing to forgive. I just want him here.

I practically run to the living room, cuddling my swollen breasts.

Like a baby.

My phone is still where I threw it on the couch.

I must be careful with it. It is filled with horrible images that will come at me without warning and send me crashing down into the abyss again.

I'm just going to check if Colin called and put it down.

I WILL NOT get sucked in.

Today, 5:24 pm:
One Missed Call:

MOM

Ugh. I am not sorry I missed that call.
More text messages:

Jennifer

Today, 2:28 pm
How is 10am tomorrow?

Nick

Today, 5:16 pm
Mom just won't listen to me. I'm sorry. The
last thing you need is her drama.

Nope and nope.
I also have two Twifagram notifications. I almost click
on it.

No. Don't.

I click on it.

The circle spinning on the screen while the page loads.

Don't do it, Sofia.

I close Twifagram. I open the App store. Select "My Apps". Twifagram. Uninstall.

Yes. That is the best thing I can do for my mental health right now.

But I'm still not safe. There's a voice mail from mom.

"You have one new message."

"Sofia, I know it is hard. I know how devastated you are (*no you don't. You have no clue.*), but you can't wallow in it. You have to get up and keep going. Get back to work and the sooner things are back to normal the sooner you and Colin can forget all about this and try again."

I press 7 to delete the message.

Trying again? Is she fucking crazy? Just the thought fills me with terror so great I feel like I'm drowning in it. Being pregnant again? I would spend the whole nine months re-living that day. Does she know the effects of anxiety on a developing fetus? God, that would be the longest nine months of my life.

I'll take my brother's invitation to vent:

Sofia

Today, 5:28 pm
She's talking about this as if I've had a
rough day. I don't understand how she can
have children and not have a clue whatsoever
what I'm going through.

I have so many more messages I should reply to, but I just can't bring myself to do it. They are all worried about me, I know, but I don't know what to say. They want me to be ok, but I just can't. I can't put on that mask. Maybe one day, but today I just want to crawl into a hole and speak to no one.

I light one of the joints that I rolled earlier and curl up on the couch, pulling the afghan around me.

The sun is getting low in the sky. Days are getting shorter. I had been concerned about how isolating it would be in the house all winter with a new baby.

I had no idea just how isolating it would actually be.

Nick

Today, 5:29 pm
She thinks that you've let what Yaya said go
to your head. She worries that you think it
is your fault and that you're cursed or
something.

Wait, what did Yaya say?

My mother's mother is full of love and support but she is also an old-world Catholic and very superstitious and

213

has some pretty crazy ideas about cause-and-effect. I could totally see her painting this as God's punishment for some sin.

If I just went to church I'd have a baby. Ha!

Nick

Today, 5:30 pm
I told her that's stupid - you don't care what anybody else thinks, you are in mourning.

Sofia

Today, 5:31 pm
Thanks for that. I really appreciate you speaking up for me. I sure as hell don't want to do it.

I should probably get off my ass and be productive somehow. I need to pump again, before I get mastitis. I should eat. I had planned to shower today, but today is almost over.

I take a long drag.

Nick

Today, 5:32 pm
I'm just glad that you're not pissed at me for telling Yaya about your abortion. I honestly forgot that she was even there when I mentioned it. You know how she just sits there staring into space and you forget that she's listening to every word. I feel really shitty about it.

Uh....

Oh.

Oh.

Yaya thinks that God took Grey because I had an abortion when I was 19.

Good thing I'm already smoking a joint or I'd be pretty livid.

However, I can't deny the thought had already crossed my mind more than once. Half a lifetime of brainwashing will do that to you. I don't believe in God, and I haven't stepped foot in a church for almost twenty years, but their bullshit way of thinking is ingrained in my subconscious like the ten Commandments were engraved in stone.

I will not carry guilt for my choices. I do not regret having that abortion. I only regret that I felt like I had no other options.

His name was Robbie. We started dating when we were sixteen. He went to my church and his Dad was a lawyer and his mom was head of the Catholic Women's League so my parents were thrilled with the whole thing. As immigrants, this sort of match meant we'd made it.

We both fell in love hard and fast. We acted like we'd invented love. Like, nobody knew how much we loved each other, and that every effort to get us to slow down was a crime against humanity. I had a promise ring on my finger after six months.

And then, of course, he wanted to have sex.

I wanted it too. God did I ever want it. I was so hot and horny all of the time. We'd sneak into every closet, bathroom and wooded area that we could find and rub each other over every inch. We'd talk on the phone late at night and masturbate. We'd write the dirtiest letters. But I was still in my parents' clutches and was terrified of sex.

On my eighteenth birthday he proposed. Our families were happy, but nobody was surprised.

We had sex that night. I wanted him to wear a condom but he said that you can't get pregnant the first time.

The next time we had sex I begged him to wear a condom, but he took it off half way through because it hurt too much.

The next time we had sex he said, "God knows we are pure of heart so he won't let us get pregnant until we're ready."

So I went to see my doctor about going on the pill.

By this point in my life I had very serious doubts about religion. I saw just how silly the whole idea of God is: like Santa for grown-ups. The only thing stopping me from being a full-blown atheist was: if God pretend it meant that all of the people I respected most in life were fools.

That, and a lot of guilt.

But the church's hold was loose enough that I wanted birth control.

My family doctor, however, was not similarly liberated. He refused to give me birth control without my parents' permission.

I was eighteen. An adult. And he refused to give me birth control.

It still makes me furious.

For a while my friend Amy sold me her pills, but then she got a boyfriend and needed them herself.

I asked Robbie again to wear condoms, but he still refused. I said I wouldn't have sex without them and he lost it.

He pestered and whined and threatened and guilted me. Day in and day out. It was all he would talk about: he just wanted to show me how much he loved me, if I loved him I'd do it, I was being stupid, I was acting like a child, I was a bitch, I was a fucking cunt...

But I loved him and I always did what I was told, so I caved and we had sex. Unprotected.

We made it almost a year before I got pregnant.

Thinking back, what pisses me off the most was that the sex wasn't even good. He didn't do foreplay, it was never about my enjoyment. I was just the vessel into which he jammed his cock. After a while I didn't even pretend to enjoy it anymore, and the bored look on my face never seemed to dampen his pleasure.

He got more controlling. More manipulative. Meaner. He put me down a lot: told me I was fat. I had stupid friends. I was stupid. He'd lose his temper more. Then he'd beg for my forgiveness. When I forgave him he'd explain how it wasn't really all that bad, it wasn't how I remembered it, and it was kind of my fault in the first place. Since I was already thinking the same thoughts, it wasn't a hard sell.

Then one day we were taking a walk along the river and I said something that pissed him off. We argued, I stormed off. Then he called my name. I turned to look, and he whipped a rock at my head so hard I heard bells. Two days later my eye was still filled with blood. The doctor said I had hyphema and without treatment I could have permanent vision damage. When the doctor asked how it happened I told the truth.

He suggested I not pick fights with Robbie in the future. One of my marriage vows would be obedience, and it is never too soon to practice that.

That was the nail in the coffin of my relationship with the Catholic Church. That it was a sin for me to use birth control but not a sin for him to hit me in the head with a rock? Well that was just too fucked up. I never went to church again.

I know what those people would say – those people on the internet who try to argue that sexism is just a few bad apples – it was just one ignorant person. But it wasn't just one ignorant person. It was almost every adult I knew. My whole life I'd listened to people tearing apart women for being slutty while men's violence and alcoholism and indiscretions were hushed and excused. It is a whole fucking system, and if you don't see it you must be a man.

I think this weed is making me angry. Or maybe I'm hangry? When did I last eat? Did I eat anything today?

My vision was just starting to recover when I found out I was pregnant. That was the nail in the coffin of my relationship with Robbie. I took the pregnancy test on a Thursday night, and laid awake all night, staring at the ceiling, watching my future parade before me: marriage, babies, violence, control, helplessness....

I didn't tell anybody about the pregnancy. I got a passport, got an abortion, and went halfway around the world for three years. Australia, New Zealand, China, Japan, Korea... I worked when I needed money, made friends from all over the world. I expanded my mind beyond my sheltered Catholic upbringing. It was the best choice I could have made.

I didn't come back until Robbie was married to Maria Avila.

My family practically disowned me. Mom and Dad were furious, because this reflected on them. My sister was super pissed, because it damaged her dating prospects. My brother Nick, however, couldn't care less. For much of the time I was gone he was the only one who'd even speak to me. He's a lazy jerk, so he'd only write once every few months, but he kept me in the loop about all of the family drama. Like how Robbie broke down the door in a rage thinking I was inside, then stalked my family for a few weeks, and then attempted suicide in our back yard.

I felt terrible for leaving Robbie without any real explanation or warning. Isn't that messed up? I felt terrible for hurting his feelings when he didn't even say sorry for nearly blinding me? How messed up is it that I carried such guilt but he only carried rage?

But my brother reassured me: "This guy is fucking nuts. We all agree you dodged a bullet. A rocket. You dodged an exploding rocket full of rusty nails and dog shit."

My brother has always been classy.

I'd never been particularly close with my brother until I went traveling. Turns out he's actually a pretty decent guy. Lazy, yes. Crass, absolutely, but decent. I hadn't noticed it earlier because I was too busy being pissed off that he got away with murder and just did whatever he wanted while I was expected to cook and clean all damn day. In high school, Nick was fucking three different girls at the same time, meanwhile Robbie and I couldn't be unsupervised for more than a few minutes until we got engaged. But, in the end, my brother got one of his girlfriends pregnant and they had to get married. They have three kids now, and he and Marlea fight all the time. They have nothing in common and Nick cheats a lot, but he never talks of leaving. Nick went down the road I ran from, but it never left him feeling trapped.

Maybe nobody threw rocks at his head. Maybe he gets his needs filled outside the marriage and everyone turns a blind eye. Just maybe.

If I had kept that baby I would have belonged to Robbie for the rest of my life. He believed that he owned me, and nobody was going to tell him otherwise. I would never have been permitted to make my own choices for the rest of my life.

I hated choosing the abortion. It really fucked me up for a long time. It crushes me, still, to think I'll never get to meet that child. But I would not wish that life on anyone. I am angry at all of the adults who failed to protect me from being trapped into that life. I am angry for all of the girls who've been sucked into the quicksand against their will.

Like Marlea, my sister-in-law. Even Nick sees how unfair it is for her. When she got pregnant, she became a mom-for-life, but he still got to go to university. She gave up everything and has been raising kids for eighteen years, while he has a cool job and a full social life. She's still folding laundry at ten pm while he's fucking Janice from down the street when he's supposed to be walking the dog. He sees how unfair it is, and he supports the choice I made. Although, he is fully willing to reap the rewards of this biased system without lifting a finger to make it better for women, let alone his own wife, so maybe he's not that decent after all....

I do not regret the abortion. I regret that I will never know that baby. I feel terrible guilt for the whole situation.

But I know it in no way caused me to lose Grey. In Yaya's day, abortions caused infertility because the girls' uterus was gouged out in some greasy back-alley procedure. When done by an actual doctor, first trimester medical abortions leave no lasting damage.

It wasn't God's punishment then, and it isn't now, because God is a made up fairy tale.

How long have I been staring out this window?

Oh, yeah. Fuck Yaya and her Catholic guilt.

I almost giggle.

But Grey is dead. And I'll never be a mom.

I can see why people want to believe in God. Everyone says, "You'll get to meet him one day in heaven." That must be comforting.

I'd like to meet them both.

I want it so badly it hurts.

But I know it never will be. They'll just haunt my dreams until I die.

Maja

He doesn't even notice I'm crying.

I don't know why I'm crying. It's silly, really. But... I guess... I just feel invisible. He talks at me, not with me. It isn't a conversation. I don't get to participate. If I try, he cuts me off or replies with something completely unrelated to what I said. He so obviously doesn't care one bit about what I have to say.

I'm an audience.

To the Nate show.

And he's so aggressive.

The girls are settled in front of the TV. I managed to calm them down, get them out of Nate's way, and put on the *Lunasaurs* movie. Since then I've finished prepping the lasagna and put it in the oven and now I'm doing the dishes, all while Nate stands over me talking loudly and increasingly drunkenly about his genius idea.

"It was fucking awesome. I mean, I'm good at poker. I get poker. I can pretty much count cards. But, Black Jack.. Well, I'm easily the best Black Jack player on there. I made two grand in the first two games. I just get systems. Like, I can see the whole game play out and I just fucking know.

"I'm like that at work too. I just see the whole system and fucking Mandy, thinks she's a manager, has no clue..."

He still hasn't told me if he really quit his job or if he's just blowing hot air. I really hope he hasn't quit his job. I honestly don't know what our financial situation is, because Nate is always moving money in and out and around, and we have so many different bank accounts. I don't understand what he's doing, and often get the impression that neither does he. It often seems like there's a lot more money going out than coming in. Could he be that reckless?

"... Yeah, Mandy is so stupid but she's telling ME what to do. Dumb fucking cunt. Now, Robert Turnival, he knew his shit. When he ran the department it was a well oiled machine. Everyone knew their job and shit got done. But that dumb fucking cunt Mandy couldn't sell freezers to Eskimos she's so fucking dumb. Everything fell apart as soon as she took over. If Robert Turnival was still my boss I'd have stayed, but with dumb fucking cunt Mandy, fuck it. I'm outta there. Like rats from a drowning ship."

I can't help but wonder if the office fell apart because Mandy is stupid or because they all call her 'dumb fucking cunt Mandy'? How the hell is she supposed to run a department when none of them respect her or listen to her leadership?

And I bet she's ten times smarter than you, you sexist asshole.

I wipe the tears from my cheeks with the backs of my soapy hands.

"I mean, I don't have a problem with a girl for my boss. I didn't have a problem with you being my boss. But you've just gotta know how to take advice, you know? You can't just..."

He's just talking bullshit. Shit is just pouring from his mouth.

He did have a problem with me being his boss. He was always telling me how to do my job, always with that same B.S. line: 'a good leader always knows when to listen and take advice from their front line'. Which I actually agree with, but he forgets about the part where a good employee accepts their boss's final decision and doesn't have a temper tantrum when they don't get their way. He treated me like a child, telling me every decision I should make, all the while patting himself on the back for how great he was for letting me have such power.

I was young and had no confidence, so I trusted him.

What a mistake I made marrying him. All these years I've held on to the hope that he'd grow up and get his shit together. It's just not going to happen.

I admit that I made a mistake. I chose the wrong partner.

But without him I wouldn't have my girls. I can't really say it was a mistake.

Hmmmmmm...... I'm not buying that. If I'd married a decent man I'd still have had awesome kids, because I'm the one who made them. Sure, he donated 50 percent of his DNA, but I grew them, birthed them, held them, nourished them, slept with them, sung to them, and taught them everything they know. I'm the reason they are who they are.

I just didn't know what to look for in a husband. I got fooled by all of that love nonsense when I should have chosen someone who had self-awareness and the slightest bit of work ethic. Humility. Kindness. Empathy... I chose someone who made me laugh, when I should have chosen someone who made me dinner.

Or did anything at all to help make my life pleasant.

"I mean, let's face it, you are just better at this than you were as a manager. And you like it better. I'm better at computers and you are better at taking care of people. I mean, you're not amazing at it. Your cooking isn't much to brag about. I think I'm probably actually a better cook than you are but you enjoy it more so I like to let you do it. Don't get pissy at me, I'm just telling the truth. No need to get emotional over facts..."

I can't even look at him. I just hate him. He sees me as staff. My job is to serve him.

And apparently I'm not good enough at it.

How do I get out of this? How do I fix this mistake? I want to leave him, but where would I go? Not to my mother and father, they won't help me. They don't care that he's drunk or violent. You put up with it: divorce is not an option. I can't get an apartment because I don't have first and last months' rent. I don't have an income and I don't have references. How do I get a job when I haven't worked in nearly six years? My training is practically obsolete now.

Lish keeps telling me to start my own business that I run from home. I would love that, but it can't work. I can't start a business here. Nate would never allow it, and I can't rent a place for my business without an income. And I really don't think I'm smart enough. Starting a business is a huge undertaking.

He has me trapped. I'm completely and fully powerless.

I could look into a women's shelter, but I don't think they'd take me. It isn't like he'll kill me if I stay, Nate isn't that bad. He just drinks too much.

"... but you still have a sexy ass, even when it is double size." Nate is behind me now, rubbing his groin against my butt. He reeks of alcohol and beer farts and his breath is wet on my neck. He reaches around to grab my breasts but I clamp my arms down on his hands.

"Please don't, they're all swollen and sore." They are no worse than usual, but if I say 'you smell like vomit and feces and I'm disgusted by you' he'll have a temper tantrum.

He forces his hands past my barrier anyways and starts kissing my neck, his mouth open and wet with beer-saturated drool. I stop doing the dishes, stepping away from him to grab the dish towel. He moves toward me again: "Come on baby, I want you. You are the size of a fucking cow but I still want to fuck you."

He says that as if it is a compliment. As if I'm the luckiest girl in the world.

I hate you. "Thank you, but I feel really uncomfortable these days. I'd really rather not." Actually I'm really horny lately. I always get horny in the third trimester. But he is disgusting and I want nothing to do with him. I would love to have sex with him when he's sober, but I honestly can't remember the last time I saw him for more than two minutes when he's sober.

Just in the morning when he's late for work and angry at the world. That is it. He's usually already had a beer or two when he gets home from work.

He is trying to rub against me again. He's so much bigger than he used to be. He dismisses the beer gut as just bloating: "it would go down if I stopped drinking beer for a week" but he denies that he's bigger all around. His arms, his chest, his back... and when he wraps himself around me I feel like a mouse caught up in a boa constrictor. I used to find his grip comforting, but now I just feel panic.

"Nate, please. I don't want to. And dinner is ready."

"Jesus, fuck you." He snarls at me, as if I'm the cruelest,

most repulsive person in the world. "You know, I work really fucking hard to put a roof over your head and food on your plate, and get toys for these kids and none of you fucking appreciate me. The kids just want more, more, more, and you look at me like I'm a fucking pile of garbage."

Well he is right about that. I do look at him like he's a disgusting pile of garbage. But I'm not sure why that is my fault.

"Do you know how easy it would be for me to cheat on you? I could fuck any woman I wanted. I could fuck that dumb cunt Mandy, she can't keep her eyes off me. But I don't. And this is how you thank me? Well, fuck you all, ungrateful leeches."

He grabs his beer and stomps downstairs to his office.

I wipe my neck with the cloth – his spit is drying and tightening my skin.

He's wrong about everything else though. I do appreciate him, and I do love him, and I do want to have sex with him, but not this drunk, angry version of him. This is not the man I fell in love with.

And I don't want to leave him. I don't believe in divorce. I believe in making it work, pushing through the hard times, fixing the broken bits.

But he doesn't. He just wants me to accommodate him. He just wants me to do more, me to try harder, me to toughen up, and he'll just keep being a cave man.

At what point am I no longer the good, loving, loyal wife and become the doormat who wasted her life on someone who didn't deserve her?

Dishes are done, dinner is ready, table is set. I turn off *Lunasaurs* and the whining commences. Both girls whine that they want more TV, that they don't want to eat, they don't like lasagna (they fucking do), they want peanut butter sandwiches, they hate lasagna, they're huuuuuuuuuuungry....

Nate doesn't come for dinner. No surprise. He'll show up when we're almost done, wolf down a serving and a half without breathing or talking or looking up, then burp loudly. He'll leave his dishes on the table, say something rude, and then go downstairs to his cave.

The girls finally settle and start eating with no sign of Nate.

In the quiet of chewing I hear retching downstairs. Then the bathroom taps running.

He's barfing in the sink.

Why can't he barf in the toilet like everybody else on the planet? It is literally four inches away from the sink. But no, his drunk, bloated face is too good for the toilet bowl. Or maybe his precious time is too valuable for bending down that extra bit. Instead I get to stare at his dried vomit chunks while I'm brushing my teeth.

I fucking hate him.

I can't eat. Two bites in and I feel bloated and gross. But watch, I'll be hungry again in twenty minutes.

When dinner is over the girls are relatively cooperative getting cleaned up and into pjs, shoes and coats to go to Lish's house. They are still crazy exhausted and very sluggish and whiney (I'm feeling pretty fucking morose myself, so I can't really blame them). They want to bring fifteen stuffies each, and since I'm too tired to argue I'm now lugging three bags plus pillows. But they are moving forward, so it is the best I can hope for. Isaac will probably just put on a movie and they'll pass out on the couch as long as he doesn't give them any sugar.

Which he probably will do because he's a stoner. I laugh.

When we were ready to go out I started to go down and tell Nate that we're leaving, but I can hear the loud rumble of his snoring all the way at the top of the stairs.

Fuck him.

6:30 pm

Alisha

I cannot believe it is 6:30 already. Maja and the girls will be here any minute and we're only just eating dinner. I haven't done the daycare billing, I still haven't folded the fucking laundry, and I'd hoped to shower and change out of these boogery clothes before going out. Ugh.

Where the fuck is Isaac when I need him?

I called him for dinner three times, but he's just in the garage smoking a joint, drinking a beer and probably watching rugby while Kai and the twins and I eat without him.

Just because we're talking by text doesn't mean we're talking in person, I guess. He'll need to get a bit wasted first. Let go of his inhibitions a bit and then we should be able to have an actual conversation. About something that happened two weeks ago.

Needs two weeks, four beers and a joint just to talk about his feelings. Jesus Christ.

And men call women high maintenance.

But at least he finally answered my question about

watching Elle and Claire. That only took six hours. I guess that is better.

I'm trying not to dwell on it because my anxiety level has come down a fair bit since this afternoon and I don't want to spoil it. Our quiet afternoon in the backyard wasn't ruined when Ruby woke up from nap. She was in a good mood and I sat in the grass with her while she explored various toys and bits of nature until her dad came.

It is nice when I just sit down and watch the children play. I have to ignore the voice in the back of my head which makes it hard to enjoy myself – that voice that is constantly calling out all of the items on my to-do list. As much as I'd like to get shit done, my body can't handle any more baby-wearing today, and my mind can't handle any more screaming. So the chores and cooking and laundry had to wait until Ruby was gone.

At least tomorrow is Saturday.

The kids and I played the tickle swamp monster game: where I lay on the ground and the kids try to get close to me without getting tickled. It is a great game for giggling, and everyone loves it. Even Ruby.

Ruby's dad was almost fifteen minutes late, so I didn't get dinner going until almost six. And even though I was making spaghetti with leftover sauce from the freezer it still took ages because the twins interrupted me 700 times. Isaac was home on time for once, and he did remember to pick Kai up. He did the dishes and then disappeared with a beer.

So here I am. Alone with children. Again. Still. Always. Sigh.

"How was school this week, Kai? Were you able to go a couple of days?" Kai is only ten but he already suffers pretty badly from anxiety. He's had a rough life so far:

his parents had a terrible relationship followed by an ugly divorce and a long, vicious custody battle in family court that only resolved when he was eight. His mom, Melanie, has always played him against Isaac and me. She treats us like an enemy in a war, and Kai is her spy and soldier and conspirator. She encouraged – no, actually demanded – Kai to lie to us about everything, even mundane details like visiting family. She has told him we are equally dishonest. She even told him my cancer was just a lie to win custody. That one actually came up in court and it helped the judge find in our favour. I say in our favour, but we still only get two days a week. Melanie had wanted to completely forbid Isaac any access to Kai, which is ridiculous. He's not a perfect dad, but he's a good person. Keeping him from his children is just vicious.

I often have a hard time reconciling a woman like Melanie with my feminism. She's exactly the woman the men refer to as proof that women are shitty people. I have to remind myself – she's shitty because she's been shat on, not because she has a vagina (and I often ask myself: how much of the shit she's taken came from Isaac? He can be a pretty selfish, inconsiderate person sometimes).

The result of all of this madness is that Kai is a mess. He doesn't know who to trust, he has no idea what a healthy relationship looks like, and he is epically insecure.

The sad thing is, Kai always had anxiety, even before the custody battle got ugly. When he was only four years old he would have a panic attack if we went to a busy mall or amusement park. He refused to use public toilets because they were too loud. We got him sound canceling headphones which really helped, but his mom threw them out because she wanted him to "toughen up". Once when he was seven we tried to take him to the zoo and he was so nervous he kept barfing in the car, so we turned around and came home.

Now he has a lot of anxiety around school and finds it very difficult to go. I don't know if there is bullying involved, but I know at least part of the problem is Kai's crushing perfectionism. He has always put such pressure on himself to do things "right". When he was five years old I tried to do a craft with him and it just ended in tears because his craft didn't look like the one in the picture.

I wish so much that I could homeschool Kai. Isaac wishes I could too, but of course Melanie would never even consider it. We get too much opportunity to "brainwash" him against her as it is. She won't even let him see a therapist about his anxiety. I think we should take her back to court about that, but re-opening that can of worms might push both Isaac and Kai over the edge.

Instead I have to sit by, completely helpless, and do nothing to solve these problems, which is very hard. I'm a doer, not a sit back and suck-it-up-er.

It crushes me that all of these adults are completely failing Kai. We're supposed to guide him, but instead we're just letting him fall through the cracks.

It makes me so sad.

Of course, I'm not completely helpless. We have him for 48 hours almost every week. For those hours we try to be as calm, stable, supportive and loving as we can. Hopefully we can provide him enough of a safe place that he gets a break from the crazy.

Except for the two year old twins. They come with a lot of crazy.

"Yeah, I went every day this week, but it was really hard. I feel overstimulated today."

Hehe... Kai has apparently been listening to me after all.

"Oh, that is helpful to know. We'll have to tell your dad you need peace and quiet tonight. Elle and Claire are coming over, so he'll have to make sure you get space if you need it."

Kai gives me a big smile and my heart leaps through my chest. That was awesome. He communicated, I let him know I heard him. Fuck yeah, I'm not completely failing after all.

Now don't fuck it up.

"When you have to do five days in a row, do you find it gets a bit harder every day? Or does it go up and down?"

The twins are both playing intently with their spaghetti "worms". Making a dreadful mess, but that is unavoidable with pasta. They are quiet, it will be worth the mess.

"Well...." Kai is thinking hard about his answer, "I'd say it gets harder until Friday. Thursday is the worst and Friday is better."

"You know, I'd say the same." This is lovely, that Kai is opening up to me. I've known him since he was only two, and I love him dearly, but as he's grown older he's pushed me away and I feel very much like "step-mom" rather than Lish. These sorts of conversations, where he opens up, are fewer and further apart every year, so I cherish them. "Sometimes, when it has been a really hard week, I start getting stressed again on Saturday evening, because the weekend is too short."

"Yeah, I've ruined an entire Sunday doing that." Kai nods at me. He is such an unusual kid, the way he talks like a grown up.

"The weekend definitely needs to be longer. Two days off is not enough to recover from five days on."

"When I grow up, I'll just have to get a job with a four day weekend." Kai smiles a great big mischievous smile.

"When I grow up, I'll have to get a job with a seven day weekend." Kai laughs at my joke. The twins laugh too.

"I'll get a job with a 365 day weekend!" Kai laughs louder and the twins copy him. The twins love Kai, and he loves them too.

It brings me such joy.

Sheba's bark scares the crap out of me.

Maja and the girls are here.

Fuck. So much to do. The table is a mess, the twins are a mess, the kitchen is a mess, and I haven't grabbed any of the stuff to take to Sofia's. I could really use Isaac's help but he's never here when I need him.

"Kai, can you help me out? Can you knock on the garage door and tell Dad that Maja is here and I've got to go?"

"Yeah, sure." He hops down from his chair. Kai is short for his age, but he has broad shoulders that suggest he'll be built like a tank, just like his dad. Add that to the black hair, dark brown skin, and dimple in his chin, he'll be the spitting image of Isaac.

I'll bet that drives Melanie crazy.

I open the door for Maja and it is like a hurricane sweeps in the door. Claire is whining, and Elle looks like she's in full-blown melt-down, Maja's arms are loaded with bags and pillows and stuffies, precariously balanced on her belly. Her face is hard, her jaw is clenched, her eyes narrowed.

"Jesus Christ, Elle, will you stop it already! I know you want a pet chicken, I hear you. But we can't. It just isn't possible. Even if it was legal, we can't just go to a store and buy a chicken. So, breathe, calm down, and shut up already."

"But I want a chicken! I want a chicken right now!" Elle

cries real tears. She is legit worked up about a chicken enough that her heart is breaking.

Maja looks like she's about to flip her lid so I jump in: "Elle, have you ever seen a movie called *Chicken Run?*"

"Is it about chickens?" her tear-streaked face peers up at me sadly.

"It is!" I hope Maja doesn't mind my interruption. I know she could handle it, but she shouldn't have to do it alone all the time.

"Are the chickens real or manimated?"

"Animated." I hope that is the right answer. Elle thinks for a minute and then nods her head.

"OK!" I smile as she dries her eyes and marches straight for the TV room. Claire follows singing *Lunasaurs* happily, as if she wasn't just wailing her head off a minute ago as well.

"Jesus fucking Christ, Lish. I'm just surrounded by madness. They are all insane." Maja drops the entire load of things that she is carrying, and she's up to her thighs in a mountain of pink things.

"I hope it isn't contagious." I laugh. Not laughing at her, of course, just that it is better to laugh than cry, I guess.

"I think it is, Lish. I really do."

"Have you recovered from your brush with the law?"

"Honestly, that wasn't even the worst part of my day."

I believe her. Poor Maja. We all have our shit to carry, but hers always seems to come directly from the people who she loves the most, and that isn't right.

Isaac comes in from the garage. He reeks of weed and his eyes are already a bit glossy from the beer.

He is in charge of five children. I really wish he wouldn't get quite so wasted. If I say anything he'll be pissed at me, so I bite my tongue. So far he's always managed to keep everyone safe while intoxicated. He even saved Hana's life once when she choked on a piece of cheese while he was baked. But if something bad ever did happen while he was wasted I would never be able to forgive him. Never.

I used to watch movies or TV shows where, after losing a child, the marriage falls apart and I could never understand why – 'don't you have so much more reason to be together?!' I would shout at the TV.

But now I get it.

"Isaac, can you put on *Chicken Run* for the kids, and then clean up the twins? I have to grab a few things and run."

"Yeah, for sure" he rubs his hands together like a man prepared to get shit done and walks off to the TV room.

I excuse myself from Maja and rush off to my bedroom to change into clothes that aren't stained with boogers and tears. I grab a baby wipe to clean my face and armpits. Shower of champions.

Back toward the kitchen. Elle is standing in the hallway outside the TV room looking like she's about to cry again.

"What is it, Elle?"

She doesn't answer, but she doesn't have to. As I crouch next to her I can see that Isaac is watching Rugby replays on the TV where she and Claire were all set up for movies.

Jesus Fuck.

Conscious effort to not use a nagging voice. "Babe, can you put on *Chicken Run* for Elle and clean up the twins, please?"

"Yeah, yeah. For sure. I'm doing it." He sits forward in his seat...

Like a man prepared to get things done.

We'll see...

Into the kitchen. I grab some pot cookies out of the

freezer for Sofia and throw them into a baggie and label it "cannabis". I started experimenting with baking my own cookies a few months ago. I find they help with both my anxiety and insomnia, and they are a lot easier to use when there are kids around than stinky joints.

I should have had one last night. I won't make that mistake again tonight.

I made these ones pretty strong. It was an accident, actually. I find it is hard to be consistent with the potency of baking weed. These ones are too strong for me, but maybe they'll be enough to numb whatever horrible thoughts must be haunting Sofia right now.

The twins are out of patience with sitting at the table and are now having a spaghetti fight.

Jesus, what a mess. Little bits of red noodle on the floor, table, walls, babies, chairs...

I grab two face clothes to clean the twins.

Maja has been on the bench in the front hall looking at her phone, but now she sighs deeply and puts it away.

I wonder what shit is pestering her tonight?

"Should I put the girls' stuff in the twins' room?" she asks.

"Yeah, that's a good place. Maybe set out what Isaac needs for bedtime? Oh, shoot, that reminds me, I need to get the sleeping mats from the daycare."

Maja goes off to the bedroom. The twins are clean so I get them out of their spaghetti-stained seats, carrying them over the saucy floor, and send them off to watch *Chicken Run*.

Isaac comes into the kitchen and starts to help himself to some dinner.

"Sorry, Isaac. I don't have time to clean this up, are you ok to do it?"

"Yeah, for sure." He nods at me while slurping up noodles.

He definitely seems to be in a better mood at least.

I'll just put the milk away. There are still four beers in the fridge.

Don't say anything.

"And, honey, do you think you can take a break from the beer and weed when you are alone with the kids?"

I said something.

"Yeah, for sure e ipo." He kisses me on the cheek and smiles as he sets down his dinner and starts to wipe the table.

If he's speaking to me in Maori, he must be in a better mood.

Downstairs. Mats. Sleeping bags. Upstairs.

"So, Isaac, I'll put these in the TV room for now. The girls can sleep on them in the TV room or in the twins' room, it is up to them. The girls' pj's and toothbrushes and stuff..." he's looking at rugby on his phone, his other hand holding the cloth, frozen mid-wipe of the table. He's not listening, is he. "Isaac? Are you listening?"

"Yeah." He nods without looking up from his phone.

He's not listening.

"Isaac. They should all be in pj's with teeth brushed and settled down by eight. If they don't fall asleep, that's fine, but just get them ready."

"Yeah, for sure." He smiles at me. "Have fun!" he looks back at his phone.

Oh well. It will be interesting to see what happens.

I walk into the TV room where Maja is saying goodbye to Elle and Claire.

I drop everything and use my free hands to flap my t-shirt open and closed to try to cool off from the hot flash that was triggered by all of this running around.

Then I set the beds up, say goodbye to Kai and the twins, who are horsing around on the couch.

"Kai, are you ok, or do you want them to back off?"

Kai laughs, "I'm ok."

Which reminds me.

Back into the kitchen. "One more thing, Isaac?"

"Yeah" still looking at his phone, but seated at the table now, on top of some noodles I don't doubt.

"Isaac?" He looks up after a moment. "Kai says he had a hard week and is overstimulated. So if he needs alone time, can you make sure he gets it?"

"Yeah, of course." He smiles and looks back at his phone.

In the front entrance, I sit on the bench to put on my shoes. I can hear Elle crying. She doesn't want Maja to leave. She is practically hysterical. As Maja emerges from the darkened TV room Elle is wrapped around her leg, pulling on her shirt, wailing, "don't leave me, Mama! Don't leave me!" Maja's face is twisted with frustration and exhaustion.

"Elle, let go!" she's trying not to shout, but Elle can't hear her over her own screams.

I don't want to intervene, because I don't want Maja to think I doubt her momming skills. However, I also know Elle is more likely to control herself when dealing with me than with her mom. That is just how kids are – a stranger gets the best behaviour, but they let it all lose with their moms. I approach the two of them in the hall and crouch down to Elle's height. She looks at me with her tear-stained face and, in my softest, most conspiratorial voice, I say, "Elle, I happen to know that as soon as we leave Isaac has a whole bunch of treats he's going to give you guys. Treats that mommies never let kids have."

She wipes her tears, "What kind of treats?"

"I don't know. He won't tell me because he knows I won't let you have them."

She grins. Then she stops grinning. "But I don't want Mommy to go."

"I know, your Mommy is awesome, isn't she? But we need to leave just for a little bit, so we can help Auntie Sofia."

"How long is a little bit?"

"Mmmmmm, two hours?"

"How long is that?" Her face is so sad.

"About as long as a movie." I say, with a glance up at Maja, who looks unhappy. I hope she's not pissed at me.

"I guess that isn't too bad." Eloise replies.

"Awesome. So, do you want to give Mommy one last hug and kiss and then when we can't see you anymore Isaac is going to get out some of those terrible treats that are bad for you."

She sobs quietly while hugging and kissing Maja one last time, and then she wanders toward Isaac in the kitchen and says, "What kind of treats have you got?"

"Oh, the best ones. They are so good that I had to hide them. Do you want to see my hiding place?" Thank God Isaac was listening to that and jumped right on the ball. Hero.

"Let's go quickly, before she changes her mind." Maja whispers.

Out the door and both of us sigh deeply with relief. It is getting dark. The air is turning crisp. The leaves, just beginning to turn colour, rustle in the evening wind.

Maja smiles sadly at me and we get into her truck.

6:50 pm

Andrea

As soon as the boys climbed into the tub I shampooed their hair (Zach had loads of sand in his) and cleaned them (Zach's fingernails are hopeless).

I'll let them play for five minutes and then it's out and bed. It is super early for them to go to bed, but Zach can't tell time and Wallace's silence can be bought if I just say that once Zach is asleep, Wallace can read until I get home. I'm supposed to be at Sofia's in ten minutes, but I can't leave bedtime for Damien. He'll just stick them in front of the TV and wander off, and they'll still be there when I get back. But TV and not enough sleep means that they'll be crazy all day tomorrow, so I'm just going to do this and be a bit late. The girls will understand.

While the boys bathe I could be productive. I could load the dishwasher or sweep the floors, but instead it's looking like I'm just going to sit on the toilet lid and check Twifagram.

More of Jessica Hammond's baby pictures. I'm going to have to unfollow her if she's going to be posting pictures of her baby every five hours.

Ovarian cancer support group: ladies posting pictures of how they decorate their bald cancer heads. Some of these ladies are really stylish. Most of them are older, but a few look much younger than me. So sad.

Not many black people, though. I wonder if that is because white people are more likely to get ovarian cancer? Or if white people are more likely to join a Twifagram group about it?

Google: ovarian cancer racial disparity

Oh, look. The first article: While white women are more likely to get ovarian cancer, black women are more likely to die from ovarian cancer. Why? Lack of awareness, socioeconomic reasons, genetics, and implicit bias among doctors.

Awesome.

I read something about this when I was pregnant: studies have found a shocking number of doctors subconsciously believe black people feel less pain, have thicker skin, are prone to exaggerate, and are more likely to lie to get pain killers. And this translates to higher mortality, and lower life expectancy for people of colour. A black woman in the US is three to four times more likely to die in childbirth than a white woman.

So, yeah, I'm not really surprised about this.

Anyway...

The boys are blowing bubbles and giggling. I love how they play.

"Five more minutes, boys."

How will Damien pay the bills when I'm gone? I have insurance, a quarter of a million I think. He'll spend that in three years, then what?

It is terrifying.

Ugh. On Twifagram Damien's dad has posted a meme mocking that little girl climate change activist.

Jesus that man is an asshole. Well educated and rich, so he thinks that makes him better than everyone.

He's not really an asshole. He does have a kind heart and thinks of himself as progressive, but he's completely blind to his privilege. He complains about paying taxes but can't imagine how much more life would suck to be so poor that you had to rely on public welfare just to live. He complains that all this talk about transgender is getting old, but can't imagine how transgender people might be tired of everything being about straight people. He is disgusted that Muslim women are forced to wear a veil, but thinks school girls should have to cover up because it's distracting to the boys.

He doesn't deny climate change, he just doesn't think we should let it threaten the economy or change the way we do anything. He wants business as usual: we can find clean energy later.

People like Ken just don't see it. They don't see that climate change is already here. It isn't some obscure event in the future, like it was when he first heard of it. It is already here. I see it when I go to Kenya: it is getting dryer every year. The wet seasons are shorter, and they bring less rainfall, and when it does rain, it comes down so hard and fast that the parched earth can't drink it in and they get floods that wash away roads, and force the sewage into people's houses. Famine and floods and oil spills are a constant and serious threat. And people are starving.

But people like Ken just see more third world suffering. Everything he knows about Africa he learned from World Vision advertisements. He thinks everyone in Africa is already displaced and starving and dying, so how is this different. 'That sucks, nothing we can do.'

But there is something they can do. They can give up a little bit of their comfort and make the changes that will fix this problem.

That is it, though. Nobody wants to give up their comfort. In fact, most of them are too busy being pissed off they don't have more comfort.

Everyone wants a bigger piece of the pie, they can't see how much they already have.

Little do they know, the pie is almost gone and then we'll all be fucked.

I am tempted to comment on this stupid meme, but I won't.

Just keep scrolling.

Fuck this is such a waste of my life.

I turn the phone screen off and look at the boys. They are stacking all of their bath toys up to make a waterfall. I love it when they work together as a team.

Basically I love it whenever they aren't fighting. Haha!

"Two more minutes, boys."

I catch sight of my face in the mirror. God I look tired. And old. When did my face get so swollen and saggy? It wasn't that long ago that I was young and fresh. I had no idea how beautiful I was, how strong I was. I had no idea how sexy and powerful I was.

Now I'm just saggy and swollen. Saggy eyes, saggy tits, saggy ass.

I could have had any man I wanted, but I didn't know it at the time.

So what happens if I leave Damien and still don't find passion? Who is going to want to date a woman who is dying? Life isn't a romance novel, where the man nurses her through to the end, and she's stunningly beautiful as she takes her last breath. My hair will fall out and I'll have a compromised immune system and get shingles and nobody's going to want to kiss me when I'm always barfing.

Damien will have a hot new wife and I'll just have a colostomy bag.

What happens if I die alone?

Jesus, I need to think of something else.

Maybe I should get botox.

I would hate myself forever. My feminist side screams "Looks aren't so important that you should inject poison into your face!" but my vagina is screaming, "yes they are!"

I need to think of something else.

I love the idea of writing books for the boys.

But what will they be about?

What do I want to say?

Everything. I want to say everything.

Maybe the first book will be about just how much I love them and how proud I am and how they are never alone. Because I'm a part of them, and because they have each other.

My eyes are filling with tears. I blink them back and smile at my boys.

How do I distill that into a book for children?

Without lying to them. I'm not going to be looking down on them from heaven. I'm not going to be reincarnated as a butterfly (my mind flashes to Lish's daycare girl who was told that butterflies were her grandma, and how traumatized she was when Sheba swallowed Grandma whole).

But I am in them. I'm in their DNA. Every cell in their bodies was made by my body. They are like limbs of my body who walk on the outside, and I will never truly die as long as they live.

Like Voldemort's horcruxes.

Ha! That could be a funny twist. If I was basically haunting them from within their own DNA. All through their lives, all these experiences growing up, but in constant battle with their mom in their DNA.

A graphic novel. One for each year of their lives into adulthood. The books mature as they do.

That could work. If I did it right. It could be funny and sweet while modeling how to handle moral...

"Zach, please don't sit on your brother's face."

"Mom, I asked him to!" Wallace protests.

"Wallace, please don't."

"Why?" he challenges.

"Well, for starters he isn't toilet trained..." that was apparently a strong enough point because Wallace immediately sat up.

I should get going. Yet somehow I'm on Twifagram again. I thought I put my phone down.

I put it down again.

That's one thing I won't think when I'm dying: I wish I'd spent more time staring at my phone. I should throw the damn thing in the garbage. Spend more time with real people, not virtual ones.

I should tell the girls tonight. Every day I put it off just makes it harder.

"OK boys, I need to pull the plug now."

"Few more mimits!" Zach bellows.

"Sorry buddy, it is late already. I have to get you out now."

"Few more mimits!" he says, his growing anger turning his cheeks red.

"I know you love the bath, my love. I'm sorry for cutting it so short. But, how would it be if I said that if you get out now you can brush your own teeth?"

"You won't do it for me?" his eyes widen.

Basically that means instead of me putting him in a headlock and his teeth getting cleaned, he can just suck all of the berry-flavoured gel off his toothbrush and go to bed with dirty teeth. I don't like it, but you've got to choose your battles.

And Zach immediately gets out of the tub.

Dry them, teeth, pj's, bedtime stories, cuddles, lights out (with Wallace's reading light on standby for when Zach starts to snore), more cuddles, and "Goodnight my darling boys".

Check my watch: 7:10.

Not bad.

Down the hall is the closed door of Damien's office. The golden strip of light at the bottom of the door is the only sign that he's still within. I haven't seen him all day. The boys haven't seen him all day.

How unfair that he gets a lifetime with them and he couldn't care less.

I force down a wave of powerful emotion and get moving.

I knock on Damien's door and poke my head in.

"Damien?"

"Mmhmm?" he says without taking his eyes off the monitor.

"The boys are in bed and I've got to go to Sofia's. If they get up, can you just put them back to bed?"

"Mmmhmm." Still looking at the screen.

"There's food on the stove if you are hungry. I didn't have time to sort the dishes, so maybe you can?"

"Yes, of course. Have a good time."

Have a good time? Visiting my friend whose baby just died? I'm sure it will be a blast.

I close his door, entirely unconvinced he heard a single word that I said, and head to the kitchen to gather Sofia's groceries.

Pizzas from the freezer. Bread, milk, butter, cheese, eggs, microwave meals, strawberries, chips, apples, toilet paper... hopefully that will do for now. I don't know how much she'll eat. She was eating really healthy when she was pregnant so I imagine she's going to want to do some comfort eating.

I should have bought some ice cream.

7:15 pm

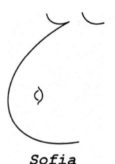

Sofia

I am in bed curled in a little ball when I hear the crunching of gravel under wheels as a Maya's rumbling truck pulls into my driveway. Even with the sheets over my head I can see the headlights briefly illuminate the room.

Well I guess it is too late to cancel.

Unless I just don't open the door.

Jingle of keys.

Unless Drae gave her my keys.

I came to my room a while ago with the intention of showering and getting dressed, but I just couldn't do it. I've been under the covers ever since.

I have to get up.

Sofia. Get up.

You can't let them find you here.

You look like an idiot.

But my arms won't move. My legs won't move. I feel like I'm made of rock, except that tears are leaking from the corners of my eyes.

7:16 pm

Maja

Lish got out of the truck much more quickly than I did, and she's already putting the key in the door.

I feel queasy.

Her baby died and I'm pregnant with a baby I once told her I didn't want. I'm the last person in the world she wants to see.

"Lish, wait." I whisper-yell in the dark.

"Oh, do you need help carrying something?"

It's almost dark, and there are no lights so Lish can't see me when I gesture for her to come closer, so I muster my courage and step forward.

"I'm just... Lish, I'm so pregnant. I don't want to upset her." I'm not sure why I was embarassed to say that.

"Oh! Yeah, for sure. We can just keep you out of sight? How about I take care of Sof while you do some cleaning behind the scenes."

I feel instant relief. "That sounds good."

"It'll be ok." She reassures me with a squeeze of my arm. And she unlocks the front door.

7:17 pm

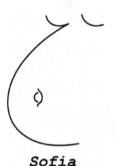

Sofia

"Sof?" Lish's voice echoes up the hall. "It is Lish and Maja. Drae told us to walk right in because you're too much of a selfish jerk to open the door. Those were her words, not mine."

I laugh and cry a bit at that. Yeah, sounds like Drae.

"Sof? Are you asleep?"

Ok, you really have to move now, Sof. They're in your house wondering where you are. They're going to think you are dead if you don't answer.

"Yeah." I squeak. My voice is lost. I haven't used it in.... Hours? Days? I clear my throat. "Yeah." Cough again. "I'm here."

I manage to toss the covers from my head when Lish walks in.

I must look pretty fucking shitty because she instantly starts crying. Not the ugly cry, but the 'I'm going to pretend I'm not crying' type of cry.

"Oh, Sofia." She comes to hug me. I fall apart in her arms. But she holds me together.

7:20 pm

Alisha

Oh, Sofia. My heart hurts for you.

She holds me tightly as she sobs. So I hold her just as tightly in return. We sit like that for a long time. I imagine it is possible that she might never stop crying. I wouldn't blame her at all. But eventually her grip loosens and she pulls away.

"I'm sorry, I just...." Sofia starts but I interrupt her.

"There is nothing to apologize for." I smile at her as we both wipe away tears. "You cry all night if that is what you need to do." She smiles sadly in return. "In the meantime, there's work to do. Do you want to shower while I clean in here?"

"Yeah, a shower would be good."

"Ok. Get up then. Go. I've got this."

7:22 pm

Sofia

My body listens when Alisha speaks. I've been telling myself to have a shower all day with no success. Lish only has to say it once and I'm shuffling out the door and down the hall.

7:25 pm

Alisha

Where do I begin?

It is a strange thing, cleaning someone else's room. There's that part of me that doesn't want to invade Sof's privacy, that doesn't want to do something wrong and make things harder for her. But I know right now I just need to be bold and get shit done for my friend. So I grab a laundry basket and start picking laundry off the floor and tossing it in. The dirty dishes I set in a pile on the dresser to take into the kitchen. Empty takeout bag into the garbage. It looks like a tornado struck in here, but it shouldn't take long to clean it up, really. Not with all of us working together.

Speaking of, Drae is almost a half hour late. She's usually pretty punctual.

But kids are assholes, so, who knows...

Maja

The kitchen isn't really that messy: empty bag of chips, empty box of crackers, empty ice cream container. Sofia hasn't been taking very good care of herself. Not that I blame her. It is hard to make a kale salad when you are crying so hard your eyes swell shut.

The sink is full of those little bottles for pumping milk. All of them have yellow curdled milk hardened to their insides. I fill the sink with hot water and bubbles while I clear the garbage off the counters.

I don't mind cleaning up this mess. This mess doesn't make me angry at all. I actually quite like cleaning when I know it will be appreciated. It is when I feel like a slave that I get pissy. When I'm working my ass off and nobody lifts a finger to help me, but I'm expected to drop everything when they need help, and be all sunshine and happiness all day without a negative thought crossing my mind.

Fuck that. I'm working so much harder than everyone else in my house, and I'm sacrificing so much, but I'm still at the bottom of the hierarchy.

7:28 pm

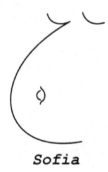

Sofia

The hot water feels so good. A million tiny pricks of pain drawing the blood to the surface of my skin. Draws my attention away from the blackness in my heart devouring me from the inside out. Washing away my tears. Washing away the dried blood, the sweat, the sour milk.

Lish might have to come and tell me to get out again too.

7:30 pm

Alisha

I'm glad to be here. I'm glad to feel like I'm actually helping in some way. It doesn't even crack a dent in the problems Sofia has, but it makes me feel less helpless.

I already delivered the dirty dishes to Maja to wash, and I piled together all of the laundry from the floor, including some blood-stained sheets that will probably be ruined forever. Now I'm stripping the bed, then I'll take it all down to the laundry room.

But I'm also looking forward to getting home and finally talking to Isaac. We used to have so much fun. We watched movies, took walks, played cards, cooked... we even had fun cleaning together. But now we rarely talk. We are too busy or too tired or he's angry at me.

We live in the same house but not in the same world. I hope tonight we can have a laugh together. Like old times.

I think this will be two loads of laundry. I'll do the clothes first, so she has something to wear. Then sheets.

I pick up the overflowing laundry basket and head down the hall, past Maja in the kitchen running dish water, and down to the basement laundry room.

7:33 pm

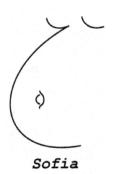

Sofia

How long have I been standing here?

I really must use soap now.

I turn the water hotter. It is almost hot enough to scald now. The pain is comforting.

7:35 pm

Andrea

I park on the side of the road and sit for a moment in my dark car to give myself a pep talk.

Drae, you have to tell them tonight. You can't sit on something like this. They'll feel like you don't trust them. Friends tell friends when they have cancer.

Deep breath.

I let myself into Sof's house without fanfare. Maja is in the kitchen washing dishes when I bring my bags of food in.

"Hey Maja. How are you doing?" I squeeze her shoulder in place of a hug, since she has her hands in the soapy water.

Maja takes a deep breath and replies in her most cheerful voice, "Yeah, I'm good." I don't believe her for a second. "You?"

I laugh in reply. "Yeah, I feel like crap too." Maja turns to look at me. She looks a bit like she might cry, or like she has been crying, and we smile sadly at each other. I really should give her a hug, but instead I start putting the food away. "How was Sof when you got here?"

"I don't know. I'm trying to stay out of sight." Maja speaks softly. "She's in the shower now. Lish is downstairs doing laundry."

Trying to stay out of sight? I guess that makes sense, but it is so sad. Maja and Sofia's babies were meant to be friends.

"I guess I should cook one of these pizzas."

7:42 pm

Alisha

I get the washing machine going without too much bumbling, and then put the blood-soaked sheets in the laundry sink and soak them with cold water and stain-remover. Then I head back upstairs.

Drae has arrived. She's unwrapping a frozen pizza.

"Oh, hey Drae. How are you?" I give her a hug that she returns with her usual stiffness.

"Maja and I have already established we feel like crap. You?"

I laugh, "Yeah, that sounds about right." Which reminds me, I should take another codeine because this headache is creeping back. I can really feel it in the muscles around my chest, where my breasts used to be. They are so tight that they're tender to the touch, and they pull my whole upper body inward and downward.

I stretch my arms up and back.

"Drae, do you happen to know where Sofia keeps her clean sheets?"

"I'm pretty sure there's a linen closet in the hall." Drae

tosses the pizza wrapper in the garbage and leads the way down the hall.

The linen closet is exactly where you'd expect it to be. I totally didn't need to ask for help with that job, I scold myself.

Drae picks a set of black cotton sheets from the top of the pile. "How long has she been in there?" Drae whispers and points at the closed bathroom door.

"Like, twenty minutes. I've been thinking we should check on her."

Drae tries the door. It is not locked. "Sofia? Are you ok in there?"

7:47 pm

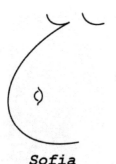

Sofia

No.

"Yeah, I'll be out in a minute." I call.

But I'm curled up in the fetal position on the floor of the tub. I don't remember doing it, but here I am.

Did I use soap?

You have to get up, Sofia.

I can't. I'm so broken.

The water runs across my face, into my mouth and nose and eyes, so I don't know if I'm crying real tears or just shaking and empty.

I'm so broken. I can't even stand up in the shower. How will I ever survive this? A lifetime of this pain?

It hurts so much.

7:50 pm

Maja

Dishes are clean. Counters and table are wiped. Floor is swept. I wish my kitchen could look this clean.

Sofia would rather have a family than a clean kitchen.

Now I feel terribly ungrateful. I'm practically wishing my family away and Sofia would give anything to have hers back. How can I be so selfish?

I should vacuum.

7:51 pm

Andrea

Sofia's bedroom smells like sorrow.

It is much cleaner than it was this morning, but we need to do something about the smell when we're done making the bed.

Lish sighs heavily as she changes the last pillowcase. "She's still in there. Should we go in?"

My sigh matches hers in weight. I flash back to just a few hours ago when I was in a million pieces on the bathroom floor. Could I have gotten up without my coworker Diane there?

"Yeah, I'll do it." I grab Sofia's bathrobe from the closet and head toward the bathroom.

I pause outside the door for a moment. I'm such a personal boundaries person. Every bone in my body screams with discomfort about this. But I know I have to do it.

Open the door. It is so steamy inside that I can hardly see.

"Sofia? I'm coming in."

A soft, unintelligible sob comes from within the shower.

I close the door behind me and approach the steaming shower. I pull the curtain back far enough to reach the taps, and as I lean forward to turn them off I see Sof's head resting on her hands, curled up in the pooling water at the bottom of the tub. Her brown hair flowing down the drain with the current.

Sof lets out a whimper when the shower stops.

"OK my darling. Let's get you dry." I look around for a towel and grab one from the back of the door. "I'm going to wrap this towel around your hair first and then I'll hand in your bathrobe, ok?" This is going to be awkward, but whatever. It is just a little water. And if your best friend can't see you naked when you are having a mental breakdown then what hope is there?

7:58 pm

Alisha

Maja has found the vacuum and is cleaning the floor of the bedroom. I've opened the window and lit the vanilla scented candle on the dresser to try to freshen the place up a bit. Here's Sofia's breast pump. I guess she's still pumping. I know she had wanted to donate to the same breast cancer charity that had arranged milk for the twins when they were young, but she would have to quit the weed to do that, and I sure as hell wouldn't be able to quit if it were me.

I'll put the pump by the bed, just in case.

Maja says something I can't hear over the vacuum. I shake my head and she speaks louder: "There are bottles for that in the kitchen!"

I give her the thumbs up and head to the kitchen to grab the clean bottles.

The pizza is sitting on top of the oven. I guess Drae was waiting for the oven to heat up and then I distracted her. I put the pizza in and set the timer. I look for plates, a pizza cutter, and a glass. I pour some orange juice.

I wonder what Isaac and the kids are up to.

I really hope he stopped drinking.

8:02 pm

Sofia

Thank God for Drae. My body listens to her when she tells me to stand up. I slide my wet arms into the sleeves of the bathrobe that she'd draped across my back, and pull it tight around me. Then, holding Drae's hand, I step out of the tub.

"I'm sorry, I feel so silly."

"Don't you dare, woman. You have my permission to be as broken as you need to be. If you are too sad to breathe, I'll do it for you. That's what I'm here for." She smiles sadly at me.

I don't know how I still have tears left, but they rise up to my eyes yet again. "Thank you, Drae." It is barely a whisper.

"Don't mention it." She hugs me and kisses me on the head. "Now let's get you dressed and fed."

Maja

Should I vacuum Grey's room?

No.

Too much stuff on the floor anyways.

We should probably throw out some of those dying flowers. It's really not smelling good in here.

I pull the vacuum back down the hall and into the living room. Just in time too: I hear the bathroom door open and Drae is guiding Sofia back to her bedroom.

This is silly, Maja. You can't hide from her forever.

But how can Sofia and I ever be friends when every time she sees my baby she's reminded of what she lost?

If there was ever a good reason for two friends to grow apart, this is it.

I tidy up the marijuana stuff on the table. I'm not sure what to do with it so I just sweep it all into the box. I'm the only one who doesn't use it. Drae only rarely does, but Lish and Sof use it daily. When they're not pregnant, of course. It just seems so gross and stinky and dirty. There's some on the floor too. I'll vacuum it up. I hope that's not a waste.

I picture Nate passed out drunk in the basement at home, my girls at Lish's house having more fun when I'm not there yelling at them. I picture Sofia and Drae and Alisha being friends without me.

I feel very lonely.

I start the vacuum and the sound numbs my sadness.

8:10 pm

Andrea

"Do you want to dress yourself or should I stay to help?" I picked out some pj's and set them on the bed next to Sof, all wrapped up in terrycloth with swollen eyes and rosy cheeks.

Imagine if she knew I was dying?

I'm suddenly filled with dread.

I can't tell her. She's already broken into a million pieces. If I tell her it will kill her.

"I think I can do it." Her voice crackles as though even her vocal chords have given up.

"That's good, because you're starting to come across as kind of needy." I joke when I'm nervous. Is she ready for jokes?

"Well, I was hoping you'd come to the bathroom and wipe my ass, but if you're going to be like that..." she croaks. Always ready for a joke. That's why we're friends.

I laugh. "Yes, I am going to be like that. Pull it together, woman." I give her a kiss on the head and slip out of the room and close the door.

I'm shaking and my hands are clammy.

Am I having another panic attack?

I have to tell them tonight.

But I just can't. They've been through enough. Not just Soph but Lish already battled cancer and it wasn't pretty. Watching me go through it will bring all of that shit up again. And Maja, living with that cave man, she doesn't need more to worry about.

I can't tell them. They have enough shit on their minds.

But I can't not tell them.

I let myself back into the bathroom to splash cold water on my face.

Fuck.

8:13 pm

Alisha

I open the freezer to find some ice or a bag of peas – anything to cool myself down. Standing next to the hot oven waiting for the pizza has triggered a hot flash so strong I actually feel nauseous.

No ice. But just standing with my face in the freezer feels better.

8:15 pm

Sofia

OK. On your mark. Get set. Go.

I let go of the robe, let it drop to the floor, and pull on the PJ pants as quickly as I can. Then I grab the top and pull it over my head, but it doesn't get far because there's still a towel wrapped around my hair. I set my hair loose and it slaps wet against my skin. I should towel it off but the urge to curl up in a ball is too strong, so I just let my PJ shirt get wet and crawl on to the bed. But the bed is made and getting under the covers seems impossible. I collapse in a lump on top.

At least I did something.

I wonder if it's too much to ask Lish to roll a joint for me.

I've taken all of the cushions off the couch and I'm vacuuming inside. Is that too much?

My first pregnancy Nate took over vacuuming. He did loads to help out when Elle was born. But not anymore. I don't even ask for help with anything anymore. He'll either complain that the job is unnecessary and a waste of time or he'll do it so poorly that I end up having to go back and fix whatever damage he's done and redo the job, which takes even longer than just doing it myself in the first place.

Maja

He's trained me to just not even ask.

On the back of the couch lies a white knitted baby blanket. That must be Grey's. My heart hurts. I fold it carefully and place it lovingly on the coffee table.

Fuck, life is too hard.

8:20 pm

Alisha

I'm pretty proud of the tray of food I put together. I couldn't find an actual breakfast tray, so I used a cookie sheet and laid a pretty tea towel across it. Then I laid out a plate with three pieces of pizza, apple slices, a glass of orange juice and a dessert plate with a pot cookie on it.`

Drae is standing outside of Sof's door.

"How is she doing?" I whisper.

Drae's face looks possibly the most serious I've ever seen it. Is Sof that bad? I feel the blood rush to my head as my anxiety rises and triggers another hot flash.

Jesus Christ, this is ridiculous.

"Sof, Lish has dinner. We're coming in." Drae calls through the door.

"OK" comes the muffled reply.

Both Drae and I take a deep breath and in we go.

8:22 pm

Sofia

I just need Drae to tell me to sit up, then I'll be able to do it.

It is like my brain and body are disconnected. Some wire wiggled loose and the messages just aren't getting through.

"Do you think you can sit up, Sof, or can I help you?"

And just like that my body starts to move. Drae helps by pulling back the covers and propping up the pillow and I crawl inside.

Lish sets the tray down on Colin's side of the bed.

I'm sitting on my side as if I'm expecting him to show up. But he won't. How long will I sit here? How long will I save his side of the bed?

How long will I save Grey's room?

Drae and Lish are sitting on either side of the bed. They are talking – fussing over me, asking questions that I don't really hear, their faces painted with worried expressions, looking at me with baited breath to see what I'll say.

I'm not sure what to say because I can't focus on the questions.

"This is perfect. Thanks so much. You guys..." I notice

how clean the room is. It no longer smells like stale milk and ash trays. Is that vanilla?

The vanilla candle Colin gave me last Christmas.

For a moment I am sad. I was saving that candle.

For what?

I guess this is as good a time as any.

I look at the tray that Lish has set before me. Pizza, apple, OJ, a cookie. It looks a bit green. I sniff it. "Is this pot?" I look at Lish, of course.

"Yeah." She smiles proudly, "Coconut chocolate chip. They're really good. You can hardly taste the weed at all, and I think they might even be strong enough for you."

Cool. This is way easier than rolling a joint. "You guys are the best." They've just taken care of everything. Swooped in and made it all happen, like a team of fairies. I feel like I might cry again, so I stuff an apple slice in my mouth.

The girls make idle conversation while I eat. They talk about the weather, about Twifagram arguments, about politics. I half listen. I feel like I should participate but I just don't have anything to say. But I'm glad for the distraction. I like listening to them talk after days of silence.

Every once in a while one of them will ask if I'm ok. If the food is ok. If I need anything. If I want to be alone. I insist that I'm fine and they continue chatting.

I am, actually, fine. Maybe it is the food. Maybe it is the clean room. Maybe it is the love. But I suddenly feel less broken than I've felt in days.

Except.

"Where is Maja?" I could hear the vacuum earlier, but now it has stopped.

Lish and Drae look at each other and then look back at me.

"I think she's worried she'll upset you." Lish says cautiously.

I frown. "She can't possibly make it worse than it already is. Can you tell her to come in here?"

Lish goes with a smile. "As you wish."

"Can I take your plate?" Drae asks.

I actually ate it all. I didn't even notice. I'm kinda proud about that. I've eaten so little lately, it's a surprise I'm producing milk at all.

I pluck the pot cookie from the tray and pass the tray to Drae.

I can hardly taste the weed.

This is not going to be strong enough.

8:35 pm

Maja

So, I vacuumed the couch and dusted and washed the TV and the coffee tables. Then I washed the windows. Next I went into the kitchen and dried and put away the dishes. Then I wiped the counters, the table, the cupboard doors. I was about to pull out the oven to wash behind it when Lish came in and said:

"Maja, Sofia says to get your butt in there."

Fuck.

"Yeah, for sure. Give me a second." I wash and dry my hands, my heart racing.

Calm down, woman. You are being ridiculous.

Drae comes into the kitchen with Sofia's empty dinner tray. With her free hand she squeezes my arm for encouragement.

Lish reaches for my hand. I am painfully aware that my palms are cold and clammy and I feel embarassed, but I take her hand and we walk together down the hall.

To Sofia's room.

I enter.

Sofia is in the bed, sitting upright, propped on pillows.

I'm so conscious of my giant belly. Of the baby shifting within, still very much alive. I try to hide it with my arms, which is absurd.

Sofia smiles warmly as her eyes flood with tears.

I'm crying too.

She holds her arms up: an invitation to hug. I climb onto the empty side of the bed and she wraps her arms around me and we cry together. We cry that moaning, shaking cry that bursts out of the deepest parts of your body. That cry that you only do alone when your heart is absolutely broken.

And my heart is broken. My poor Sofia. To lose a child. Is there anything more cruel? It is like having a piece of your heart torn out and destroyed. She will never heal. She will never be able to take joy in pregnancy or childbirth or children or family. Christmas and birthdays ruined. Family reunions, first day of school, children laughing in the park... all of these things that should be joyful instead will inflame the wound and her heart will feel freshly torn. The 18th day of every month. Thursdays... life will be a minefield of things that could send her back to that moment when she held her dead baby in her arms.

Curled together on the bed, arms around each other, her wet hair plastered against my cheek, Sofia and I cry together.

8:37 pm

Sofia

My heart is already so broken, but it breaks a bit more for Maja. I didn't imagine that was possible.

She must be so scared.

32 weeks pregnant should be joyful. She should be excited and relaxed but instead she's probably terrified of something going wrong.

I sob deeper that Maja has to suffer because of me.

8:39 pm

Alisha

I'm still able to unload the washing machine through my sobs.

I'm sobbing for Sofia and Grey and Maja. I'm sobbing because life is fucking hard and I'm so glad we have each other.

And, while I'm overcome with sadness I might as well examine my own life, with a husband who used the word 'divorce' today.

Load the clothes into the dryer.

Will he really want a divorce if I'm never going to have sex again?

How do I feel about that?

Horrible. No, not horrible, just really sad and full of regret. I regret that it has come to this.

But, at the same time, if the only alternative is having sex, then it will have to be divorce.

I drain the rust-coloured water from the laundry sink and squeeze out the blood-stained sheets as well as I can. Then I put them into the washing machine.

I wonder if that would make sense to him?

I suppose that might sound terrible. That I'm making a choice that could ruin our marriage. Maybe it already has ruined it. But to me, it just isn't a choice. I just can't do it. I just can't have sex with him any more.

But would he leave me?

I don't think so. But... I just don't know.

I guess it depends on why he's married to me.

Lifetime companion? Or guaranteed shag?

8:41 pm

Andrea

In the kitchen, I'm washing the dishes, but my mind is not here. It is just swirling around the same thoughts over and over.

I should have told them before. If I'd told them two weeks ago everyone would have dealt with it and moved on by now.

If I tell them now it will be too much.

But if I don't tell them they'll feel like I don't trust them.

But I do. I trust them more than I've ever trusted anyone. I can't begin to say how much I value these women.

Pizza dishes are cleaned and put away. The house looks, and smells, much better now.

Lish comes up the stairs from the laundry room. Her eyes are wet from crying.

I hug her.

I should hug my friends more often if I'm dying.

8:44 pm

Maja

"Maybe we both..."

"I needed a good..." we both speak at the same time as we pull away from our hug. We laugh at our gaff and wipe our tears.

"My tits are killing me," Sofia frowns, "Can you hand me all that crap?" she points to the bag with the breast pump and the mess of bottles and lids. I hand her what I recognize as Drae's industrial-grade breast-pump.

"The last time I visited my uncle in Spain he was showing off his fancy new milking machine. I can't help but identify with those cows whenever I use this thing." Sofia jokes but she has to force the smile.

I laugh at her joke. Maybe too loudly. I'm so awkward.

"With the amount of milk in your freezer, woman," Drae says from behind me, I hadn't realized that she was there, "I feel like you are as productive as a cow, too. What are you going to do with all of that?" Lish is behind Drae. She looks like she's been crying, and Maja and I are a mess, but Drae looks immaculate.

"I don't know," Sofia sighs, "Do you know anyone who

wants to feed THC-laced milk to their newborn? Could be a niche market."

"Maybe we can get Gwyneth Paltrow to declare it prevents Autism. Then your milk will be more precious than gold." Drae jokes.

We all laugh.

Wow. We all laughed.

"Don't mock it, Drae. That vaginal steaming changed my life." Lish jokes.

"Is that what cured your cancer?" I jump in on the banter.

"Ha! You know it. The chemo was just so I could lose weight."

"Maybe that will be the next fad diet – the Chemo Diet." As I say it I see Drae frown. I wonder what she is thinking about?

Nobody laughs that time. I guess we're done with that.

8:51 pm

Alisha

Drae takes a seat on the large trunk by the window and I sit at the foot of the bed. Maja is still beside Sofia, on Colin's side of the bed. The three of us make idle conversation over the swish-suck of the breast pump. It seems insensitive to talk about mundane, superficial things when Sofia is bogged down by such an epic tragedy.

But maybe we're a nice distraction?

I'll tell myself that.

"You'll like this one, Lish." Drae begins, "I left work early and picked Wallace up after school today. One of the other moms said to me, 'Oh, I didn't even know Wallace had a mom.'"

"Are you kidding me?" Drae gives me a look that says she is not. "In this day and age people still shame working moms?"

"Absolutely." Drae's brow is furrowed.

"Do you know what else is bad, though?" Maja jumps in with a bitter tone, "I have people try to shame me because I don't work. Like I'm a freeloader setting a bad example for the kids."

"Oh, yeah," I've experienced this myself, "Remember when I quit my job at the University and the Chair of the department called me a 'breeder'?"

Drae's face comes alive, "I remember her. Doctor Orlov, right?"

"Yeah, that's her."

"I don't remember her!" Maja looks to me to explain.

"She created the Gender Studies department. She was an old-school feminist who refused to get married or have kids and became a hard-ass to make it in such a male-dominated university."

"She had a reputation for hating the female students." Drae added.

"But I don't think she really did, I think she just pushed them harder because she believed women needed to be smarter and tougher than the men to succeed." I explained. Even as an undergrad I was torn over how to feel about Dr. Orlov. She was so mean, but then, once she believed I was working hard enough, she'd be so kind.

"And she was probably right." Drae shrugged.

"But she called you a breeder?" Maja looked horrified.

"Yeah, she saw it as a betrayal to the feminist cause, giving up a career to have kids. That was what her generation fought against, and here I was bowing to The Patriarchy. But it is really just an example of the difference between her feminism and mine – to her, feminism was about proving women are just as good as men, but to me feminism is about doing what is right for me, regardless of what is expected of my gender."

"That's stupid. You can't shame another woman for her choices and call yourself a feminist." Maja frowns.

"I just don't see why this is still an issue." Drea is sitting on the windowsill and the street lights cast shadows across her face that make her look very tired. "My mom worked. All of her friends were working moms, growing up most of my friends' moms worked. All of your moms worked. So why is this still a big deal?"

I think about this all the time: "I've always just figured that it is a part of this B.S. where no matter what a woman does it isn't good enough. We're too sexy, or not sexy enough. We're too angry but too submissive. We are supposed to bring in the bacon like a man, but still have a house like the pages of a magazine and kids that look like a photo shoot and do exactly as they are told the first time, every time. Anything less and you shouldn't have had kids."

"And then nobody likes you because you're too perfect." Drae cuts in.

"And then you have a mental breakdown." Maja mumbles.

"I just think, there's never been a generation of moms like us before." Here I go, ranting again... "Helicopter parenting is the norm, and with social media, the whole world is just waiting for one of our fuck-ups to get caught on film. Nobody has ever had that pressure before."

Maja nods her head, "And of course, a fuck up is now, just, like, the stupidest little thing. A few weeks ago I got told that I shouldn't leave my kids in the car when I go in to pay for gas. Like, seriously? They are in so much more danger crossing a busy gas station than they are in my truck for, like, four minutes."

"No you didn't!" Drae's voice lowers dramatically.

"Was it hot?" I don't think that matters, but maybe it did to the nosy good samaritan.

"No, it was 8:30 in the morning and, like, ten degrees."

"I hope you slapped the person." Drae is joking, of course.

"And then you get caught on video slapping them. The video goes viral and suddenly everyone is telling you you're an unfit parent!" the girls all laugh as I bring the conversation around full-circle.

Sofia smiles. I wonder how closely she's following the conversation?

"But you're right, Lish," Drae looks serious, "about how no generation of moms has had it like this. So much has changed about parenting. No parents before had to contend with Netflix and YouTube and unlimited data and 24 hour a day screens."

"True." Maja nods, "When I was a kid we only had 3 channels. Cartoons were on for an hour in the morning and an hour after school. And half the time they were re-runs so we often didn't watch TV all day. But now I'd say 50 percent of the battles I have with Elle are over TV time. She's totally addicted, and it makes her crazy."

"I read a thing about how all this screen time is a huge factor contributing to the rise of anxiety in kids." I'm pretty sure screens are giving me anxiety too.

Maja frowns, "And it doesn't help them any when their parents have anxiety too."

I nod my head, "Yeah, what is that about? My mom raised two kids, worked a full-time job, worked on the farm and battled cancer, and when I ask her about anxiety she just shrugs as if the whole thing was a piece of cake. I don't do half of that but I am a so stressed I feel like I could die from it sometimes."

Drae is looking out the window thoughtfully, "I wonder if it is because they had less to worry about. They didn't have Amber Alerts screaming in their faces every time a kid went missing, they didn't have sexual predator databases."

"They didn't have school shootings," Maja adds.

"They didn't know spanking causes aggression and anti-social behaviour. They didn't know letting your baby cry-it-out gives them brain damage, or yelling at your kids gives them low self-esteem and depression." I can feel my body tingling, a warning of another hot flash about to start, so I roll up my sleeves to ward off the heat.

"They didn't know when you are pregnant you have to sleep on your left hand side or else you might kill your baby." As the words come out Maja realizes what she's saying and panics, looks toward Sofia. Sofia doesn't seem to react, so maybe she's not really listening.

Drae jumps in, redirecting the conversation, "And we're expected to play with our kids. My mother never played with me."

"Mine either." I nod.

"Mine either." Maja's face is still blushing from her moment of panic. "We just went outside and stayed there all day."

"And did loads of crazy dangerous shit with no supervision at all. You don't see kids doing that anymore." Drae laments.

"That is the thing, eh? Children are never out in public anymore. Nobody plays on the streets anymore, parks are usually empty. Kids are always put away somewhere: daycare, school, summer camp, teams and clubs every night of the week..." As I say this I become aware that Drae has her kids in a lot of activities. I hope she doesn't think I'm judging her. I'm not. I know she does it because she wants what is best for her kids. I know she didn't get to join any groups or clubs or teams when she was a kid, and she wants to give her boys what she didn't have...

Maja doesn't notice I've put my foot in my mouth: "When we do go out, it is almost like people have forgotten how children behave. I get dagger eyes any time my kids run or jump or laugh. I can't figure out if they hate kids or if they hate moms."

"Maybe it is both." Drae frowns.

"And with all of this," I move on, "all of these ways that parenting is harder, we're also doing it in more isolation than any generation before us. People used to have their family closer, they used to have relationships with their neighbours, they used to have a community of people they could come to for help. Now we're supposed to do it all alone. When people see us struggling they don't help, they just point out our mistakes." I'm clearly thinking of my grumpy neighbour when I say this.

"When we put it that way," Maja mumbles, "it's no wonder I'm having a mental breakdown."

9:02 pm

Sofia

These are all things I used to care about: the decline of parenting, sexism, mental health in modern society...

I know they are important.

I just don't care.

They might as well be talking about the stock market. Or makeup brands.

But it is nice to hear voices. After days where the only sound is my crying.

I need to switch the breast pump to the other side. At first I try to do it without flashing my nipples to everyone in the room. But it is impossible. Who cares. Drae just picked me up off the shower floor, a bit of nipple isn't going to ruin our friendship.

I was adamant I wouldn't cover up when I was breastfeeding Grey.

The girls should be here to cuddle him. They should be cleaning because I'm busy taking care of a little person. Instead they're cleaning because I'm too broken to take care of myself.

An hour ago my brokenness terrified me. Now I hardly care. I've accepted it.

Irreparably broken.

I'm not sure what changed. Is it the presence of other people? Is it these specific people? Their love and caring when I'm down?

Or am I just so broken that my feelings have actually run out. Like an empty gas tank: no sadness left for today.

Sorry. The sadness store is closed. We're all out of sadness. Try again tomorrow.

For now, all we have in stock is cold, numb, objectivity.

9:08 pm

Andrea

"I finally saw that movie, Jilly." Lish announces. We had been talking about seeing that movie together, but then life got crazy and none of us had time.

"What movie is that?" Maja must have forgotten all about it.

"That is the one everyone was raving about: raw and honest portrayal of motherhood, blah, blah, blah." Lish waves her hand in the air dismissively.

"Oh, no. Was it not good?" I had been really excited by the trailers. There were a few lines that rang true for me.

Lish sighs. "No. It was just more of the same old patronizing crap: 'I'm tired, my husband doesn't think I'm sexy anymore, the other moms make perfect cupcakes' bullshit." She's rubbing her chest again, where her breasts were. And stretching her arms. I feel like she's doing that a dozen times a day. It must be so uncomfortable.

We all are damaged. In so many ways.

"Oh, that's disappointing." Maja wrinkles her nose.

"So it is basically the movie equivalent of a pat on the head and a 'there, there, isn't life hard'?" I put on a mocking voice to mimic fake pity.

Lish laughs, "Yeah, basically. I was really hoping the underlying idea was going to be about how important it is to have a support network, and about moms helping each other through hard times, but instead it was basically 'women are crazy and doctors can help'."

"Oh, God." Maja and I roll our eyes and groan in unison.

"That's bullshit." I almost spit the word.

Maja adds: "I wish that not being sexy was my biggest problem."

"And I wish that doctors could help." Lish says.

"That's bullshit." I say again, with more force this time. "The women I know are all getting their asses kicked by real, serious problems. Death and disease and betrayal and violence and poverty... and we're pushing through it practically alone, with no help from our partners, no help from the people around us..." I realize I'm ranting but I can't rein it in. "But nobody talks about that. They talk about the 'Mommy Wars' as if women have nothing better to do than fight with each other about who is more perfect."

"Why is the world so preoccupied with pitting women against each other?" Maja's brow wrinkles.

Sofia is finished pumping. She's holding the bottle and the suction-part and looking a bit lost. Lish notices and reaches out and takes it from her while she talks: "It was the same before we were married: this idea that women are always fighting each other over men. And any time a woman says something about another woman it's 'meow, catty, jealous much?' And as soon as we're married the narrative changes, now we're fighting over who is a better mom. I don't give a shit if you had a homebirth or a hospital birth, or if you use formula or breast milk. Why does the world want us to hate each other?" Lish makes a good point.

"Maybe they want us to hate each other, because if we didn't we'd just get together and talk about how much we hate men?" I smile and the girls all laugh at me. I rise from my spot to take the filled bottle from Lish, and twist the lid on while she packs away the parts of the pump back into the bag.

Lish nods her head in agreement, "It's funny because it is true: every time I get together with the women I know, sooner or later we end up talking about how much the men in our lives are fucking up. We're all shocked by how difficult life is, so much more difficult than we were prepared for. How we're working harder than we ever knew we could while the men in our lives are just dropping the ball. Even my mom complains that my dad is dropping the ball."

"Ha. Not my mom." Maja shakes her head, "My mom doesn't expect him to carry any balls at all. The balls are all her responsibility. He goes to work every day and she does literally everything else. But she doesn't complain because that is just how it is supposed to be."

"Do you think that is why we are all so angry? Because our generation was raised in a world where women were supposed to be equal, and it turns out that we are not at all. The odds are still stacked against us?"

Maja cuts Lish off, "Or are we angry because we thought men were supposed to be better than us and it turns out that we are clearly better at pretty much everything and yet they still have more than us?"

I excuse myself from the room to put the milk in the kitchen.

I'm struggling to follow the conversation. Every time

there is a lull I suddenly think: I have to tell them. And then I start to sweat and it takes a minute to get my mind back on track.

I find the freezer bags for the milk on top of the fridge and pour the contents of the bottle in.

I have to do it.

I label the bag with the date.

The first break in the conversation. I have to do it.

9:16 pm

Alisha

"None of these movies talk about that." I'm easily worked up when it comes to talking about gender in movies, "about the men dropping the ball. Men in movies are either perfect, or raging alcoholic abusers. There's no middle ground."

"Ah, I wouldn't say that is true." Drae has returned to the room carrying a bowl full of chips, "You forget about the bumbling nice guy. The Homer Simpsons and Seth Rogans of the world. They are always dropping the ball, but then they apologize and the women forgive them and then the women have to clean up their mess."

"Oh, yeah, you are totally right. I fucking hate that guy." I groan. I wonder if I hate that guy because he is basically Isaac? He has a good heart but puts absolutely zero effort into anything.

Drae demonstrates, "Isn't he so charming and lovable but clueless? He half-asses his way through life, creating more work for everyone around him, but he's a good guy, so we should all learn to relax a little bit and have more fun, like him."

"Oh, my God, I get that. Whenever Nate fucks up, the

lesson isn't that he should try harder, it's that I should chill out and care less. Except I'm the one that has to fix everything while he just laughs it off." Maja seems extra sullen today. I am worried about her.

"Related to that guy is the guy that raves about how his wife is such a better person than he is." Drae takes a handful of chips and hands the bowl to me, sitting back down on the trunk by the window, "He's all 'she's such a great mom, I let her do all of the parenting because she's better at it than I am.'" We all groan, "OR, buddy, OR maybe she's better at it because she's practicing all the fucking time. Maybe if you just tried a little bit you'd be better at it too!"

"That was Russel Brand in his stand-up." I actually wrote a whole rant about this for Twifagram when I saw it last week. Then I remembered that I'm trying not to rant on Twifagram anymore so I deleted it. "I just wanted to scream at the TV 'We're not naturally better at parenting just because we have a vagina, we're better because we're working our fucking asses off. You should try it!'"

"And if the men tried harder, we might be less pissed off and less tired and might even want to have sex with them at the end of the day." Maja grumbles.

Should I ask her if she is ok? She usually doesn't answer anyway.

Drae speaks before I can decide, "I saw this meme on Twifagram, it said something about how much more parenting women do than men, even when the women have full-time jobs. And all of the trolls were commenting: 'if she didn't want to do the work she shouldn't have had kids.' As if babies are gifts men give to us, and we are ungrateful for expecting them to participate in raising them."

"So, like, they're saying that men never want kids?" I raise an eyebrow, "or that raising children is just women's work and we're supposed to do it all alone?"

"Nate was determined to have kids. And he'll still want more when we have another girl. But he shouldn't have to make any sacrifices for them."

Did she just say 'When we have another girl'?

"Isaac wanted us to have kids. He's the one who talked me into saving my eggs before chemo." And I'm so glad he did. The hormones that they gave me to harvest the eggs meant for a few terrible months, and I had to delay my treatment in order to do it, but it was so worth it. I say that because it worked. It could have easily gone the other way.

"Damien didn't want kids. He said he did when we met, but then I had to talk him into it." Drae's face is so tight when she speaks about Damien. Something is definitely up there.

Sofia speaks for the first time, her voice small and scratchy: "Colin swore that he wasn't ready for kids yet, but he refused to use a condom and didn't pull out...."

We all look at Sofia and then burst into laughter.

9:24 pm

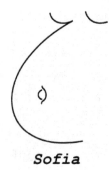

Sofia

It feels good to make everyone laugh. But now they are staring at me as if I'm growing horns.

Are my tits hanging out?

I check. Nope.

Oh, wait. I think I'm really stoned. That explains the emotional detachment.

That cookie was really strong.

9:26 pm

Andrea

There's a lull in the conversation. Now is your chance. You have to say it now.

I take a deep breath.

But Maja speaks before I can open my mouth: "You know, I wonder about that. Nate wanted kids so badly, and I know that if we separated he'd fight for shared custody, but then when he got it, I don't think he'd know what to do. He's never spent more than two hours alone with the girls. He doesn't know anything about how to take care of them. And when he is with them he just ends up losing his temper as soon as they don't obey his every command."

My face is still hot from fear. I almost told them. Almost. My heart is racing.

"He wants the privilege but not the responsibility." Lish nods.

"Yeah! Exactly! The girls are 50 percent his but the work that goes into them is 100 percent mine."

This is what I've been thinking about all day. How will he cope with 100 percent of the responsibility? At least I think Damien will be better than Nate. At least he's not a drunk.

"Isaac is definitely better than that. With my anxiety and migraines he's had to learn how to do it himself. It was really messy at first, but the more he did it the better he got. Now I'd say that we're 50/50 outside of daycare hours."

"Damien will have no idea what to do." I can hear how dark my voice is, speaking these words. "He dressed the boys in each other's clothes last week, completely oblivious to how badly they fit. He had to fill out this funding application and he didn't know the boys' birthdays. Or their middle names." It is so fucking unfair. I hate this. It is so fucking unfair.

"Are you ok, Drae?" Sofia cuts me off. She's staring at me with sad eyes.

Maja and Lish look at me too.

My heart skips a beat.

Jesus fuck. I have to tell them now.

I burst into tears.

I cover my face.

Breathe, Drae, breathe.

Swallow.

Smile.

I know it is the sad smile. I know that sad smile. That sad smile has been flying around all over the place tonight.

Their faces are frozen. Stricken. I don't think they've ever seen me cry.

Oh, God.

"It's just... I..." Breathe. My face is hot again. "I think I need to leave Damien."

Fuck, Drae.

You didn't say it.

You're such a coward.

But I just can't tell them. I'll tell them later. It isn't a
good time.

Will there ever be a good time?

Sofia's sad eyes are still fixed on me. She's waiting for me
to say more.

"Oh, Drae!" Lish gasps, "What happened?"

"Did he cheat?" Maja's eyes are wide.

I sigh.

Sofia's sad eyes.

"I... I just don't love him. I don't think I ever loved him.
And I just..." Deep breath. Isn't a total lie. Just a partial
truth. "The thought of living my whole life and never
knowing love? I've never had good sex. I've never had
passion. Heck, we've never even had a fight. It is mediocre.
I deserve better than mediocre. The thought of spending
the rest of my life with him...?" I trail off. I don't know what
to say. What are they thinking? Sof knows I'm not telling
everything. She's like a hawk, that one. Lish knows cancer,
I half expect her to be able to smell it on me. And Maja is
probably shocked I'd give up so easily when she is fighting
so hard.

Maja is the one who finally breaks the silence: "I've got
to be honest, I've never understood how you two
happened. It is like Princess Leia marrying Rain Man."

Everybody laughs. I laugh. I appreciate being compared
to Princess Leia, but I'm not sure I'd compare Damien to
Rain Man. Although, come to think of it, I have
considered before he might be on the spectrum. It would
explain a lot.

I'd prefer Han Solo, the sexist alpha-male, talking dirty
to me.

"But Drae, this is serious." Lish's face shows honest
concern. "How long have you been feeling this way?"

"Ehhhhh...." Since I got my cancer diagnosis? So, two weeks pretty much exactly, "It's been nagging at the back of my mind for some time, but I just can't ignore it anymore. Life is too short to just keep pretending."

"But I'm confused," Maja's face definitely looks confused. Can they see right through me? "If you never loved him, why did you marry him?"

Sigh. Good question.

How could I have been so stupid?

"I just don't think I knew who he was? I imagined he was someone else. I think. Or maybe he pretended to be someone else."

"I can see that." Lish nods. "Like, he acts like he's a really interesting person. He likes interesting things and knows interesting people, but he himself has actually never done a single interesting thing in his life."

"Except marry Drae!" Maja jumps in.

Is that true? "No! Damien was interesting, wasn't he?"

The girls all stare at me.

"He wrote a book!" Which nobody ever read. But I remember being in awe of him. All the fascinating stories he told. Except, now that I think about it, the stories always were about other people. People he knew who did cool things. And cool books he read or cool movies he watched. The random, obscure, trendy music he listened to...

Oh my God, she is right. He pretends to be more interesting than he is, and I never figured it out.

"Well, anyway. I was an idiot. I married him out of some messed up desire to please my mother, and that is a stupid reason to marry a person. I just didn't know it until... now."

"So.... Is there another guy?" Maja asks with caution.

"Oh, God, No! I could never cheat. Damien doesn't deserve that. I won't do anything while I'm still married to him."

"But you want to?" It was more a statement than a question.

Apparently Maja knows me too well.

I can feel my cheeks flush. "Hell, yes, I do." I smile, remembering flirting with Hot Spin Instructor. The girls laugh. "I just want some big, sexy, hairy man to throw me around a little. I just want to fuck someone. A messy, sweaty, wild fuck. Just once in my life..." before I die. Isn't that supposed to be a teenager thing: 'I don't want to die without having sex'. Well I don't want to die without having good sex.

"So you and Damien never had crazy sex? Not even when you were new?"

"Oh, God, no. No passion with Damien. We were dating for weeks before he even made a move to kiss me. I thought he was just being a gentleman, but now I wonder if he just doesn't really have any sex drive. I mean, the first time we had sex he stopped to fold his clothes neatly and lay them on the dresser."

"Oooooow." Maja and Lish wince in unison.

"It is always missionary. It is always in the bedroom. I suggested we watch porn together and he just laughed as if it was a joke."

"Oh, Drae. That sounds horrible." Maja's face betrays a legitimate horror at the story. We all know that Maja has a great sex life. Nate brags about it. He jokes that the stereotype about horny Asians is true, and it makes me want to punch him in the face. But Maja has, in the past, expressed surprise that not everyone has had multiple orgasms from penetration alone, as if it is no big deal.

"It sounds like a chore." Lish nodded. And there's Lish, at the other end of the spectrum, who has given up on sex for life. She has the cancer to thank for that.

All the more reason for me to act now: before it is too late!

"That is it, Lish. That is exactly what it is. With Damien, sex is treated as a chore. An obligation."

"Ugh, who would want that?" Maja grimaces.

Not me.

9:35 pm

Maja

"If the sex with Nate was like that I'd have left him ages ago. Sex is pretty much the only thing we have going for us." And even that is shit lately.

"Maja, I've got to say it," Lish raises an eyebrow. "You thought that Damien and Drae didn't make sense, but you and Nate don't make sense to me."

"You guys think I'm a fool for being with him." I feel small. I feel like a child. A stupid child.

"Oh, no, no!" both Drae and Lish insist.

"I just figured there must be something good about him I don't know about it. You must have your reasons." Drae says softly. Warmly.

I sigh deeply.

"It is like you said, Drae. I don't know if he was always like this and I just imagined he was someone else. Or if he's changed. Or maybe I'm the one who has changed. I used to be so happy. We used to laugh so much. Now we are both angry and resentful and mean."

"Oh, Maja. That sounds unbearable." Lish reaches across the bed and squeezes my hand.

"Does he hit you?" Drae's voice is strong and firm and cuts me like a knife and I draw my hand away from Lish's as if it were burned.

Immediately my mind flashes with the memory of him punching me in the spine when I was pregnant with Elle. We were in a roadside motel on the way to Florida. He'd had too much to drink and was shouting about something, I don't even remember what, and I asked him to keep it down before someone called the police. And he punched me.

And that time he locked me out of the house. Dragged me out by the neck and locked the door, the girls sleeping inside with him, drunk and angry, and me unable to get back in. I keep a key hidden outside since that day.

Drae and Lish are staring at me, expectantly.

"He has hit me, yeah." I've never told anyone that before. I'm so ashamed with myself for putting up with it. I'm weak. If I was a strong woman I'd have left ages ago. They say people can only abuse you if you let them, and I let him. "But he doesn't make a habit of it. And I've hit him too. I'm not innocent."

"But when you hit him, is he afraid that you'll hurt him? Is he scared of you?"

No. He laughs.

"What about the girls?" Drae pushes.

"No! He's never been violent with the girls..." I picture this afternoon when he swore at the girls and knocked them over. "Except he is mean. And scary. He throws things and punches things, but he's never hit them." It makes me feel weak. Like I'm a rabbit and he's a grizzly bear. I can't imagine how weak the girls feel.

"That is really scary, Maja. Like, that must leave you

feeling powerless." Lish's pity makes me feel even more shameful.

"So, why *do* you stay?" I can't help but think Drae wouldn't stay. She would have marched out the door the first time a man laid a hand on her. She is just so much stronger than I am.

"I don't know." I'm looking at my hands: dry and cracked from doing too many dishes, purple from lack of circulation because I've been clenching them. "Sometimes I think he will change once he realizes how bad it is. Sometimes I think if I change enough it will inspire him to change. Mostly I think I just don't know how to leave. I have nothing. Where would I go? How would I pay the bills? I have a new baby coming, I haven't worked in years. I'm completely dependent on him." And part of me wonders, would he let me leave? I mean, I think he would. He's not a monster.

"Maja, if money is the reason you are staying, we will help you. Between the three of us we can find you enough for first and last month's rent, I'm certain." Drae means it. I can tell.

I want to cry.

"Absolutely." Lish reaches out to squeeze my hand again, "If you want to leave, if you decide that is the right choice, don't worry about money. We will help you."

I'm definitely going to cry.

Fuck Nate.

"But I can't. The girls need..." what? The girls need their father?

"The girls need to see how a man should treat them. They need to see what a healthy relationship looks like."

Lish is right. Fuck.

"If your girls were with a man who treated them the way Nate treats you, how would you feel?"

Horrible. I would feel horrible.

I don't say anything though because I'm too busy trying not to cry.

Lish hugs me.

After a moment I pull away, wiping away my tears, and say, "I remember my dad hitting my mom. But she wouldn't care that Nate hits me. She thinks that is just how it is. Men hit women. I should get used to it."

"That must make it even harder for you to stand up for yourself. If it is normalized by your parents and they won't support you. That's got to mess you up." Lish says.

I laugh. "Lish, I love the way you always let me blame my parents for my mistakes." The girls laugh with me.

"I've gotta refute your mom, though. Damien has never hit me." Drae says.

"Isaac hit me. Just once. He'd been drinking, of course. No, wait, he also pushed me into a wall once. I didn't even consider leaving him. I blamed myself. I'd egged him on, pushed him when he was clearly losing his temper, so I decided it was my fault. I don't blame you for staying, Maja. We know it is complicated."

"But we won't judge you for leaving, either." Drae adds.

"Colin never hit me," Sofia is paying attention after all, from her cozy spot curled up in the pillows a few feet from me. "But my high school boyfriend did. My brother did. So did my dad."

"Yeah, my brother did too. Like, not your usual sibling rivalry violence, but scary abuser violence." Lish frowns.

"Oh, well," Drae adds, "If we are including relatives, yeah, I've been hit. But my uncle lives in Kenya, and I don't have to talk to him or even see him anymore. You have to put up with Nate every day. Would you say he is ruining your life?"

"Yeah, I would." He is. He makes every day worse.

"When you are on your death bed, will you regret the time you spent with him?"

"Yeah, I will." I already regret it.

"So when do we go apartment shopping?"

I laugh. That is a thrilling idea. Apartment shopping. I love it. I'm grinning through my tears.

But then what? I get a job? Put Elle in school and spend all of my wages on daycare? Send my newborn to be with someone else all day? I'd have to get a lawyer. Would Nate pay child support?

He'll call me a freeloader.

A golddigger.

I'm not smiling anymore.

There's an awkward silence.

I don't want to talk about me anymore. I feel raw and drained.

"Sofia, what happened with Colin, anyway?" I throw the attention toward the most vulnerable person in the room.

I'm a shitty friend.

When the spotlight turns to Sofia I feel all of my strength drain. I would love to curl up in a ball under the covers like Sof is right now. My hands are shaking and I feel queasy.

9:41 pm

Sofia

I don't know.

I know that thought scares me, the not knowing what happened, but I feel that detachment that comes with being really baked. My emotions are still there, but they are dulled. Like the volume has been turned down. I was at a ten and now I'm at an eight. Maybe even seven. That cookie was good.

"I don't know what happened." I clear my throat. It is tight. I'm clenching my whole body. I try to relax but my body just doesn't listen to me yet. I should get Drae to tell my body to relax. That might work.

"He just said, 'It's too much' and he left. Put some things in a bag and left. I just watched him. I didn't know what to say."

"What the hell does that mean, 'it's too much'?" Lish's face looks like she is growling. Is that a weird thing to think?

It's too much.

"I don't know."

"Like, there's too much sadness in this house and he's too overwhelmed to be here?"

"I guess, maybe. I sort of thought he meant that I'm too much. Too broken. And he doesn't want to deal with me."

"Oh, Sofia! Who wouldn't be broken by this! You can't blame yourself." Lish's face looks so distraught. I think she might be the most empathetic of us. But also the least. I don't know if that makes sense.

"I just thought he was broken too. He puts on a strong face, but I assumed underneath he was hurting as much as me. But maybe I was wrong."

"He didn't talk to you at all about how he was feeling?" Drae asks.

"No. He didn't even really cry. And then he hid all of Grey's stuff in the bedroom."

"Oh, I wondered what that was all about." Maja's face seems older. I think we aged her five years with that last conversation.

"Surely that is a sign that he is hurting too, but just doesn't want to face it?" Drae wonders aloud.

"I don't know. He just didn't talk to me. I feel like I fell into this huge black hole and he just let go of my hand and left me there."

"Oh, Sofia." Maja's sad, aged face.

"You haven't heard from him at all?" Lish's sad face.

"No, not since he left. Was that Wednesday?"

"Today is Friday! That is shameful. What a horrible thing to do to you." Maja's sad, angry, aged face.

"I'm sure he's hurting too. He just doesn't know how to cope." Lish's sad, empathetic face.

Drae's face looks distant. I think it is the saddest of them all. She just hides it better. A lifetime of hiding her sadness. A chameleon.

"Sofia doesn't know how to cope. Nobody does. But you stick together. That is what marriage is. For better or for worse. You stick together and you help each other, that is how you cope." Maja has a very strong moral compass when it comes to other people, but talks herself out of it when it comes to her own life.

I want to defend Colin. But also, Maja is right. I need him, and I thought he needed me. But I guess not.

9:44 pm

Alisha

I hear the buzzer on the laundry downstairs. I don't want to step away from the conversation but it is almost ten o'clock and we need to fold the laundry and get home. God knows what Isaac and the kids are up to.

As I slip out into the hall and down to the basement I check my phone. Isaac has sent me... four, five, SIX pictures of the kids. Looks like they are having a blast. He also writes that Hana got poop all over the bathroom again and Ari fell face-first down the stairs again, and walked away with barely a tear. In the pictures there is candy on the table – looks like Isaac found the Halloween candy. Life with a stoner...

Clothes out of the dryer.

Oh, my heart. Sofia alone when she needs Colin most. Maja trapped in a marriage with no respect. Me in a marriage that is crumbling.

Wet sheets into the dryer.

And then there is Drae. Putting her happiness first for once, after a lifetime of doing what she's been told to do. I'm so proud of her.

I lug the basket of clothes up the stairs.

Now we just need to get Maja to put herself first. I don't think she'll ever do that. She might put the kids first, but she has been beaten down her whole life to the point where I don't think she believes she deserves to be first.

As I re-enter the bedroom Drae and Maja are laughing.

"How about you, Lish?" Maja turns to me, "Do you want to join a sex club with Drae and me?"

The conversation took a dramatic turn while I was downstairs. "I can't think of anything in the world I would enjoy less." That is an exaggeration. Not by much, though.

"Maybe Isaac is just lousy in bed, and with the right man you would change your mind."

"Or the right woman." Drae throws in.

I'm completely embarrassed by this conversation. I force a smile and drop the basket of laundry on the bed. Drae and Maja move closer to help with the folding. "No, it's not Isaac. It is me. I'm just not interested. I don't even want to masturbate. I'm just done."

"And Isaac is ok with that?" Maja seems incredulous.

"No. He told me today that he's thinking of leaving me."

"What?!" Drae starts a pile for unmatched socks. "But you told him he can sleep with other women. That is, like, every married man's dream. What more does he want?"

"He says it isn't the same. He only wants to have sex with someone he loves."

"Well that is sweet." Maja is a sucker for a romantic gesture. "Can't you just fuck him now and then just to save your marriage?"

"I did that. For years I did that. I don't want to do that anymore." I feel myself getting defensive: that panic rising up in my chest. I take a deep breath and start again, calmer. "I was thinking about this earlier. Imagine that what turned Nate on, what really got him going, was poking you in the eye. And he wants to poke you in the eye, repeatedly, once a week or so. Maybe at first you'd be like, ok, if it is important to you, you can poke me in the eye. But after a while you'd get fed up. First of all, it hurts, and you don't like it. But secondly, it is kinda fucked up that he gets joy from doing something that causes you pain. I don't think anybody would fault you for saying no, never again to that. Yet for some reason I feel like I'm a shitty wife if I say no to sex, when for me sex is absolutely no different to being poked in the eye."

"Wow, you really don't get any pleasure from sex at all?" I wonder how crazy that seems to Maja, who gets such joy sexually.

"No. I hate it. I want nothing to do with it. It was ok when I was younger, but I haven't taken any joy in it for years. A part of me is envious of the two of you and how much pleasure you get from it, but that is just not a reality for me."

"Well then I'm glad you put your foot down and put yourself first for once." Drae announces.

"Do you think he'll leave you?" Maja wonders.

"That is the question of the day!" I smile. "Although I don't think he will. I don't think Isaac is a leaver. He might talk about it, but I can't see him following through. It was Melanie who left him before. She cheated on him, and he threatened to leave, but he didn't."

"Well, if he does leave you, and Drae leaves Damien, and Sof still hasn't heard from Colin, we could all just move in together." Maja winks.

9:50 pm

Sofia

"Once we've folded your laundry we'll go." Drae pulls a shirt from the basket, "You look like you are ready to sleep."

I have slowly sunk down in the bed under the weight of the world. "Yeah, Lish's cookies are strong enough to sedate a horse."

"Oh no!" Lish's eyes grow wide, "Are you ok? I should only have given you half!"

"No, no. Sedating a horse is exactly what I was looking for. We're good."

Lish laughs. "Oh, well then! There's a whole bag of them in your freezer!" She smiles kindly.

I fucking love my friends.

They are chatting, smiling, laughing. Their presence is like a warm light in the room. When they go it will be cold and dark and empty again.

I feel myself looking forward to it. Being alone in the dark feels right. Like I belong there.

And nobody to see how ugly and broken I am.

9:58 pm

Maja

"Well it sure doesn't take long to fold laundry when all three of us work together." Drae is putting the t-shirts in the top drawer of the dresser.

"Yeah, I should invite everyone over tomorrow. I've got like five loads cleaned but not folded." Lish jokes and everyone laughs.

But, really, that is a great plan. I hate doing laundry, and there's always so much of it because Elle changes her outfit every 45 minutes.

"I'm in." Drae jokes, "Folding your laundry will distract me from thinking about fucking Hot Spin Instructor. I can do spin class in the morning, masturbate all afternoon, and go over to your place after dinner."

Laughter.

"Please shower before you come?" Lish laughs and we all laugh again.

"So, this guy teaches spin class tomorrow morning?" I ask once the laughter has died down.

"Yeah, he also does Tuesday and Thursday, so I usually

go during work. But he specifically invited me tomorrow...
it seems rude to say no."

"Can I come?" I'm grinning. I've never done spin, I'm
more of a runner, but I'm willing to try if it means I get to
check this guy out.

"You're eight months pregnant!" Alisha laughs.

"That's ok!" Sofia calls out from her spot curled up on
her pillow, "As long as she's been exercising regularly and
consistently, she can keep working out right until she goes
into labour."

"There you go, my midwife OK'd it." I smile, satisfied.
I won't mention that I've been dropping my runs pretty
often as the pregnancy progresses, but I'll be good. I know
my limits. "My parents are taking the girls apple picking
tomorrow, so I'm free. What time?"

Drae smiles slyly "10:15."

"I'll be there." I grin. I'm really excited about this.

"Anyway, we should really go. Sofia, you really do look
like you're half asleep." Lish smiles warmly at our friend.

She looks so small lying there.

I hope she'll be ok. I mean, I know she'll never really be
ok, but I hope she finds a way to make a good life, despite
this.

We all hug her. We fuss over her. Fill her water. Plug
her phone into the charger. Adjust her pillows. Lish puts
another cookie on a plate beside the bed, "for later" she
says.... Then we kiss Sofia good night and Drae locks the
front door behind us.

10:03 pm

As soon as the door closes I turn off my light and sink down in the bed.
I welcome the darkness.
The emptiness.

Sofia

10:04 pm

Maja

Man, it got cold out.

By the time we've hugged Drae goodnight and climbed into my truck my hands are shaking so hard I can hardly get the keys in the ignition. I crank the heat, but I know it probably won't kick in until right before we get home. Piece of crap truck.

"Jesus Christ it is cold!" Lish exclaims as she sits on the icy seat next to me.

I can't stop shivering. My teeth are chattering and my shoulders are up to my ears. I put the truck into gear anyway. Lish's house isn't far, I can leave the truck running while I get the girls.

"Are you ok?" Lish asks my shivering self.

"Yeah, just cold."

"That was a really emotional visit. I feel totally overstimulated. Like, I'm twitching. And the cold doesn't help."

It was a bit of a roller coaster. So much sadness. So much pain. But also so much love and support. I feel completely drained.

I am shivering too hard to talk. It makes it hard to drive.

Thankfully it is late and the roads in this suburb are pretty quiet.

So much to process. Sofia. Nate.

Lish puts a hand on my arm, "Seriously, are you ok? That must have been a lot."

"Lish, I have already cried too much tonight, don't you go make me cry again!" I pretend like I'm joking but I think she knows I'm not.

Lish laughs, "OK, I won't. You've got it. I'll talk about something else entirely. Did you see how much gas went up today? Twenty cents since this morning!" She smiles at me.

I'm still shaking. My belly hurts. The shivering is more than my overstretched abdominal muscles can take and they ache immensely.

"I'm glad Sofia hugged me. I was so worried we couldn't be friends anymore. I mean, I'm still worried. I'm worried about her, about our friendship, about my baby, about her and Colin. But that hug put my mind at ease, you know?"

"Yeah. I do. I mean, I feel totally helpless when I see how much pain she is in, how much pain you are in, how much pain Drae is in. It is all so shitty, and there is nothing I can do to help any of you. But it feels better knowing we are in this shit together, no matter what. That is comforting."

"Thanks for the offer to get me an apartment, Lish. That is really amazing of you guys."

"It isn't just an offer, Maja. We are serious. I won't push you to leave or stay, but whatever you choose, we'll help you the whole way. If you need daycare, I'm here for you, for free if you need it." I suspect that Lish can't really afford a client that doesn't pay, but I love that she offered anyway.

"Thanks, Lish."

"You know, though, you were talking about Nate, and how you don't know if he was like this all along or if he's changed. It could be both. I've read stuff about men who are abusive – and not just physically abusive, emotionally abusive too – and they say that generally abusers are masters of disguise. They pretend to be who you want them to be, until they get what they want. And they will switch back and forth between different personalities, to keep you lost and confused. Does that sound like Nate?"

I have often thought it is like living with two different men. Or more. Just when I get so fed up I can't stand another day with him, the other Nate shows up, loving and affectionate and understanding. "Yeah, maybe."

"Another thing, is often abusers claim they were abused when they were young. Has Nate said anything like that?"

"Yes. He said his mom was really violent, and that is why he doesn't trust women. When he hit me once he was so apologetic afterward. He said for a moment he saw his mother and all of his childhood trauma came up, and when he hit me, he was hitting his mother. But I don't know... I just find that hard to believe. She is so quiet. She is practically a doormat to his father. But I guess if Nate can hide his dark side from outsiders, maybe she can too?"

"Or he's full of shit."

"Yeah, or that." Which I already know he is. I've caught him lying so many times I've lost count.

We pull into Lish's driveway. I'm still shivering. The truck hasn't warmed up one bit. I'll leave the engine on and maybe it will be warmer when I bring the girls out.

When we go in the door we are immediately bowled down by the dog excitedly greeting us. She is whining and wiggling and licking. I like Sheba, but she sure can get in the way! When she calms down I can hear the twins squealing and giggling in the TV room. I take off my shoes and follow Lish to the TV room. The twins are there, jumping on the couch, and Isaac is there, passed out on the recliner. Actually passed out and snoring. So much for Isaac being more reliable than Nate. Kai is there too, with his headphones on playing a game on his phone. He gives Lish a look that says he is not impressed.

"Oh, for fuck sake." Lish sighs when she sees. "Kai, you are amazing. Thank you for being the responsible adult in the house."

He half smiles at her and goes to his room.

"I'm thinking Elle and Claire are sleeping in the twins' room." We head further down the hall and peer into the dark bedroom. By the glow of the night-light I can see my girls sprawled across the two mats on the floor, close enough that Claire's hand is across Elle's neck and Elle's feet are across Claire's legs. Oh, how I love to look at them when they are sleeping. "Do you want me to help you carry them to the truck? Or do you want to let them sleep here and I can bring them to you in the morning."

"Oh, you've got enough on your hands. You don't need two extra kids." Although I hate the idea of waking them, carrying them to the truck, they'll cry the whole way home, and by the time they get home they won't want to go to bed at all.

"Are you kidding? Your two peacefully sleeping kids are currently my favourite people in this house. They can stay as long as they like."

That would be a lot easier.

"Are you sure? I can come get them in the morning."

"No, no. I'll bring them to you. I don't mind at all. You deserve a good night sleep." Heading back toward the door we pass the TV room again, where the twins are now crawling on Isaac. They are sticking their fingers up his nose and he's giggling with his eyes closed.

"What will you do with him?"

Lish sighs. "We used to draw a penis on the face of whoever fell asleep at a party. Should I do that?"

I laugh. "Make sure to use permanent marker!"

10:22 pm

Andrea

I take the elevator from the parking garage up to our condo on the 8th floor. I always thought I would one day have a house with a backyard in a neighbourhood with lots of kids just coming and going from each other's houses. BBQs and pool parties...

I didn't expect to have so many regrets in life. I just thought I had more time.

Down the hall. Past the door that always smells of weed and blares Marilyn Manson. Past the door with the little wooden welcome sign, hand-painted with sunflowers and a little red bird. Past Harrison's door. Harrison is the dog. I have no idea what the people's names are.

Our door.

Will this be the last home I ever know? I hope not. I've hated this place for so long. It was fine for two adults. It was fine when Wallace was a baby. But the minute he started walking we outgrew this condo and I've been desperate to move on. But Damien has been dragging his feet on this the way he dragged his feet about having kids: it's not so bad, we can't afford a house until his business is going, we save money here, houses are so much maintenance. A million excuses.

I don't think he wants a house. Or a backyard. Or the suburbs. Just like I don't think he wanted kids. In fact, I suspect he regrets almost everything about the last seven-or-so years. But he won't say it. If he was just honest about how he felt in the first place, neither of us would be in this situation.

Taking off my coat I can hear the TV is on. Both boys are on the couch, in the dark, faces glowing by the light of the TV.

Are you fucking kidding me?

"Why aren't you two in bed?!" I should have started with hello.

Wallace sighs and, without taking his eyes off the TV says, "Well, I got up to get some water and then Zach got up to ask Dad if he would read us a story and Dad said that he was busy but we could watch TV instead."

Fucking hell. "That was three hours ago. Have you been watching TV for three hours?"

"Well, we paused it to get a snack." He points at the cheerios in a bowl on the table. And on the floor. And on the couch. There's actually one stuck to Zach's chin.

For fucks sake. "OK boys. I hope you had a fun night, but I'm going to have to be the party pooper who turns the TV off and sends you to bed."

"Few more mimits." Zach hasn't taken his eyes off the TV since I walked in the door. He is like a zombie in front of that thing.

"I'm sorry buddy. You will have to watch the rest in the morning. I've got to turn it off now. It is very late."

The instant I press the button on the remote Zach loses

it. "Nooooooooo!!!!!" he cries. "Turn it on! Turn it on! TURN IT ON! TURN IT ON!"

And this is why we don't watch TV in the evening.

I hope Damien can hear this. I hope it is completely ruining his concentration.

"Wallace, do you want to go brush your teeth again please?" I mime toothbrushing in case he can't hear me over the screams, and off he goes toward the bathroom.

"TURN IT ON! TURN IT ON!" Zach has picked up the remote and is winding up to throw it at the TV. I grab it. He reaches for a bowl of cheerios. "TURN IT ON! TURN IT ON!" I grab that too.

"Zach, calm down." I say firmly but he is still screaming. Everything from the coffee table on the floor with one sweep of his little arms.

Motherfucker.

I put down the remote and cheerios and scoop him up into my arms. He's squirming and kicking and screaming "TURN IT ON! TURN IT ON! TURN IT ON!" I hold him tightly and, making sure to breathe deeply, I carry his wriggling body to the bedroom. Trying to get him into bed is like trying to pack an octopus into a can, but eventually I get there. I lie down beside him, pinning his angry body to the bed, and continue to breathe deeply and loudly while he struggles against me.

He has been having these epic freak-outs more often lately. Lish says he is having them at daycare too. Her advice was... oh, what was that word? Co-regulation. If I stay calm and speak calmly and breathe deeply it will help him do the same. I've got to say it has worked pretty well. Already I can feel the fight in him weakening. Now he's sobbing instead of screaming, "turn it on, Mama," which is very sweet and very sad but I keep breathing until he is silent.

Wallace comes into the room and climbs the ladder to the top bunk and turns off his reading lamp without a fuss.

"Mama?" Zach says in his sweetest, saddest voice.

"Yes, Bean?"

"Can I watch TV when we wake up?"

"Sure you can, my love." He wraps his sweet little arms around my neck and plants a wet kiss on my cheek and rolls over to sleep. I kiss the back of his head and get out of his bed, pulling the covers over him.

To the top bunk I whisper, "Good-night Wallace. I love you."

"I love you too, Mom."

I slip out of the room.

There's that fucking light under Damien's fucking door. I want to yell at him, tell him that he's a shitty father and a shitty husband.

Instead I go to clean the living room. And then I clean the kitchen. He didn't do the dishes. His dinner is still on the stove.

Surely that isn't healthy? Spending all day and all night in there. Not eating, not sleeping. Surely there is something wrong. Does he have depression? Anxiety? OCD?

I don't know. He never talks to me anymore. When we do talk it is about his work, not about anything real.

No, reality is my responsibility. Bills, children, cooking, cleaning. That is my job. Chasing dreams is his gig. My dreams? Nope.

Damien's door opens.

Holy shit.

"How were the girls?" his voice is so casual. He has no idea....

"Sad. Angry. It was a difficult night. And I've got to say it didn't get any better when I came home and found the boys watching TV even though I put them to bed before I left."

"Yes, they have an agenda of their own. I can see how you might find that frustrating."

What the fuck does that mean?

Shake it off.

"Would you be able to take Wallace to swimming lessons tomorrow morning? I am hoping to go to spin class, I missed it today."

"I'm afraid you'll have to make other arrangements. I have a meeting with a client tomorrow. I'm hoping you and the children can go out. It doesn't look very professional."

Seriously?

He continues, "And I don't know why this condo always looks like such a pigsty. I feel like every time I clean it just gets messy again as soon as I close my door. Maybe we can tidy up before you three leave tomorrow."

Damien I have cancer. I've got two years to live. I'm leaving you so that I can enjoy the rest of my life. I'm giving the children to Sofia because she will take better care of them than you will, you self-absorbed, pompous twit.

"Who keeps eating all of the brie? I really wanted a prosciutto sandwich, but there's no foccacia and now there's no brie. I thought you went shopping today?"

"I went shopping for Sofia. You'll just have to lower your standards to ciabatta and mozzarella."

He pauses to look at me. "I'm not sure why you are so angry all the time, but I've got to say, it really doesn't suit you. You come across as a bit of a stereotype."

Did he really just fucking say that?

I don't even...

I can't even...

"I'm going to bed. Enjoy your dickhead sandwich."

Dickhead.

My face is hot as I walk down the hall to the bathroom.

Not sure why I'm angry?

Splash water on my face.

A bit of a stereotype?

Floss teeth angrily.

Yeah, no. This is over.

Make-up remover.

How fucking patronizing.

Brush out hair.

I hate this bathroom. It is so small. There is no counter space. And I hate that picture in the hall. From our wedding. That photographer cost a fortune but she took great pictures. They look like something from a magazine. Right down to the stiff poses and total lack of passion in our eyes.

I suddenly can't stand looking at it.

I take the picture down.

Where can I put this thing so I never have to look at it again?

I grab my keys. Out the door. Down the hall. Past the weed and Marilyn Manson apartment, down in the elevator, and into the parking garage.

I toss the whole thing, custom $200 frame and all, into the dumpster.

Heading back to my apartment I feel giddy. I don't think I'll sleep tonight.

10:35 pm

Maja

The house is exactly how I left it. Complete with Nate snoring in the basement.

At least it is clean.

Hanging up my coat and taking off my shoes I make an extra effort to be quiet. I would just rather not deal with him tonight.

I am literally tiptoeing around him.

I don't really know what to do with myself. No kids. Clean house. No Nate... what else do I do if I'm not cleaning or cooking or being bossed around?

I make myself a cup of tea, checking my phone while I wait for the kettle to boil.

I scroll through memes about Canadian weather, articles decrying cancel culture, as if calling for an accused rapist to NOT have a job where he has power over rape victims is some violation of freedom of speech? I don't get it. I see more images from the flooding in the Philippians: it looks even worse than the floods in 2009 when I was there. People abandoning their homes, with whatever valuables they could carry piled on top of makeshift rafts. Homes completely wiped away by mudslides.

Mom is probably worried. I should call her tomorrow.

Oh, there are some more comments on Lish's Twifagram Post:

twifagram

Heather

@Jake, I actually do know a man that was accused of rape and went on to be President of his company while she was blacklisted from the industry completely. I also know a woman who was raped by someone that she could identify and the police wouldn't even follow up on it. I also know a woman who was arrested for loitering (because somehow that is a crime?) and the cop offered to let her off if she gave him a blow job. I'm sorry, Jake, but my 3 anecdotes trump your one made up anecdote.

René

@Jake I actually knew a girl who got suspended from high school for bullying after accusing a guy of sexual assault. There was a video of the incident, but SHE got suspended.

Ellen

@Jake, we know that you don't intend to hate women, it is just an accidental side effect of not seeing women as equal to you.

Damn, girls. Take him to school.

I've never been raped or sexually harassed or anything, but I know a lot of women who have been. I don't know how I got so lucky.

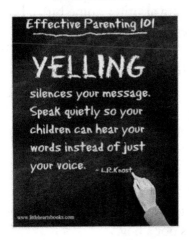

Oh, come on. Are you kidding me? I'm not supposed to yell at my kids? If I didn't yell they would literally never hear me. Those kids are as loud as jackhammers.

Ugh, I'm such a shitty mom.

I take my tea to the living room, stretch out on the couch and put on an episode of Call the Midwife.

Oh, God. It feels so good to put my feet up. They are so swollen that my socks have left a deep gouge where the elastic is. I take them off and wiggle my fat toes. They look so funny.

And my vagina hurts. I think the baby must have dropped into my pelvis this week because the pressure on my bones is immense, and my vagina feels stretched. And the ligaments around my belly feel like they are torn. And my back. Oh, God, my back. I can't wait for this pregnancy to be over.

But at the same time, I am getting increasingly anxious about this birth.

I'm sure it is, at least, in part, to do with Sofia and Grey. I suspect the rest is about Nate. Will he be any help at all? I've been planning another home birth, but maybe that is a mistake. I mean, I loved my home birth with Claire. It was a beautiful, peaceful thing compared to the violent and disrespectful hospital birth I had with Elle. But after the midwives went home Nate started to celebrate, and at 4am he was passed out on the couch when I was calling to him for help, juggling a newborn and a stitched up vagina while putting Elle back to bed. It was not fucking cool. And this time there will be TWO older siblings that need to be managed.

I can almost guarantee he'll be very pissed when he sees that this baby is not a boy.

I fucking hate him.

The girls are right. I should not put up with this.

I hear Nate's heavy footsteps coming up the stairs. A belch. A fart. He's in the bathroom peeing with the door open. He's in the kitchen getting a beer.

He belches again as he enters the living room. The whole couch moves when he drops on to it.

"Call the Midwife again, eh? Any babies die? Any white ladies having black babies? I swear that happens every time I watch this show. When are these white ladies going to learn to cheat with white men so they don't get caught?"

I don't reply.

"I don't know why you watch this show. How many times can you watch a screamy, sweaty woman who lives in a slum push out a baby before it gets repetitive?"

I can't hear a fucking word they are saying. I turn up the volume.

"Oh, you trying to drown me out? I see how it is. Here I am trying to enjoy some quality time with my wife and you just try to drown me out?"

Oh for fuck sake.

I turn the TV off, put down the remote, and turn to face my husband.

His eyes are still glossy, which means he's still a bit drunk.

"Quality time with your wife? Maybe you could start with 'How are you?' or 'How was your night?' or 'Where are our children?' or 'What did you get up to while I was passed out drunk?' before you..."

"Jesus Christ, you just never stop. I just can't do anything right with you!" He chugs his beer.

"You keep saying that as if it is my fault. How is it my fault that everything you say to me is belittling me or degrading me?"

"Oh, fuck you." He picks up the remote and puts on an episode of Brooklyn 99 and starts laughing excessively loudly.

I guess I'm going to bed.

Getting off the couch takes monumental effort. I'm so heavy. Everything hurts so much.

As I waddle out the door Nick shouts: "And get me a beer while you are up, will you?" and he laughs as if he's the funniest man in the world.

10:48 pm

Alisha

The twins are in bed, Kai is in bed, Claire and Elle are still fast asleep. Kai says they put themselves to bed shortly after Isaac passed out. They moved their mats themselves, brushed their own teeth, and went to sleep holding hands. Very sweet. Somehow I don't think they go down that easily at home.

Now to clean the kitchen.

Isaac put some of the dishes in the dishwasher. And he sort of wiped the table, but the highchairs, walls, and floor all still have spaghetti sauce crusted all over them.

But I'm too tired to be angry. I'm just going to imagine a world where I came home to a clean house, sleeping kids, and a conscious, sober husband. If I pretend hard enough, maybe I'll believe it. Willfully delusional is the only way forward.

This has been a challenging day. I am just completely emotionally exhausted. I'm going to need some time off this weekend or else I'll totally burn out. I hope Isaac can take the twins somewhere tomorrow. I really need a whole day. Fuck, I really need a whole week, but I'll take a few hours if that is the best I can get.

I'm envious of people who have family nearby. My parents are in Belize, Isaac's are in New Zealand, neither of us have grandparents or siblings (well, that's not entirely true. I have a brother but having him watch my kids is not an option). I only have my girlfriends when I need help. And, yes, they are always willing to help whenever I need it, but I try not to ask unless it is an emergency. They have so much of their own shit going on, my anxiety seems pretty lame by comparison.

Although this migraine is getting worse again. It has been only three hours since I took pills and the pain is already pushing through. I should take some more before bed. And I should take a pot cookie out of the freezer. If I have that at eleven pm it should help me sleep through until morning.

"Woah. What happened?" Isaac wanders into the kitchen looking lost and confused. "One minute there's a party going on and the next thing I know everyone is gone!" I pause from scrubbing spaghetti sauce off the walls and throw him a dirty look. "Is everybody good?"

"Yeah, everybody is ok. Elle and Claire are sleeping over. You might want to apologize to Kai for making him babysit and to Maja for putting her kids in danger."

"Yeah, of course. I can do that. I thought tomorrow I'd take them all out for something fun. So you can have a break." He grabs a mop and starts to clean the floor.

"That would be nice, thank you. Although Kai might need something quieter. You should ask him before you make plans."

I grimace at the way he mops the floor, just pushing the food and dog hair around, depositing it in little clumps in the corners and under the table.

Whatever. I'm too tired to care. At least he's trying. Half-assed. And I'll have to fix it later.

Seth Rogan-ing it. I laugh to myself, thinking about Drae's perfect catagorization of my husbands' behaviour.

Leaning the mop against the wall (not where it goes) Isaac smiles, "Wanna smoke a joint with me?"

What I want is to go to bed, but my anxiety is too high for sleeping, so... "Yeah, why not." Maybe we'll get that quality time after all.

The garage is cold, but Isaac has it all set up: a poor man's man cave. There's a space heater and a laptop with a speaker on top of a little table that he filched from the neighbour's curb on garbage day, and a mini-fridge that he took from work.

"Check this out. It's the trailer for the new Taika Waititi film." He smiles excitedly as he presses play on the laptop.

It is nice to see him smiling and talking again. It's like the last week of being completely ignored never happened.

The trailer plays while he rolls a joint. It looks funny, for sure, but I just don't really watch movies that much anymore. By the time the twins are in bed I just want to sit in total silence in the dark staring at the ceiling trying not to have a panic attack that I have to do it all again tomorrow. Movies don't fit that schedule.

"Pretty funny, eh?" the trailer ends and Isaac sparks up the joint. "A lot of people are offended, but I think it looks brilliant. It's really subversive."

I smile and take the joint from him.

"How were the girls? How is Sofia doing?"

I sigh. "She's doing exactly the way anybody would be: She's a fucking mess. And Colin left."

"He what?"

"He packed a bag and left. On Wednesday."

"Man, that is not cool. Their baby died and he left? Even I know that isn't ok, and I'm an idiot."

"And something is up with Drae."

"Like what?"

"I don't know. She's acting weird. She hugged me."

"Is that weird?"

"Yeah, Drae is famous for not hugging. She is a personal space person."

"Oh, I thought all women were huggers."

"You also think all women want to sleep with you."

He laughs so hard he spits his beer.

"You have a point." He smiles that smile that I fell in love with. With those dimples.

I pass the joint back. "So are we good, you and I? Are you ok?"

"Yeah, it's all good. I was just stressed at work. No big deal."

Just stressed at work? You ghosted me in my own home for a week and then said that you might leave me for lack of sex and now it is no big deal? What the Fuck, Isaac? That is what I want to say. But instead I go with: "So what about the texts you sent me today? You seemed to suggest that our marriage was doomed."

I can feel the weed working it's way through my body. The muscle tension weakening ever so slightly, my tightly-wound brain unraveling just a tiny bit.

"Yeah, I was just stressed at work. There is a lot going on."

"So you are ok with never having sex with me again?"

"I mean, it sucks. I'm bummed about it. But whatever. It is what it is."

"Do you think you will date other women?"

"I don't know. I just can't be bothered. It is a lot of work."

He hands the joint back to me and I take a deep drag. If I wasn't so worn out I'd be really pissed right now. What the fuck? Is he crazy? He was so angry for a week that he couldn't look at me and now it is nothing?

I wish he would be honest with me. Tell me what is really going on. I wish he would talk to me.

Slow exhale.

"So what is going on at work that has you so stressed?" He finishes his beer and opens another.

"Oh, nothing." He's staring at his computer now, scrolling through trailers. "I.. Just.. You know, the usual shit."

The usual shit. Of course it is.

"Is it Chris? Is he making life difficult?" Chris is the asshole manager. Every workplace has one.

"Yeah, he's definitely pissing people off, but I heard that he went for a job interview at the Marriott, so maybe he'll be gone soon."

"Well that's cool. Maybe you'll get promoted to his job."

"Nah, fuck that. I don't want that job. Everyone comes to him with their problems."

"But wouldn't you get a raise?" I pass back the joint.

"Yeah, not worth it. There, this is what I'm going to watch tonight."

He puts on a Seth Rogan trailer. I laugh, but not at the jokes.

Much more relaxed now.

"Did you hear the story about this movie? The director got fired because this picture surfaced of him going black-face at a party like, fifteen years ago. So they gave the job to this other director to finish, but it turns out HE was accused of sexually harassing dozens of women. And they knew that when they gave him the job. Like, what the fuck? That is fucked up."

"Yeah, that is."

"I mean, yeah, there's a picture of the brown face and there's no physical evidence of the sexual harassment, but, this world is fucked up. Like, really sexually harassing a woman should piss us off as much as black-face, shouldn't it?"

"Yeah, did you see my..."

"It is a shame because the first director was way better." I find it funny that Isaac can be so woke about feminist issues yet at the same time constantly cut me off and speak over top of me... "The reviews of the movie say it is pretty bad, that the second director tried to do something totally different and it just doesn't work."

"When you watch it you'll have to..."

"I mean, yeah, I get pissed off when somebody that I admire does something so disrespectful, but I also kinda feel like, if we're going to fire every guy that ever did something racist, every white person over the age of 25 is going to be unemployed." He laughs.

"I do find it funny..."

"This weed is good." He says as he exhales a large cloud and passes the joint to me. "I got this weed from that place by the highway, the "Smoke Signals" place? Canada's First Nations grow good weed. I hope New Zealand legalizes it soon, then we can check out some quality Maori bud."

I don't even know why I'm here.

About a year ago, we were hanging out in the basement, and I started coughing. He just kept talking. I coughed so hard that I had to run to the bathroom and I vomited. He just kept talking, followed me to the bathroom and talked while I barfed. He didn't stop to ask if I was ok, he didn't offer to get me water, he didn't wait for me to be able to breathe. He just kept talking.

I just don't even know what to make of that.

I take one last drag of the joint and pass it back to Isaac.

"You gonna watch with me?" he asks as he presses play on the movie.

"No, I've got to go to bed. The twins will be up in six hours."

"Hey, I'll get up early tomorrow, do breakfast, and take the kids somewhere all day. Give you the whole day off."

I smile and give him a kiss. "That would be lovely." I know he means it when he says it, but when it comes time to wake up he just won't. He'll sleep in until ten, they won't leave until after lunch, the twins will nap for a half hour in the car, and they'll come back three hours later exhausted, overstimulated, full of junk food, and I'll be left to deal with the fallout while Isaac sneaks off to the garage to smoke a joint, patting himself on the back for what a great dad he is.

Fuck my life.

11:08 pm

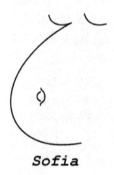

Sofia

I wasn't actually sleeping, I don't think. I was just daydreaming in bed. I was imagining I was still pregnant, and picturing the person Grey would become. His first steps. His precious smile. His hazel eyes. His wild giggle. I was deep enough into the fantasy that I could feel the joy and the love. I was glowing. Warm. Full.

My phone buzzing the arrival of a text message brought me crashing back to reality.

To darkness. Cold. Empty.

I don't want to look at my phone. It will be my mother making me feel weak. Or Yaya making me feel guilty. Whoever it is probably wants something from me. And I have nothing to give.

Or it could be Drae. Or Lish. Or Maja.

I reach for the phone.

My heart skips a beat.

Colin.

It is from Colin.

COLIN

Today, 11:08 pm
"I'm sorry. I fucked up. Can I com home?"

I'm crying again.
It is hard to text when you are crying.

Sofia

Today, 11:09 pm
Of course.

I stare at his message for a full minute at least. I've been fantasizing about that message all day. It is hard to believe that it is real. Should I pinch myself or something?

I don't need to. I can tell that it is real because he misspelled "come" and my fantasies would never allow a mistake like that.

The girls will be so relieved.

Oh, I should send them a message:

Sofia

Today, 11:09 pm
He texted. He's coming home.

————————

No, actually, one more.

————————

Today, 11:10 pm
And thank you. You have no idea how much I
love you women. As long as I have you in my
life I still have hope.

————————

11:11 pm

Andrea

I knew I wouldn't be able to sleep.

It just keeps rolling around my head. Tell them. Don't tell them. I'm a coward. I'm insensitive. Round and round and round.

My phone buzzes.

It is Sofia.

Sofia

Today, 11:09 pm
He texted. He's coming home.

Oh thank God.

I really do think Colin is a good guy. Of all the husbands he is the most respectful, the one who tries the hardest. I can see how he might not know how to cope, how he might panic and run away. It sounds like the kind of thing I would do. But he also really loves Sofia, so I was pretty sure he would do the right thing in the end.

Sofia

Today, 11:10 pm
And thank you. You have no idea how much I love you women. As long as I have you in my life I still have hope.

Jesus.

I start to cry instantly.

Two more years. She has me for two more years. And then what? She goes through all of this pain again?

My thumb leads the way through my phone to Twifagram and to the cancer group that I joined this morning.

twifagram

Andrea

How did you all tell the people that you love? There has already been so much tragedy, I can't bring myself to tell my friends. This is the last thing they need in their lives. Did any of you just keep it to yourself? How did that turn out?

And now I wait and hope that some total stranger out there holds the answer to my problems.

11:13 pm

Alisha

I've set myself up in Isaac's bed with my laptop to do billing for the daycare. Well, it is actually my bed too, but I usually rotate between here and the twins' bed and the daybed in Kai's room, and this is the only unoccupied spot tonight.

I also shouldn't be looking at screens this late at night, but the invoices need to be sent out, so I'll just have to rely on the joint I smoked and the cookie I ate to get me to sleep tonight.

And I hate doing billing. It is depressing. I nearly kill myself all week and at the end of it I only make $600. And I'm one of the most expensive daycares in the city. There are women out there making $75 a day. Brutal.

Imagine if we valued child care as much as we valued, say, soldiers or doctors?

Maybe we wouldn't all grow up to be damaged and full of anger yelling at each other on Twifagram.

My phone buzzes.

Sofia

Today, 11:09 pm
He texted. He's coming home.

Oh, thank fuck. What a relief.

Today, 11:10 pm
And thank you. You have no idea how much I love you women. As long as I have you in my life I still have hope.

My heart swells. I'm so glad that we could do something. I reply right away:

Alisha

Today, 11:13 pm
I love you ladies! How anybody gets through life without friends like you, I don't know. I feel so blessed!

As I'm about to set the phone down I get a Twifagram notification:

twifagram

Andrea has posted to your group Breast and Ovarian Cancer Warriors Canada

---

What the fuck is Drae doing in my cancer group?
I follow the link in the pop-up.

Andrea

How did you all tell the people that you love? There has already been so much tragedy, I can't bring myself to tell my friends. This is the last thing they need in their lives. Did any of you just keep it to yourself? How did that turn out?

Holy fucking Jesus Christ Holy fucking Jesus Christ Holy fucking Jesus Christ.

I'm pretty glad I'm high right now because the pain in my heart might kill me otherwise.

So that is what was up with Drae. I thought there was something more she wasn't telling us.

Oh, poor Drae.

I'll bet she hasn't even told Damien.

That is a heavy thing to be carrying all by yourself.

Oh, Drae. My poor, strong, Drae.

Fuck this life. This is bullshit.

11:15 pm

Maja

I'm lying in bed scanning Twifagram instead of sleeping (why am I such a loser? When am I going to get my shit together? How could I even run a business when I can't even manage my own internet addiction?) when I get the three messages, one after another.

Sofia

Today, 11:09 pm
He texted. He's coming home.

Today, 11:10 pm
And thank you. You have no idea how much I
love you women. As long as I have you in my
life I still have hope.

Alisha

Today, 11:13 pm
I love you ladies! How anybody gets through
life without friends like you, I don't know. I
feel so blessed!

I feel overwhelmed by love! Like, it is swelling up in my
chest and creeping into my throat and leaking out my eyes.
God, how many times can I cry in one day?

Maja

Today, 11:15 pm
I love you ladies too! I feel so lucky to have
such strong, brave women in my life. I feel
stronger and braver because of you!

That doesn't even begin to capture how I feel. I wish I was
better with words.

I have to piss again. I've been trying to ignore it because I
literally JUST pissed five minutes ago, but that is the third
trimester for you.

I set down my phone, roll my giant body over, swing my
legs off the bed, and lift myself up. My feet are still sore, my
pelvis, my back. It all aches tremendously.

God, pregnancy sucks.

But it could be worse.

I might as well get some water while I'm up. So I can pee it out again ten minutes from now.

I walk as softly as I can so Nate doesn't hear me. I've had enough of talking to him today.

Trying to be nice. That was trying to be nice? What a dick.

I fill my glass up and turn to leave when I see Nate standing by the door.

"You look beautiful standing there." He speaks softly. "I don't tell you that enough. Is there anything more beautiful than a woman growing new life within her?"

Oh, God. What is he up to now?

"Thank-you, Nate. That is very nice of you." I step past him to head back to the bathroom. I can hear him following me.

"I should say it more often, how amazing you are. You are an awesome mom, our girls are the best, and it is all your doing."

He wants something.

I set the water glass down on the bathroom counter and Nate is right there, right beside me. He is so much bigger than me. I used to like that. It made me feel safe. Now it makes me feel claustrophobic.

"Honey, I need to pee."

"Yeah, of course." He steps aside so I can get to the toilet, but he continues to hover over me.

"We used to have so much fun together, didn't we? Remember that time we fucked in that elevator in Niagara Falls? Remember that time you gave me a blow job on the 401?"

"Nate, I already told you I don't want to have sex."

"I know that. Your body hurts. You are growing a person. I understand, you don't want to have sex. I'm not

361

trying to have sex, I'm just trying to have a nice conversation about happier times."

"OK, fine." I needed to pee so badly a few minutes ago, but now, nothing. I lean forward while lifting my baby belly with my hands, hoping to clear some space for my poor bladder.

"Do you remember the hand job you gave me under the table at Christmas at my parents' place? That was wild. We had such a good time."

Oh, finally, the pee comes. It is the stupidest little trickle. I'm glad I got out of bed for that.

I lean back and reach for the toilet paper but Nate is right in front of me.

And he has his dick out.

It is still a bit soft, getting harder as he shakes it in his hand.

"Jesus Christ, Nate, get that out of my face."

"Just suck it, baby. I know you don't want sex, but just suck it. Suck it like you used to." He's stroking it vigorously now, and leaning toward my face.

"I should have known. You are only nice to me when you want something." I reach around him to grab the toilet paper and wipe. "You don't remember all the mean shit you say to me, but I do, and it doesn't exactly leave me longing for your cock in my face."

"Just do it. Like old times. Don't you miss how things used to be? Just suck it."

"Nate, please, leave me alone. I want to go to bed." I try to stand up but it's too awkward with this big belly and Nate standing in the way.

"Just lick it baby. Just kiss it. Just for a minute. Just show me you still love me."

Maybe I don't love you.

I don't say that out loud.

"Nate, I don't want to. Please get out of the way."

"You want to. I know you do. Once you start you won't be able to stop." He's stopped rubbing his cock now and he's ramming it toward my mouth.

"Nate STOP!"

"Not until you suck it. I'm not letting you leave until you suck it." He rubs it with his hand again and then, with the other hand on my head so I can't move away, he rubs the head of his cock on my lips. "Suck it baby. You know it will be so good."

I give up.

I open my mouth and he thrusts his dick in with a sigh of relief. He slides it in and out, holding my head with both hands so that all I can do is hold my tongue across the back of my throat to protect my gag reflex.

"Oh yeah. Oh baby. You know what I like. Rub my balls."

I rub his balls. The sooner he comes the sooner he'll fuck off and leave me alone.

In and out. He's getting rougher as his excitement builds. I try to control my own head but he's got both hands twisted up in my hair and I'm no match for his strength. My jaw hurts and the back of my throat hurts and I'm still sitting on this fucking toilet with my pj pants around my ankles and the baby's head is so low in my pelvis that it feels like it is going to fall right into the toilet and would you just fucking come already so I can go to bed and pretend this shit never happened.

"Oh yeah. I love you baby. I'm going to come in your mouth and you are going to swallow every last drop because you are a dirty fucking slut and you fucking love to suck my dick." And with that he ejaculates and it floods down my throat and I can't breathe.

"Oh, yeah. That was amazing. Thanks for that." As he puts his dick back in his pants I'm still struggling to breathe. "I love you but I'm not kissing you until you brush your teeth. You're fucking disgusting."

He laughs and walks away. Back to the kitchen and opens another beer.

11:32 pm

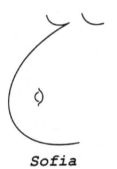

Sofia

I hear a vehicle outside. Is that him? He asked if he could come home, but he didn't say when. I don't even know where he's been staying.

I hear a key in the door.

My heart races. I sit up in bed. It looks good in here. I'm glad the girls came. If Colin had seen how nasty it was in here before he might have turned right around and run away.

And there he is at the door. Average height, broad shoulders, skin deeply tanned and freckled from working outside all summer. His curly blonde hair pulled back in that handsome bun that his brothers always make fun of him for. His ginger beard, usually immaculately groomed, looking shaggy and unkempt. It is the only sign that anything might be amiss.

As he steps closer I can see the tears in his eyes.

I hold my arms up to him and he crumbles like a sail when the wind dies. He climbs into bed beside me and, with his head on my chest and his arms wrapped tightly around me, we sob together for the first time since our baby died.

1:23 am

Andrea

I sit up in bed so suddenly that it scares me wide awake.

My heart is beating a million miles an hour. My groin is on fire, and wet with excitement.

Holy fuck that dream was hot.

I feel like I was literally about to orgasm in my sleep. Can women have wet dreams?

I want to finish.

Damien is in the bed beside me. Wow. He actually came to bed.

I could wake him.

I almost laugh out loud. No, not going to happen. He would shut me down without hesitation.

I reach into my bedside drawer, grab my vibrator, and sneak off to the bathroom.

3:00 am

Alisha

"Meow. Meoooow. Meeeeeeeeow." The cat leaps onto the bed, landing squarely upon the sleeping toddler beside me.

"Get the fuck out of here!" I hiss at the creature and push her away, praying that she won't wake the babies. After some resistance the cat leaps back to the ground and proudly walks away, throwing me an angry glance over her shoulder.

And then the migraine hits me like a sledgehammer in the back of the skull. That spot where your spine turns into your brain-stem. Then the pain shoots around the right, causing my entire right side to flinch and retract, and my right eye flashes with cold white light, then goes blind.

I'm going to barf.

I scramble out of bed as quickly as I can while trying not to stick my elbow in Ari's trachea. I can find my way to the bathroom even with my eyes closed, but it still isn't fast enough and I only just manage to avoid making a mess of the hall floor. I retch again and again, trying desperately to keep control over the powerful impulse. Trying to be quiet so I don't wake anybody. Again and again, until my stomach is empty and the emptiness amplifies the pain in my stomach and my head. I can't tell how much of the wetness on my face came from the splashing toilet water or from my tear ducts.

At last the retching fades and then stops. The entire right side of my body is still pinched, as if half of me had been electrocuted, and panting to catch my breath is making my head throb. Throb isn't the right word. It isn't big enough. I once saw a picture of a whale's heart and it was the size of a minivan. My head feels like that thing if it were plunked upon my shoulders, still beating.

At least I still have my imagination.

I lean back against the wall beside the toilet paper roll. I breathe. I try to relax. I'm completely focused on my breathing and I try to imagine my muscles melting like butter. After some time, I have no idea how long – did I fall asleep here? – I become aware that the pain has dulled. I open my eyes. I check my watch.

3:39am. Again. Seems to be my new favourite hour of the morning.

So much for the pot cookie getting me through until morning. I definitely shouldn't have smoked that joint with Isaac. Something about smoking a joint always makes my migraines worse.

I should have known better.

One more thing that Isaac and I used to do together that I can't do anymore.

I slowly climb to my feet. As I rise to full height, the blood rushes to my head and with it a wave of pain grips my right hand side again, but it fades after a moment and I am able to wash my hands and my face. I rinse out my mouth, but it still feels terrible, so I brush my teeth.

Without turning on my electric toothbrush, because it is too loud and the last thing I need right now is company.

I tiptoe out to the livingroom, since all of the beds in the house are occupied.

I need to eat some food so that I can take some pills so that I can fall asleep again.

I grab my box of "headache crackers" from the pantry, and my bottle of pain-killers from the counter, and then I prop myself up on the couch in the exact right position: with my back straight, my chin tucked down, and my pelvis curled under. It has taken years of physiotherapy, osteopathy and self discipline to learn how to compensate for my misshapen spine. Finally I cocoon myself within my favourite blanket and stare out the window into the night.

It is snowing.

Are you kidding me? It is only October! I was outside with no coat on only 12 hours ago!

Shit.

It is pretty though. Huge, fluffy flakes delicately swirling in the lamplight. They look like they are dancing with each other. So graceful and silent.

The kids will lose their minds when they see it. There is enough coming down that it might even stay for a few hours.

I watch the snow while gently munching my crackers in the dark.

Drae has cancer. I still haven't decided what to do with this information.

She must be so scared.

I can totally understand why she didn't tell us. It is already all-hands-on-deck to help Sofia. And Drae is a helper, not an 'ask for help'-er. I think that being strong and independent is just too much of a core belief for her.

I grab my phone from the coffee table and go straight to Drae's post.

Andrea

How did you all tell the people that you love? There has already been so much tragedy, I can't bring myself to tell my friends. This is the last thing they need in their lives. Did any of you just keep it to yourself? How did that turn out?

There are a dozen replies now. Almost all of them urging her to tell her friends. Friends are what get you through, they all say.

It is true.

I sigh deeply and start to type:

Alisha

A very dear friend of mine is in the midst of an epic personal tragedy, and today she described it to me as being sucked into a giant, black hole, being all alone in there, and not being able to get out. It is true, that she is in that black hole alone, it is true that none of us (her friends) can be in there with her, or get her out. That is work that she has to do herself. But we can bear witness to her struggle, we can shower her with our love and our faith in her strength. So, while the fight is hers and hers alone, she does not have to be alone while she fights it.

That is why you tell your friends. Because the black hole is certainly a lonely place, but you don't have to be alone. When I had cancer, only I could take the chemo, but you held my hand while I did it. Only I could have the surgery to remove my breasts, but you could feed me and entertain me while I recovered, and love me while I rebuilt my life.

You see, we are stronger together. And you should just tell us.

Perfect. I press 'post'.

I reach for my pill bottle, take two tablets, and return to staring out the window at the snow swirling gently in the pale glow of the street lamp.

THE END

Resources

If you or someone you know are experiencing domestic violence, there are resources that you can access for help.

In Canada

Please visit the Canadian Women's Foundation website to be connected to services in your area.
   "https://canadianwomen.org/support-services/"

In the US

Please visit the National Domestic Violence Hotline
   "https://www.thehotline.org/resources/"

Ezmé Purvis

Ezmé Purvis was born and raised in rural Ontario, Canada, in an old farmhouse three miles from nowhere. Like many a stereotypical small town girl, Ezmé took off as soon as she graduated high school. In eleven years Ezmé lived in ten cities in four different countries, doing almost every job imaginable. From packing peppers to catering $500/plate fundraisers. From making hotel beds to lecturing at an international conference on the Middle East. From performing on stage with some of the greatest names in Canadian Theater, to being barfed on by three different kids in one day while running a daycare.

Ezmé has always wanted to be a writer, ever since she wrote her first story about an alien invasion, with full-colour illustrations, when she was eight. Unfortunately, Ezmé has mostly found herself too busy trying to pay the bills to finish a whole book. Oh, and sick. She's spent way too much time being sick, and having surgeries: Ezmé has had lots of bits removed and a few extras put in over the years. She's not quite cyborg yet, unfortunately. But we can cross our fingers: who knows what the future might hold.

F*ck the Mommy Wars is Ezmé Purvis' first book.

Website: ezmepurvis.com
Email: ezmepurvis@gmail.com
Facebook: ezmepurvis.author
Twitter: @EzmePurvis
Instagram: ezmepurvis

Coming Soon

THE RELUCTANT FEMINIST

In the year 255 of the Matriarchal Era, life is better than it has ever been. Women hold exclusive power and men are confined to the only place where they can be trusted: in cages. Without men there is no crime, no addiction, no murder, no abuse, and no rape. Women are not judged or shamed, there are no laws telling them what to do with their bodies, and empathy and kindness are so normal they aren't even words anymore. Life is good.

But Aphra knows that not everything is as it seems. The women in charge are hiding something about the past, and she is determined to uncover the truth.

UNTITLED 14TH CENTURY PLAGUE NOVEL

Yaqut is a black slave who has inherited not only his freedom but also his Egyptian masters' Mediterranean shipping company. He is on a trade mission to Europe when the mysterious and horrific deaths begin.

Adelie is a French noblewoman who has lost everything to the plague and is left with no choice but to cross the Mediterranean to find her missing husband.

The two of them make an unlikely pair but together they set out on an adventure that will change the course of history.

CPSIA information can be obtained
at www.ICGtesting.com
Printed in the USA
LVHW010352170920
666201LV00026B/598